CW01426121

WASTING

THE BOOK OF MALADIES

D.K. HOLMBERG

ASH PUBLISHING

A JOB OFFER

Sam hovered in the shadows, her cloak wrapped around her, shielding her from sight. She had no intention of getting caught, but if anyone were to suspect she was here, it would be Marin. The woman was too well connected, almost as if she knew Sam's plans even before Sam herself.

At least Tray watched from a nearby rooftop. If she didn't make it out, he'd know and would come in for her. Her brother had a unique relationship with Marin, and he trusted her much more than Sam ever could.

"Is this the map?" she heard Marin whisper across to another, though she remained in shadow.

The woman was compact, only a few inches taller than five feet, but still taller than Sam. She hated how small she was, hated the way it limited where she could sneak, but it wasn't like she could choose her height. She'd been born small, and supposedly took after her mother, though Sam barely remembered her. All she knew was that others who *had* known her mother said she took after her. Even Marin had mentioned it when they'd first met.

"This is the map. You know what they would do if they knew I shared this with you?" the man said. He stood along one of the dozens of canals that ran through the city, close enough that he could probably feel the spray off the water from the eels swirling beneath the surface. "I'm only doing this to repay the debt. After this…"

Sam couldn't make out who the man was, nor did she recognize his voice. There seemed to be an accent to his words, but in the city, there were nearly as many accents as there were sections to the city. People came to Verdholm for safety.

"We're even, I know," Marin said. She remained near one of the buildings lining the canal, enough distance from the man that she could move quickly if needed. It was a good position. Marin tapped her canal staff on the hard stone path that ran along the canal, almost a warning to keep the man away.

"You understand that it's not usable in its current form, even for you?"

Marin cut him off with a wave of her hand. "I understand that we haven't had anything like it in the city in many years." Her voice had trailed off as she spoke. "I don't know why they would risk it now, but it's to my benefit they do."

Marin took something from the man—a scrap of paper or a bundle?—and slipped it into her pocket.

"And the payment?"

"The same place I promised before," Marin said.

Sam knew Marin traded in information, but thought that was it—that she traded, not bought what she needed.

"If this is inaccurate, you know what will happen." Marin's threat held menace, enough that Sam almost took a step back, but she was shielded in the shadows. Wearing her cloak—one she'd borrowed from Marin long ago—no one could see her.

"It's real enough. You won't have much time."

Sam shifted her position. The moon was high overhead, gleaming along the rundown buildings in this section of the city. They were far enough removed from the central part of town that she didn't fear getting caught by the guards. Marin catching her might not have nearly the same consequences, but there *would* be consequences.

What was she thinking following her here? Just because she found work as a thief—and good work, most of the time—didn't mean she needed to risk that by opposing Marin.

She turned her attention back to the conversation. What had she missed?

"You plan to go after it today?"

Marin nodded. "There won't be much time before it's transported beyond my reach. The rest of the preparations are in place. If I don't make my move now, I don't know if I'll be able to. What of you?"

"I have to return. Otherwise, all of this will have been in vain."

They said something else, but too softly, so Sam couldn't hear it. She knew not to move. Movement now would disrupt the silence, and with Marin, she didn't want to risk that exposure. The woman would not be forgiving.

The man moved away from Marin, leaving her standing alone.

She remained motionless for long moments before turning in Sam's direction, as if she knew she was there. "You can come out of the shadows, Samara."

Kyza! How had Marin detected her?

Sam stepped forward. "You knew?"

"I think I'd recognized my own cloak," she said, eyeing Sam up and down before her gaze settled on her in full. She had hard eyes, and they looked at her in a way that demanded she do as instructed. Sam suspected that any who fell victim to that gaze would do the same. "How much did you hear?"

Sam shrugged. There was no use denying that she'd overheard everything. "Enough. What sort of prize are you going after?"

She smiled, but Marin's eyes never changed. "I'm not going after any prize."

"But I heard you say that time was important. I heard you tell him you needed to act—"

Marin gave a single shake of her head. "I'm not the best person to reach this target."

Sam's heart fluttered even before Marin said anything else. She didn't need her to say anything more to know what she intended.

"Since you seem to have heard everything, I think you'll be a good fit to go after this."

"I don't work for you, Marin." She didn't want to work for anyone, though Bastan had the best claim on her, as much as she wanted to get away from him. Sam didn't want to spend all her days thieving. There would be something else for her, even if there were times it seemed that she would never find it. Thieving was a means to something else—someplace better—and Sam was determined to find it.

"No, but you have, and you will again. Now."

"Give me a reason why I should?"

She eyed Sam strangely, almost appraising her. "How much do you need to pay off Bastan?"

"There is no paying off Bastan," Sam said. Even if she had enough money to pay him off, she doubted she could completely separate from him. Once her mother died, Sam had taken all the jobs she could to keep her and her brother safe. It just so happened that most of them were tied to Bastan, and he took his cut. Each job she took drew her deeper into his web, and she was tied to him more and more. In some ways, Marin was still worse. At least with Bastan, you knew what he wanted and where you stood. With Marin, there was always a sort of uncertainty.

"Oh, I don't know about that. For the right job, you could get your independence back, and no longer be dependent on him for jobs. What do you think about that? Would you like to be able to take only those jobs you choose? Would you like to not pay a cut on everything you pull?"

It was as if Marin knew all the annoyances she felt. There was only so much she'd managed to do to keep both her and Tray safe. Bastan helped, but he had a price, and she gladly paid, to ensure her brother's safety. Other than in dreams, she'd given up thinking she could ever get away from it.

"Why give up a job like that?" she asked. "If what you have is so valuable, why not do it yourself?"

Marin tipped her head. "I could. But I think I'd prefer to have you do it."

"And if I don't?"

"That won't happen, so I won't bother telling you what could happen if you don't do this for me. Why should I describe the way Tray would suffer, or the way your jobs would suddenly become more difficult?" Marin offered a false smile.

Sam was stuck. She didn't *want* to work with Marin— she already had one person who pushed her hard enough —but she feared that if she didn't, Marin would do all the things she promised. Her brother needed her help. Sam needed to keep him safe. She couldn't do that without money, and without the support of someone like Bastan —or Marin.

"What's the task?"

Marin fished something out of her pocket and passed it to Sam. She unfolded the slip of frayed paper, revealing a hand-drawn map. It was the diagram for a building, and from the way it was depicted, Sam could tell it was a high-born house.

"No."

"You don't know the job."

"I know it well enough. I'm not breaking into some highborn fortress."

"Fortress? That seems a bit strong, even for you, Samara. This is a house, and what you're after is incredibly valuable. Enough that when you manage to acquire it, I'll see any debt you owe to Bastan wiped clean. How does that sound?"

She hated to admit it, but that sounded great, and if there was anyone who would be able to afford to pay what Bastan would require to wipe away her debt, it would be Marin.

Worry tickled at her. Why would Marin offer her this opportunity? It wasn't that Marin was any slouch when it came to sneaking around. She was as good or better than Sam. She was the person who'd taught Sam most of what she knew, back before Sam understood the way Marin worked, and the expectations she would have for that knowledge.

If she did what Marin asked, she'd be trading one sort of service for another. And even then, she wasn't sure she'd be completely free of Bastan. He appreciated her skills far too much to let her go easily.

Marin watched her, and her eyes hardened. "No strings on this one, Samara. You do this, and you're free. Not only of Bastan, but of me. I won't require additional service of you."

Sam sighed. She wasn't sure she believed her, but that wasn't the point, was it? The point was to tempt her, to coax her into helping, regardless of whether she wanted to or not.

"I'll think about it." She handed the map back to Marin, but she didn't take it.

"Keep it. If you decide to do this for me, you'll need it."

"When do I have to decide?"

Marin quirked a smile. "You'll have until tomorrow

night. After that… then the offer disappears and will be made to another."

Damn her. First the temptation, then the time limitation.

She knew what Tray would say. He already liked Marin well enough that he took her jobs without Sam. There weren't many jobs Tray could do, not on his own—with his size, he didn't have the same quiet to his steps or the same understanding of silence—but by using her brother, Marin bound him ever more to her, and in turn, risked binding Sam to her, as well.

"I do this, and you leave Tray alone."

Marin actually smiled at that. "Your brother can make his own decisions, can't he?"

"My brother doesn't see what you are, but I do. If I do this, you leave him alone. This pays for both of our freedom."

Marin chuckled. "So dramatic. It's not as if I intend to use your brother in some nefarious way, Samara. He does the occasional odd job for me, nothing more."

"And those will be over." She tried to say it as fiercely as possible, but wasn't sure if it came out as she intended or if she only sounded amusing.

"You'll have to be the one to tell Trayson what you've told me, but I will agree."

Sam should have questioned more. Marin agreed far too easily, but the idea of not having Bastan on her ass all the time and not worrying about Marin harassing her brother was too much for her. The appeal was too great.

"What is it? What are you after?"

Marin shook her head. "You'll know it when you see it."

"That's not how I work."

Marin shrugged. "Know that it's valuable to those in the palace, which is why I must have it."

"That still doesn't help."

"If you choose not to do this, I can't have you knowing what I'm after, but if you *do,* then know that there won't be anything else of value in the room marked on the map."

"Like gems?" Everyone knew about the collection of gems the Anders family had in the palace. The famed gem collection kept the royals in power, mined from deep beneath the city in flood tunnels. They did more than that, though. They bought protection to others in the city.

Marin laughed again. "Sure. Like gems. Collect this *gem* and bring it to me."

Sam unfolded the map and studied the page. "Where is it in this place?"

"Top floor. Look in the room at the end of the hall. You will find this on a table in the center of the room."

"And you need this claimed by what time?"

"I'm not unreasonable. I'll give you two nights to make the arrangements. After that, the task goes to someone else." She crossed her arms over her chest. "Do you think you can do this, Samara?"

Sam sighed. Why did she keep letting herself get pulled like this?

"Where will I find you when this is done?"

Marin shook her head with a laugh. "Don't worry, Samara. I'll find you."

2

FINDING THE PRIZE

Sam crouched on the rooftop, ignoring Tray standing next to her as she stared into the darkness, until the shadows in the window began to take on a shape. If the information from Marin was accurate, the prize *should* be there. Her mind offered a dozen different possibilities about what Marin might be after, but with Marin it could be difficult to know. What she deemed valuable was often *much* different than what Sam prize.

Marin wasn't alone in how secretive she could be with jobs. Bastan, in particular, feared that her knowing would make her more likely to try and keep what she stole. Without his connections, there wasn't much she could do to move those items, anyway. She *needed* Bastan—and hated that she did.

If this worked, maybe she wouldn't. Maybe she could be free of him entirely. Then she *could* choose her jobs without being reliant on others.

The soft sloshing of water through the canal was the

only noise in the silence. The canals separated the various sections of the city, winding off Ralan Bay and spilling into the Piare River. Some were naturally occurring streams that were then fortified, such as the Central Canal, but a many were dredged specifically to reach parts of the city that weren't otherwise accessible by water, with the Palace Canal being the prime example. The sound of water running through the canals carried throughout the city, giving it a sort of hum and energy.

And a stench. It was worse in the outer sections of the city—lowborn sections. Merchants and highborns did a better job of keeping filth from stagnating along the canals.

Sam let out a soft breath, steadying her nerves. In and out. That was all this needed to be. Anything more than that, and she risked failure. Success meant freedom, not only for her, but for Tray. That was the only reason she did this.

But if she failed… She tried not to think of what would happen, but she couldn't help that she did. Failure meant she'd be tied to Marin *and* Bastan.

"How did I get into this again?" she muttered to herself.

"You don't have to do this. Marin said—"

"I know what Marin told you," Sam snapped.

Tray raised his hands, trying to placate her. His thick brown hair caught a gust of wind. She wondered which side of the family his hair came from. Hers was dark and wavy while Tray had thick brown hair. So much about him was different than her.

"You don't need to do this for me," he said. "If that's the only reason—"

Sam shook her head. "That's not the only reason."

She wouldn't tell him it was the main reason. Tray wouldn't understand. He'd never *really* understood. His memories were only of a time *after* Sam had secured Bastan's support. Prior to that, they had lived on the street, begging for whatever charity they could get. Being lowborn meant they didn't get much.

She ignored Tray, making a point of *not* looking at the way he hulked over her, his muscular frame so much larger than her petite one. That was another difference between them. She had always struggled with being the smallest, or looking the youngest, while Tray's size and sharp angular chin gave him an appearance older than his years.

Another breeze gusted through the streets, fluttering the curtains in the open window across the way. The shadows in the room moved, and she counted three.

"Kyza," she swore softly. Had Marin known there would be three others in the home? Was that why she'd offered the job to her?

"Come on, Sam, you can't use a god's name like that."

This time, she *did* turn to him. Tray was two years younger than she was, but given his size, she was thankful for his protection. Still, it got tiring having her brother always admonishing *her*.

"Yeah? Who else am I supposed to swear at? Marin never said anything about the number of people watching the inside."

"Did you ask?"

She considered hitting her brother, but it wouldn't matter. Likely, she couldn't hurt him, anyway. The big idiot would stand there and take it, too, which took all the fun out of the attack. It had been years since she'd been able to actually intimidate him with her size. These days, he just shrugged it off.

"I was more focused on finding out the details of the job." She touched the map in the pocket of her cloak. It had to be palace gems inside the house, didn't it? What else would make Marin offer so much?

"Don't the details involve who you might encounter?"

Tray said it calmly, but Sam felt the way he mocked her. *Kyza!* Had her brother gotten to the point where he didn't need her? She couldn't say the same, especially tonight. She needed him to observe. If something went sideways... Sam prayed nothing would, but if anything went wrong, having Tray watching her back gave her a little sense of peace that she would get help. There wasn't anyone else willing to help her.

"Regardless of what she might have said, it doesn't change the fact that there are three people inside."

"You sure? Marin wouldn't send you anywhere that you'd encounter that many people. And she told me there would only be one, and all we had to do was wait her out—"

"What do you mean she told you?"

Tray shrugged.

Sam jabbed him in the chest. He rubbed where she poked him but didn't even bother to take a step back and give her the satisfaction that she might have hurt him, if only even a little. "You talked to her about the job?"

Tray tried to look defiant. "Why wouldn't I talk to her about the job?"

"Tray—you know we're doing this to get *away* from people like Marin and Bastan."

"That's why *you* want to do this, but I don't think they're as bad as you'd like me to believe. Marin isn't, at least. I don't know Bastan the same way you do."

"Trust me, they're the same. And they only do something for you if they intend to use you. I'm through getting used, through with risking myself so that others can get rich."

"I don't think that's what Marin is after."

"No? Then why does she have me breaking into this house if not for wealth?"

He shrugged again. "She didn't share that with me, but I doubt it's for money. You've seen where she lives. There's nothing lavish about it, not like Bastan—"

She jabbed him in the chest again. "Nothing lavish? I haven't been inside Marin's home. Have you?"

Tray finally managed to look appropriately chastised. "She's invited me a few times," he admitted. "What was I supposed to do, considering all that she's done for me?"

Sam hated that they were having this conversation here, on the top of the roof, in view of the stupid highborn house toward the center of the city that Marin wanted her to break in to, but it was a conversation they'd needed to have. Tray didn't see anything wrong with the connection he'd made to Marin, not the same way that she did, but Sam had seen parts of the city in ways he hadn't—and maybe he couldn't.

"She's not done anything for *you*," Sam said softly.

"Anything that she might have done has been for herself. Never think for a minute that it was for you." She shook her head. "You've got to look deeper, Tray. There's *always* another agenda."

"What's your agenda?" he asked.

She wanted to smack him, but restrained herself. "My agenda is keeping you safe. That's no different from what it's always been. Why would I have an agenda when it came to you?"

"I don't think you have one with me," he said, "but you have one with Marin. You know she said she knew our mother. Why wouldn't she help us?"

Because no one ever *really* helped anyone else in their part of the city. It was all about keeping away from the highborns and their sections. If lowborns got too close to them, highborns found ways of making it painful for them. And those in Caster were the lowest of the lowborns.

There wasn't any way for her to move beyond this section, not without wealth. It was possible to buy your way into one of the nicer sections of the city, but it took far more money than Sam had saved. It was the reason she kept taking jobs.

The only other option was leaving the city altogether, but that meant trying to get beyond the swamp and then the mountains that bordered the city. There was no crossing the steam fields to the west. She could try heading by sea, but even that took money she didn't have. They were isolated here in Verdholm, separated from the rest of the world.

And she was trapped.

She didn't say any of that to Tray. He wouldn't have listened, anyway. There was a part of her that appreciated his simple belief that others would look out for him. In his case, that was true. Sam had always watched out for him. Maybe that was why he didn't understand. He'd never *had* to try to do it on his own; she'd always been there for him.

Sam sighed. "Let me just do this and get us our freedom from Marin and Bastan. Then we can get away from them and not worry about what they might do to us."

"Marin wouldn't hurt me, Sam. I'm sure—"

Sam raised her hand and he cut off. At least she could still end an argument between them, but this time, she didn't feel like she ended it in a way that left her feeling like she had the upper hand. When had that changed between them?

"I'm going to get the job done. In and out."

"Marin said this shouldn't be a problem for you," Tray told her.

Sam decided to let the first part of that statement roll off her. There was no use arguing with him about Marin anymore. It didn't get them anywhere, especially not standing on a rooftop overlooking the canals.

"Fine. That might be what she *claimed*, but I've gotten plenty used to ignoring most of what she says."

"She said—"

Sam jabbed him in the chest, silencing him. At least her two years on him could still overrule him. Probably not for much longer, but she'd take all the time she had left. "If she was wrong about the number of people in the house, what else do you think she's wrong about? What if what she's after is not even there?"

Sam didn't want to think of what would happen to them if Marin had been wrong about that. Marin had only given her a few days. If she failed, then the job would go to someone else. And she wouldn't have the freedom she wanted.

"What do you want to do then?"

Sam did *not* want to get caught. If they were caught sneaking into a highborn's house, the penalty would be a barred cell for her, but for Tray, it might be worse. Thieves weren't treated well in Verdholm. Women were treated better than the men—the stupid royals and all the imbeciles working with them seemed to think the men were responsible for corrupting the women—but she didn't care for the idea of the cell. No thief did, but then, there weren't many alternatives available for most. Why else would she have taken up thieving?

Well, Sam knew why *she* had taken it up. Maybe not the reason she'd started, but she continued thieving because she enjoyed it. And because she was good at it. And because there was a part of her that believed she would one day find a job that would get her free of Caster. Maybe not to one of the highborn sections of the city like this, but better than Caster.

The wind gusted again, and the curtain fluttered once more. This time, she saw no shadows on the other side. Once she sneaked in through that window, then it would be a matter of finding her way to the room at the top of the stairs... and to the prize.

If it *was* a gem, maybe she'd keep it for herself.

"Sam?"

"I'm thinking," she said.

"Don't hurt yourself."

She glared at Tray. Sometimes, he could be obnoxious. "I'm going in. You wait out here and—"

"You're kidding, right?"

"I'm not. I'm quieter than you, and I'm the one who knows what Marin is after. And if you're caught…" That was the reason she used him for protection, but not much else. If she got pinched, she'd end up in prison, and she trusted Tray would at least try to break her out.

"I know what happens if I get caught. I'm not letting you go in there by yourself."

"I'm not letting you risk your butt when it means you might die."

"Sam—"

She shook her head. "Tray, you *know* I'm better at this than you. Watch me from here, come in for me if you think I'm in danger, but let me get in there. Kyza! I could have been in and back out in the time you've spent arguing with me."

"I doubt that."

"Well, it wouldn't have taken *much* longer."

Shooting him another glare, she started down the side of the building without giving Tray a chance to argue. It wouldn't be the first time he'd gotten it into his head that he had to come after her, though she'd never needed it. She wouldn't put it past him to do it again, especially if he really thought she was in danger.

There wouldn't be any danger. This was an in and out

job, nothing more than that. It wouldn't take her long to find what Marin wanted.

Sam grabbed the canal staff she'd leaned against the side of the building. There had been no sense carrying it up to the rooftop with her, it'd only make noise.

The staff was about an arm's length longer than she was tall and made of flexible ewe wood. She dipped it into the canal, pushing it as far as she could to the other side, before bending it toward her. This was the other reason Tray couldn't come with her; he was just too heavy to leap the canals. When they were younger, and he was lighter, he had followed her, but it had been a few years since he'd managed to chase her through the canals.

Once comfortable she had the staff fixed in the bottom of the canal, she jumped.

There was a skill to canal jumping. When she was young, her mother had taught it to them as a sport, one of the few memories she had of her mother. Most were difficult to recall. Sam often wondered what their mother would say if she learned how Sam now used that skill.

She sailed over the canal. The air was cooler over the water, though she wondered how many ever recognized that. It wasn't anything she ever thought much about, other than when she soared over the canal. It wasn't terribly wide—maybe fifteen feet, allowing two barges to pass each other—but wide enough that to cross, you either had to leap the canals like she did, or you trekked until you found a suitable bridge. In this part of the city, the bridges were few and far between, and gated at each end to prevent unsavory types from getting in. Those like her.

Like most of the buildings along the canals, the house was set only a few paces back from the water. She ducked low as she pulled the staff from the water and rested it in front of the house. On this side of the canal, there wasn't much risk of anyone else finding it, and if they did, they'd likely think it was nothing more than a push stick for one of the barges. It wasn't stiff enough for that, and not quite long enough, either. Close enough that it would pass for it, which was all she needed.

Sam crept along the front of the home, the brick catching her deep gray cloak. The cloak as much as anything else she wore labeled her a thief, but she wasn't about to risk entry without the concealment. Besides, a cloak like this was expensive, the fabric enhanced so it let light slip past it, hiding her, some magical cloth from a place Sam would never visit.

When she got to the open window, Sam ducked back down, surveying the water and the line of buildings on the other side of the canal. She saw Tray outlined on the roof, but nothing else. A barge moved in the distance but was heading away from her. It would pose no danger.

Sam flipped herself over the windowsill and into the empty room she'd spied from the other side of the canal.

She remained behind the curtain, wrapping both it and her cloak around her, keeping hidden as she took stock of what she detected around her. The years she'd spent prowling the streets had given her almost a preternatural sense, one where she noted sounds and smells and sometimes even the slightest shifting movements, and was able to react. It didn't always work, but when it did, those reflexes kept Sam safe.

They had also taught her how to achieve almost total silence. She'd learned a way of walking that was practically silent. In some ways, it was more a state of being, a way of knowing silence, of embracing it. When she was younger, it had been mostly the way she walked, but as she'd grown older, she'd discovered silence in other ways. Control your breathing. Steady your nerves so your heart doesn't beat too wildly, soften your steps so your joints don't creak. It came naturally to her in ways it didn't for her brother.

There was nothing that seemed out of place. That in itself made her a little nervous.

Hiding here didn't get the job done, and it didn't get Tray off the roof any faster. Her brother might be many things, but she worried he'd come barging in after her if she took too long. He'd have to cross the canal, but she wouldn't put it past him to figure out a way to get over here.

She peered out from behind the curtain to inspect the room carefully. She'd already determined that no one moved here, but what if she had misread the situation. At least by the window, she could hop back out and be across the canal faster than most could chase her.

Her eyes adjusted to the light of three lanterns in the room. It seemed cozy, with two plush sofas, each long enough to seat three people, on either side of a table in the middle of the room that had two glasses resting on it, the remnants of the others she'd seen here through the curtain. One of the glasses had a smear of red around the rim.

Sam grinned to herself. She'd never be caught dead

smearing that paste on her lips like so many of the high-born women were wont to do.

At the door, she paused once more, listening. Here, she watched the floor for any shadows that would indicate movement on the other side of the door. If anything moved, she'd head back and hide behind the curtain, or even leave the house altogether. The longer she was here, the less comfortable she felt with what Marin told her and the more she wanted to know what Marin had sent her here to get.

Sam pulled the sketch of the floorplan from her pocket and unfolded it. She saw the room she was in, and saw where Marin had marked where she *should* find the item, but that meant going down a short hall until she reached a stairway. From there, she needed to go up two flights to the upper level where there was apparently one massive room. That much she believed. Only these rich highborn types would waste space like that.

She stuffed the map back into her pocket.

Taking a deep breath, Sam pulled the door open a crack. The hall on the other side was a little longer than it appeared on the map, but a wide stairway stretched up at the end of it just as shown on the map.

Sam crept forward, keeping her cloak wrapped around her, ready to turn and run at the first sign of a problem. It was times like these when she wished she had a weapon of some sort, but weapons—if caught—posed more problems than she was willing to risk. It was better to run, and pray that she wasn't caught, than to risk having something with her that would result in her being imprisoned for longer.

At the stairs, she paused, listening. Was there a scraping above her?

No. Nothing was there other than the soft creaking of the building, almost as if it settled. Many of these older homes along the canal *did* settle, and they often had a strange groaning sound to them, as if they were alive.

She took the stairs two at a time, her feet padding across the wood, barely making any sound. That was one benefit to her size.

When she'd gone up two flights, she found the door indicated on the map.

Testing the handle, she found it locked. Strange. Why would they leave it locked in a place like this? Anyone who got to this point in the house would normally have to be invited in. The only person not invited in would be those like her.

Bypassing locks was one of the first skills she'd mastered when she'd taken to running the canals. There were plenty of doors where she had to get past, often times needing to use this skill so that she didn't get caught, so she didn't think this door would pose any real challenges to her.

Sam pulled a slender rod from her pocket and slipped it into the lock. This was actually one of her favorite parts of sneaking around the way she did. There was a certain satisfaction to pressing on the barriers meant to keep her out, and finding the right way to put *just* the needed amount of pressure on the lock so that she could feel the lock *click*. And then she would be in.

This lock proved a little more challenging than most. There seemed to be a few different tumblers, and she had to contort the rod in such a way that she could hold the others in place while triggering them. Sam counted as she did. Could there really be ten tumblers?

When the last fell into place, the lock popped open, and Sam pumped her fist. Tray wouldn't believe her, and she wished there was some way to bring the lock with her to prove what she'd done. He wouldn't be able to get past a lock that complicated! Not yet, at least. Then again, he might never work to become skilled at locks, preferring brute force as a way in.

Whatever was on this side would have to be *incredibly* valuable.

Maybe there really *were* gems. If she found other items of value here, she would have no choice but to take them, right? She'd give Marin whatever it was she was supposed to deliver, but the others could be for her. Selling them might be a little tricky, especially since Bastan controlled the smugglers able to get gems and other valuables out of the city, but she'd find a way.

When she pushed the door open, she found... nothing.

That wasn't true. In the massive room, there were rows of shelves, and books stacked along them, almost like this was some sort of highborn library. One table in the middle of the room had blank sheets of paper. The texture to them told her that they were well made, and likely valuable, but there wasn't a market for anything like that.

Sam scanned the shelves. Where were the valuables? Why had Marin sent her here?

This... this wasn't anything like what she'd been hoping to find.

As she looked at the shelves, she wondered if maybe there was a hidden room of some kind. These highborns often had rooms like that, and if she could only find it, then she'd surely find what Marin believed was here.

Other than a narrow door along the wall that the map showed led to the roof, there was nothing. The size of the room matched what showed on the map. There was no indication there might be some hidden area they'd walled off.

A library?

What in Kyza's name had Marin been thinking?

The table in the middle of the room. Wasn't that what Marin had said? There was only paper on it.

This had to be some sort of joke.

Well, she could play a joke too.

Grabbing a pen that lay next to the blank pages, she dipped it in the inkwell. She wrote in a flowing script on the top page, spelling out Marin's name in full.

As she wrote, the ink faded, then disappeared completely.

Sam studied the pen. Had the ink been watered down?

She tried again, dipping the pen into the ink. This time, she pulled it out and studied it, staring at the deep black color. She tapped it on the back of her hand, and the ink didn't fade at all, leaving a smudge that remained, and grew larger.

Sam wrote out Marin's name on the page. Like before, the ink faded quickly, then disappeared, leaving nothing behind, no evidence that she'd been there.

As she stared at it, she heard the sound of footsteps below, the steady thumping of boots on stairs.

Kyza!

She'd taken too long.

She hurried to the door and shut it, twisting the lock into place. Now she had to find a place to hide, or get out. She found neither.

A key slipped into the lock.

Kyza!

Sam scanned the room again, and her gaze fell on the narrow door in the far wall. She didn't have much choice.

She raced toward it, deciding to grab a few pages of the paper along the way. She stuffed them into her pocket, then hurried to the door. This one was locked from this side. She thumbed open the lock and stepped through the door just as the door into the library opened across the room.

Leaning on the door, she breathed out, studying this side.

Another stairway, this one leading up.

Sam heard voices on the other side of the door. They seemed to be coming closer.

Swearing under her breath, she climbed the stairs as quietly as possible. If she was caught, she'd blame Marin. It was possible this was some sort of plan she'd had all along. First, the difficulty reaching the stupid house, and finding nothing of value—at all—inside the room she'd sent her to. Now she'd get caught! All these years spent thieving throughout the city only to get caught in the library of some highborn house. At least she could get caught with something interesting.

Her mind started working through the different penalties she might face. Entering a highborn home was bad enough. That might get her a few months in the cells. Then there was the map she had on her. That might add a few more. Taking the pages—even though they were blank—meant that she'd stolen from one of the highborns. That would add a few years. Enough time that she'd not see Tray until he was old enough to have gotten married. Enough time for her to worry that he'd do something stupid and try to break her out.

There was another door at the top of the stairs.

At the sound of the door at the bottom of the stairs opening, she pushed this one open.

As she suspected, it let out onto the roof.

Sam stood in place a moment, transfixed.

The moon shone brightly in the cloudless sky. Sam closed the door, pushing it as silently as she could. She hurried to the edge of the roof. From here, she *might* be able to climb down, depending on how smooth the side of the home was. She hadn't thought to scope that out, but she'd scaled plenty of walls in her time.

The door opened behind her, and she threw herself over the edge.

Sam clung with her fingers holding on to nothing more than the lip of brick.

She wouldn't be able to stay here for long, but she wouldn't need to.

She hugged the wall and looked over her shoulder, searching for Tray. He should be there, still standing guard for her, ready to race over and help. If she made it down, she might even take his help.

He wasn't there.

For a moment, she wondered if maybe the person

who'd come up the stairs might have been Tray, but then she heard voices.

"There's no one here." It was a deep voice with a strange accent.

"You heard the warning the same as I did."

The first person sighed. "That's all it was. A warning. You knew the risk with this assignment."

"They shouldn't have found us so soon. Or so easily."

"They shouldn't be in the city," the first man said softly.

"We shouldn't have taken it from them so openly. We've had a decade of calm."

"With this, we can finally be rid of them. So much was risked for this."

"Out of necessity."

Sam felt her arms burning, but her curiosity was piqued. What were they talking about?

"There was someone on a nearby roof."

"One of *them*?"

"No, but possibly a sympathizer. It wouldn't be the first time they've been sent to the city."

"Then we find out what he was after."

"If he talks."

"If he talks," the other agreed. "Though there are ways of coaxing even the most reluctant into talking."

Sam's heart hammered so loudly, she thought they might hear it.

If what she'd heard was correct, Tray had been caught.

Her fingers started slipping, and she dug in with her toes, trying to grip the side of the building. Even they started to slip. If she didn't find a safe way down, she wouldn't have to worry about the noise. She'd need to worry more about dying.

As the grip in her fingers gave out, she thought of something she could try.

Sam kicked off the side of the building. If she could get enough of an arc, she *might* be able to reach the water. If she did, it wouldn't be pleasant. This high up, the impact on the water would *hurt*. And she had to hope the canal was deep enough to keep her from hitting bottom, possibly injuring her further.

She hit the water with a loud splash.

There wasn't anything she could do to prevent that.

The water enveloped her, and she sank. She tucked her knees into her chest, but still crashed into the bottom of the canal. When she did, the impact pushed all the air out of her lungs.

Kyza.

She couldn't pop up here. They'd see her. And if they'd grabbed Tray already, she had to worry about what might happen if she appeared from the water. Sam was a decent swimmer, but she preferred jumping across the canals, especially given what swam in here.

That thought got her moving.

She pushed off the bottom of the canal and swam as long as she could below the surface. When she couldn't hold her breath any more, she surfaced, taking only enough time to fill her lungs, and then she dived again.

This time, she was able to control the swim better. She flipped her legs and tried not to think about the things swimming along next to her in the water. There were some of the canal carp, and some bass, as well as other fish that weren't harmful, but there were the larger creatures, those that lurked along the bottom of the canal, like the eels. Kyza knew they were rumored to jump out of the water and grab people walking along the edge of the canals before carrying them back below the surface. That wasn't how she wanted to go out.

When she thought she'd swum long enough—and far enough—she popped her head back out of the water. She'd been staying close to the edge, and was about to crawl up the side, but as she began to reach up, she heard voices.

Sam dipped her head below the surface of the water.

She held her breath as long as she could, trying to maintain her position. She didn't want to drift too far down the canal. If she wasn't careful, she could end up in some section of the city she might not know. She needed to escape the canal and see if there was anything she could do to help Tray. Maybe he was fine and the men she'd overheard *hadn't* done anything to him, but if they *had*, she would find out, and she would do whatever it took to get him free.

With lungs burning, she poked her head up for some air. A barge moved in the distance, slowly coming toward her. It wouldn't do for one of the barge captains to find someone swimming in the canal. That might draw as much attention to her as anything else that she'd done. Besides, the stupid captains talked, and they'd find out what happened soon enough. She either needed to get herself out of the water—which she *wanted* to do before one of the eels started getting a sense of her—or hold her position beneath the surface until the barge had passed. She didn't like the prospect of staying in the water.

Sam grabbed one of the stones that formed the walls of the canal. Before pulling herself from the water, she looked up and down the row of buildings situated here. She didn't see anything that moved. At this time of night, there shouldn't *be* anyone else out. If they were, they'd likely be working some nefarious job, just like she was doing.

Something touched her foot.

Sam fought the urge to kick. If it *was* one of the eels, kicking would only draw its attention more. No… it was better to remain calm, but that was hard to do when something as big as her torso might be near enough to clamp on to her. She could all too easily imagine that double row of sharp teeth catching her leg and clamping down…

Sam swung herself over the edge of the canal, witnesses be damned.

The water where she'd been swimming splashed slightly, just enough for her to believe there was something there, and then settled. Sam prepared to jump and run, anything to get away from the edge of the canal, but the water stopped moving.

Her breathing began to slow.

That had been close.

Too close.

Damn Marin and this assignment. There hadn't been anything in the damn highborn house, certainly nothing of value like she'd been led to believe. Finding nothing, she had wasted her whole night, risked capture, and ended up taking a swim in the canal. She *hated* swimming. Not as much as Tray, but then, she hadn't nearly drowned the same way he had.

Had Marin sent her to get caught? That seemed unlikely, but what other reason was there for sending her into the highborn house?

Sam started along the row of buildings, drawing her cloak around her for concealment within the shadows. Now that she was wet, it wouldn't work quite as well, especially not with the water dripping down the sides and leaving a wet trail behind her, but she needed the warmth as much as she needed the cover from the night.

When she reached a side street, and one of the bridges leading over the canal, she ran across and raced along the street until she neared where she'd left Tray. The building here was taller than she remembered, and without the canal staff, which she'd left across the canal, she'd have to work a lot harder to get up, but years of climbing had giving her a good grip and strong enough muscles to make the climb. When she reached the top of the roof, it was empty.

Could he really have been pinched?

Sam didn't like to think of the possibility. It would be her fault if he had. Her brother wouldn't have been here if not for her.

Crouching on the roof, she stared across the canal, watching for movement inside the home. There was nothing. Even the lantern light that she'd seen before was extinguished.

What was going on here?

She was tempted to go back for her staff, but that

risked her getting caught too. Better to come back in the daylight, when she wouldn't be quite as conspicuous. Then she'd only have to deal with the strange glances from others as she carried it along the street. A good thing it came apart, making the two halves easier to conceal.

Sam studied the home again, watching for any sign of movement. There was none.

Kyza. She'd failed Marin, and Tray had been caught. Sam didn't know which of those would end up being worse for her.

3

THE MASTER THIEF

The back room of the Sornum was too nice for the rest of the tavern. Oiled paneling created a nice separation, and a few paintings hung on the walls, each worth probably as much as the tavern itself, though long ago stolen from some highborn. Bastan kept them well-maintained, and even employed a man to make certain the soot and smoke from the rest of the tavern didn't contaminate the paint. Now he perched in his ornately carved chair, gilded with streaks of gold across the top of the back making it appear like some sort of poor man's throne, staring at a painting Sam had never seen before propped against the wall.

Maybe it was one he'd painted himself. He had a talent for forgery, and though he'd never painted originals before, she wouldn't put it past him to do so.

"Where's your brother?" he asked without pulling his gaze off the painting.

She'd given up wondering how he always knew. He'd

always been able to tell when she came and went, even without looking. That talent was what had made him such a skilled thief in his time.

"That's why I'm here."

He turned away from the painting and looked right at her. Bastan had strangely pale eyes, almost a faint purple, and a sharp chin that always made him seem angry. Black hair had begun showing hints of gray over the last few years. Sam liked to think she caused that.

"Your brother isn't here, Sam."

She tamped down the fluttering in her chest. She'd known it wasn't likely that he'd come here. If anything, he would have gone to Marin, but she knew he hadn't done that, either. That was the first place she'd checked. The stupid woman had the good fortune of not being at home. Otherwise, Sam might have hit her. Marin *liked* Tray so why would she risk an assignment—and a useless one at that—that would get them caught?

"I didn't think he was." She managed to keep her voice steady. What she asked next would be harder. "I think he got caught. I need help getting him free."

Bastan tapped his first finger on that sharp chin of his, his brow knitting as he did. "No."

"No? How many of these paintings have we gotten for you, Bastan?" There were other things she'd gotten for him, but the paintings were what he valued the most. "I need my brother. Without him, I—"

"Will do just fine. You're skilled enough that you don't need him. I half believe you'd do better without him. There are times you refuse my suggestions because you're afraid he can't reach the same places as you. That wastes your talent, Sam."

"It doesn't *waste* anything. My brother keeps an eye out for me. He's the only one who looks out for me."

"I look out for you."

"You look out for yourself."

Bastan shrugged. "That's mostly true, but seeing as you manage to bring me such lovely things, looking out for you has the same effect as looking out for myself. So, you see, I *do* care."

"Then you'll help me find my brother."

"If he was caught, then you'll have to check the cells. You know the punishment thieves face... especially men. Highborns are stupid enough to think that kind of punishment will keep the city safe." He shook his head and looked back toward his painting.

"Outside the city is dangerous."

He flickered his gaze to her. "It is, but inside can be dangerous, too. Why begrudge a man the ability to protect himself, especially with people coming from all over for the protection of the city?"

She wasn't about to argue with Bastan, and she didn't need to remind him that her brother wasn't a man. He was younger than she was, and she barely claimed herself a woman. That made Tray a boy in her mind. A boy who was her responsibility, regardless of how he might see his responsibility to her.

"He wasn't thieving. Only watching."

"Then he should not have been captured."

Sam hadn't considered it that way. Why *had* he been captured, other than because he was sitting on a rooftop.

It's not like there are many legitimate reasons he would have been there. It's not like standing watch was anything subtle.

"Well, he was."

Bastan tapped his chin again. "It's possible they only want him for questioning. If that's the case, they will release him soon enough. You have to be patient."

"I have to keep him from getting killed."

"You said he wasn't thieving."

"When have you known the highborns to care? All they care about is their sections of the city and keeping us out."

"If they begin to act without evidence, and they fail to follow the law they established themselves, there's a risk of a different kind of upheaval. They will follow their law, Sam."

She wished she could be as confident as Bastan, but she'd seen too much badness happen to those she'd worked with over the years. The highborns didn't care about those in these poor sections of the city. Places like Caster weren't important enough to them. "If they don't let him out, I'm getting him free. I'll need your help."

Bastan met her eyes. "No."

"Stop saying that!"

"I can't get involved if your brother is questioned. I can't draw attention to myself and have the highborns discover me."

"They already know about you. They just can't pin anything on you."

"Which is how it will stay."

"What about these?" she said, sweeping her arm

around the paneled room. "If one of the highborns finds this place, and sees all the paintings you have here, what are they going to think?"

"Why would they think anything? Why would they even *be* here?" He leaned forward with the questions, menace dripping from his words. "They would have no reason to even come to the Sornum, and even less to find their way back here. If they did, I would do everything in my considerable power to discover who led them to me."

Sam threw up her hands. "Fine. I'll get him free myself. You have to deal with Marin and her terrible intel then."

"What's that supposed to mean?"

"She's given me bad information more than once. Tonight was the last straw. If I didn't have to find Tray, I'd be chasing her down. Maybe I'd feed her to the eels."

Bastan offered a hint of a smile. "The eels are nothing but a myth."

"Yeah? What grabs people off the streets then?"

"Me."

Sam swallowed, averting her gaze so that she didn't have to look into his strange, pale purple eyes. He wasn't the strangest type of person living in the outer sections of Caster, but he was one of them. "Anyway, you let her know that I'm coming after her."

"What did she claim you'd find?"

Sam twisted her hands together. Admitting why she'd gone into the highborn house would be dangerous, especially as she'd been working on something Bastan hadn't approved, which meant moving it with another fence, but he had to know he wasn't the *only* one in the city who used her services.

"I don't know. She didn't tell me what it was."

Bastan's laughter cut her off. "You didn't ask what she was after?"

"That's not how it works, and you know it!"

"If you accepted the job, you should know *all* the terms. Haven't I taught you anything, Sam?"

She glared at him, but Bastan seemed nonplussed. She hated that about him.

"Going in without knowing the objective is a mistake. With a mistake like that, maybe *you* deserved to get caught."

"I almost did," she said. "I had to jump in the canal to get away."

Bastan's smile made the memory of what she'd gone through all that much worse. "See? No eels."

"There was something in the water."

Bastan shrugged. "We both know there are fish in the canals. Kyza knows I serve them in the Sornum. If you found anything, that was likely what it was."

She wrinkled her nose. The fish in the canals were disgusting. How could Bastan serve them? She *thought* he served fish caught out in Ralan Bay. Besides, whatever had brushed up against her leg hadn't been a fish.

"What *did* you find?"

Sam pulled the pages from her pocket. She'd worried about how they'd dry, and whether the swim through the canal would leave them useless, but when she'd laid them flat, they had dried nicely, looking no different from when she'd first grabbed them.

"I found these. There were more, but this was all I grabbed."

"You lost Tray for *paper*?"

Sam wanted to throw him in the canal and see how he liked the sense of eels swimming alongside him. "They aren't anything of value, so I don't know what Marin was after. The paper is weird, though. I tried writing on it, but the ink didn't stick."

Bastan laughed. "Why would you try writing on it if you were going to steal it?"

She gave a sly smile and admitted, "I was going to leave Marin a little treat."

Bastan shook his head. "You should be careful about the kind of enemies you're willing to make, Sam. Some are more powerful than you realize."

"Marin?"

He cocked a brow and paused. "Even I have to admit there's something intriguing about that woman. Best not poke her too much, or she might be like one of those eels you're so afraid of."

"I'm not afraid of them. I went in the water, didn't I?"

"It sounded like you didn't have much choice in the matter. But yes, you went in the water."

He reached for the pages and Sam pulled them back.

"What are they worth to you?"

"It's paper, Sam. It's worth nothing until ink is placed upon it. Then it can still be worth nothing, or it could become incredibly valuable."

She clutched the pages tightly. "Give me a price."

Bastan laughed softly. "Let me have a look and I'll decide. Maybe I'll at least give you something to make your trouble worthwhile."

She doubted there was anything that would make

what she'd gone through just to get those pages worth-while, especially with her brother missing, but maybe she could get something out of it.

Bastan took the pages and set them on the table in front of him. He ran his hands across the edge, and she noted how the corners of his eyes softened slightly. She recognized the surprise there. She'd seen it from him before. Maybe he'd find the useless pages worthwhile, and maybe he'd even pay her enough that she could bribe her way into the cells to get information about her brother.

Bastan dipped a pen in a jar of black ink and wrote in a neat hand along the bottom corner of one of the pages. At first, his writing looked like it would remain, that the tight way he wrote his name would remain, but then the ink faded much like it had when she'd tried implicating Marin, fading into nothing.

"Interesting," he said.

He ran his hand along the page again, this time using only the tips of his fingers, as if to feel for some imperfections in the page. When he was satisfied, he dipped the pen into the ink bottle again, and started writing, this time with more force than before, and pressing along the bottom edge of the page. As before, the ink took hold for a moment, long enough for her to note that he wrote in a language she didn't recognize, and then the ink faded again. This time, more slowly before disappearing.

Bastan reached beneath his table and pulled out a tray of ink. A dozen bottles were on the tray, each in different colors. Some appeared like they were only slightly different shades of the same color. He took a maroon ink and tapped his quill into it, letting it sit.

"Where did you say you came across these pages?" he asked without looking up.

"The highborn house where Marin sent me. There was supposed to be something valuable on the top floor, but there was this huge study, a library of sorts, full of books and a stack of these pages on the table. I grabbed these before the men came up the stairs."

"Hmm." He scrawled with the maroon ink, writing again in a different language, and this time, the ink stayed. It remained visible for longer than the black ink, but then it disappeared, as well, leaving the page looking as if he'd never done anything to it. "Fascinating. Do you think it would do the same with paint?"

"I don't know. I didn't exactly experiment on it. I grabbed it when I couldn't find anything else. I didn't think there was anything special about it."

That wasn't completely true. She knew that the ink hadn't stuck to it, but thought that might only have been because of the ink the highborns had in their house. Some ink had to work. Otherwise, what was the point of having paper like this?

Bastan stood and went to a cabinet in the corner of the room. Inside, he grabbed a different tray and brought it over to his table, setting it down. On the tray was a brush, and Sam realized that he had a variety of paints on the tray.

"Let's try blue first," he said, though it was mostly to himself.

Bastan dipped the brush into the paint and scrawled a few words across the page. The thick paint clung to the paper, and his words seemed to practically protrude from the page. Sam shook her head, chuckling softly.

"Guess you're painting something new," she said to him.

The paint started to congeal and thicken. Bastan tapped his chin with the end of the brush and then pulled out a piece of paper from a drawer in the table and touched the brush to it. The paint spread across the page, performing differently than it had on the paper she'd stolen.

Bastan focused on the stolen paper with the thick lettering. The paint seemed to avoid sticking to the paper, almost as if it could be shaken off. He dipped his finger into the paint, and with a quick flick of his wrist, Bastan wiped his hand across the page.

"What are you doing—"

The paint failed to stick to the paper, instead smearing onto his hand.

Bastan brought his hand to his face and stared at it. "I wondered if the paint had gotten too thick, but that's not the case now." He continued staring at his hand, eyeing the paint that now stained it, as if it would change. Sam wasn't entirely certain how to interpret the look on his face. Finally, he tore his eyes away from his hand and gazed at her. "You've done well, Sam. This paper is quite unique."

Sam started laughing. Leave it to Bastan to find something as stupid as this paper valuable. "I think you mean useless."

He frowned. "Perhaps it will eventually prove to be, but I can think of some uses for paper like this."

"If ink doesn't stick to it—"

"Then we cannot be caught sending messages. When I discover the secret to this paper, then we have a safe way to send word to others we work with."

"What makes you think there's some trick to it?"

He pressed his hands on the table and fixed her with a wilting glare. Sam ignored it. She'd seen Bastan try to intimidate her often enough that she knew better than to pay it much attention. Maybe it had worked on her once... Fine, it *had* worked on her once upon a time, but now, she knew to ignore him.

"The highborns had this for a reason, Sam. Don't you think they have worked out how to use it?"

Sam grudgingly agreed that made a certain sort of sense. Not that she'd ever tell him that. "Good luck figuring that out, Bastan."

He leaned forward, and this time, she actually took a step back. "You're going to help me with this, Sam. I need you to go back to the highborn house and... Why are you laughing?"

Sam was shaking her head. "You won't help me with Tray, yet you want me to help you?"

"You haven't heard what I am willing to pay."

"I don't think the pay matters. I'm not going after anything for you until I get Tray out of the cells."

Bastan sat down in his chair and crossed his arms over his chest. He studied her, a bemused expression on his face. "That's your price?"

She had started to turn, ready to leave, when she paused and turned back to him. "What?"

"The price. I want to know the secret the highborns

have that lets them use this paper. I could send someone else, but I suspect you won't tell me which house you found this in, and even if you did, you probably wouldn't share with me where in the house you discovered it. So, I think you have to be the one to do this. Tell me, Sam, is that your price?"

"I thought you said you don't want to get involved when it comes to the highborns. Isn't that what you said? That you don't want them to know about you, so you won't help?"

The corner of his mouth twitched. "That is what I said."

"Then why are you willing to get involved now?"

"I told you the reason."

"No. You told me what you want me to believe is the reason, but you could just as soon ask Marin which house it was. You don't *need* me to discover that. What you're after is something else. And if you're not going to tell me, then I'll just go after Tray myself. It might be better if it was me, anyway. I wouldn't want you to risk any highborns learning about you. Besides, you said they were likely only taking him in for questioning."

"That is what I said. But it's possible they have other reasons, especially if there's something more about this paper than either of us realizes."

There *was* that conversation that she'd overheard, but she didn't know anything about what it meant. The only thing she knew was that she had broken into a highborn house and come out with paper, losing Tray in the process. She had to get to him, somehow, and the only person who *might* be able to get her access was Bastan.

"Fine. Tell me what you intend to do, and I'll decide if it's a worthwhile price."

Bastan laughed softly. "You're a challenging woman, Sam. Has anyone ever told you that?"

She shrugged. "I might have heard something similar from others. Seeing as how we both want something here, I need to make certain it's the right price for me."

Bastan looked as if he didn't want to answer, but then he leaned his elbows on his table, fixing her with that pale-eyed stare that he had. "I have an asset in the prison."

"An asset? What's that supposed to mean?"

"It means what I said. I have an asset. I will find out what the highborns intend with your brother, and then we can make a decision."

"You should do that, regardless! Why wouldn't you use this asset even if I didn't risk myself going back into this highborn house? After everything we've done to help you over the years—"

"You."

"What?"

"*You* have helped, Sam, not your brother. I have no special place in my heart for him, so it matters little to me whether the highborns decide to punish him."

"You say punish as if it doesn't mean execute."

He waved a dismissive hand. "I doubt it means execute. As I've said, they will follow their laws—"

"Why won't you help him?"

"Using my asset is risky, not only for me. I do this, and I use up my favor with him."

Sam tapped her toe. "That's not good enough. I don't

only want to know what they intend with him. I want to make certain that he'll be safe."

"That… will be difficult."

"That's my price."

Sam thought Bastan would refuse. After all, this was only *paper* they were talking about, not any of the usual things he'd hire her for. Why would he risk himself for paper?

There had to be more to it than she realized, but what was it? What reason would Bastan have for wanting the paper? Unless it really was all about finding a way to send messages secretly.

It *had* to be more than that.

And it *was*.

It dawned on her that Bastan didn't only want to find some way to send messages, he wanted a way to read what the highborns sent. That had to be the reason he wanted her to do this. Maybe that was what she'd overheard those men talking about.

"I'll do everything in my power to see him to safety if you find the secret to the way the highborns use the pages. Is that a deal?"

Sam thought about returning to the highborn house. The first time, she'd been lucky to escape. Returning for another time only asked for trouble, and she *should* be smart enough to avoid that, but if that was what it took for her to get Bastan's help, what choice did she have?

Besides, now that she'd been there, it wasn't going to be nearly as difficult getting in the second time. She knew the layout, and she knew she could survive the jump into the canal, even though she had no desire to repeat it.

"It's a deal," she said.

Bastan reached across the table and shook her hand. She could tell he tried to keep his face neutral, but she thought she noted a hint of a satisfied smile, and worried that she'd ended up on the wrong end of the bargain with him. With Bastan, you never really ended up on the *right* side of a deal.

4

A SECOND CHANCE

T he outside of the house appeared no different than it had the other night, but Sam's heart raced more than it had then. Before, at least she'd had Tray waiting, and there was a certain sort of comfort in knowing he was out there. Without him, she wasn't in any more danger than she would be otherwise, but it *felt* better knowing he was there, and knowing he would be waiting for her, even if he never did anything that helped.

She could see her canal staff still resting against the front of the building. Sam had been surprised to see that no one had taken it. She couldn't tell if it had been moved, which made her even more nervous. If they knew about her brother, and they knew she'd been there, wouldn't they have searched around the home?

They likely had, which made her wonder if the staff had been left as a way to draw her back out. It was a good thing she didn't have any intention of going back in the way she had the first time.

Instead, she crouched on a rooftop—a different one than she and Tray had sat on before he'd been snagged— and held the smooth handle of a crossbow. The bolt she had nocked had nearly two hundred feet of tightly woven Valun rope attached to the end, strong enough to hold both her *and* Tray were he here. Getting Valun rope might be about the only good thing Marin had done for her. As isolated as the city was, getting *anything* from the outside world was valuable.

Had Tray not gone missing, she wouldn't have risked the crossbow and the rope. The highborns would view this as a weapon, but she needed a quick way of getting across the canal without her staff.

Sam took careful aim at the roof of the house she wanted to target. She'd get one good shot here. If she missed, she'd not only lose her Valun rope, but she'd lose the easiest way into the house. While she might be a good shot, the addition of the rope would present a different challenge.

She'd have to aim high. With the rope attached, the bolt would come down faster than it would otherwise. Too high, and she'd soar over the house. She didn't want to hit anything on the other side, even if the rope was long enough to reach.

With one end looped around her ankle, she fired the crossbow.

The bolt soared across the canal. Rather than going too high—even though she'd aimed much higher than she thought she would need to—the bolt dropped. It sank into the side of the building, but probably about ten feet below the roofline.

Kyza!

She could cross, but reaching the roof would be difficult.

Of course she'd have to make it harder on herself. Sam secured the rope to a metal post on the roof, wrapping it tightly enough that it would hold her, but not so tightly that she couldn't unwind it from the other side with a sharp jerk on the line. If it worked, she wouldn't lose the rope. She'd lost enough lately.

Sam took a deep breath, wrapped her cloak around herself, and started across the rope going hand over hand. As she hung over the middle of the canal, the distant form of one of the barges moving toward her spurred her to move faster. It was a dark night, without much moonlight, and thick clouds prevented what light there was from peeking out for long, but she still didn't want to get caught on a rope above the canal.

Hurrying forward, she moved steadily, not wanting to jostle the embedded bolt free. A light flickered in one of the windows of the highborn house, and Sam froze. Her hands twitched, and she could feel her grip begin to slip.

She started forward again, but moved too suddenly. The rope slipped from the other side, and she swung down, toward the canal.

Kyza!

Sam braced herself for impact. It didn't hurt quite as much as she expected when she hit the wall. She bit back the grunt as she struck, hoping they hadn't heard anything inside. If someone came out and looked to see what had struck the side of the building, there wasn't anywhere she could go to hide.

When satisfied no one was coming out after her, she climbed up the rope. Her hand reached the crossbow bolt. She couldn't go any higher here, not without trying... something.

There weren't many times when she considered it a good thing she was so short and light, but this was one. She pulled herself up and hung from the crossbow bolt. Climbing carefully, she got her knees onto the thick bolt, and then—as carefully as she could—stood on it, balanced on the bolt.

Sam pulled the rope free from the bolt and wound it around her arm. Then she started up the face of the building, gripping tightly to the brick.

She moved slowly now, holding carefully, fearful she'd fall. If she fell from here, she doubted she'd have a chance to make it into the canal, and would likely end up dropping to the hard ground below. She was high enough that she wasn't sure she'd escape without injury.

Her fingers ached, burning with the effort.

A little higher. She could see the lip of the roof. All she had to do was let go with one hand and reach for it, but if she mistimed the reach, she'd fall. It could be worse. She *could* end up in the canal with one of those eels again. She didn't care what anyone else told her—they *were* big enough to eat a man.

Sam released her grip with one hand and reached for the lip of roof.

Her fingers scrambled for the edge, grabbing it, and then slipped off.

She started to fall.

As she did, she flailed her arms, almost as if she

intended to fly. By chance, her cloak hooked on the crossbow bolt sticking out from the side of the building. It jerked, and she stopped falling. Sam held her breath, expecting her robe to rip and to fall the rest of the way, but the stout wood held, as did the unusual fabric.

She let out a shaky breath.

Maybe all that swearing at Kyza hadn't made the gods turn a blind eye on her. Most of the time, she *wanted* them to turn away from what she did. Better that than have the gods know what she did, the way she snuck in and stole. This time, she was happy enough to take a little extra observation from the gods, especially if it kept her from falling.

She unhooked the crossbow from her belt and secured the rope to the end of another bolt. This one wasn't quite as stout as the one she'd used to make the crossing in the first place. That one had been designed for things like this, whereas this one was only meant to go inside of someone, usually in some sort of messy way.

Sam took careful aim and loosed the bolt. Even from this close of a distance, it dropped more than she would have expected, sinking into the stone about a foot below the top. At least that was a distance she could reach by climbing.

Tugging on the rope to make certain it was secure enough for her to climb, she started up once she was satisfied she wasn't going to fall. She couldn't count on her cloak catching her again.

Sam was tired by the time she reached the roof.

When she pulled herself over the edge, she reached over and untied the rope, wrapping it around in a careful bundle in case she had to run away quickly. Better to be prepared now. When she pulled back over the edge, she noticed the door to the roof was open.

Kyza!

She should have been more careful. If she made it all the way here, only to get caught before she could even attempt to sneak in? There wouldn't be another chance at this. Getting broken into twice meant that they would increase their security. At least, she would have.

She should have looked to see if there was anyone up here before she pulled herself up onto the roof. Sam pulled the cloak around her. The fabric protected her if the shadows were just right. It didn't work in the middle of the day, but on a cloudy night like tonight, with barely any moonlight coming through the clouds, she *might* be able to hide within the cloak.

There wasn't anyone out here.

Sam remained hidden for a moment, letting the cloak billow around her as she stared at the door leading back into the highborn house. All she needed was to find the secret to how they used the pages. That was all Bastan asked of her. That couldn't be too hard, could it?

As she stepped through the open door and down the stairs, she tried to calm her mind, but found it difficult. If the highborns came across her, she would suffer more than jailing this time. Her punishment would be death. With Tray now missing, there wouldn't be anyone to come for her. Bastan might mourn, but he wouldn't feel all *that* bad about it. No... she couldn't let herself get caught here.

The wooden stair groaned softly as she took her first step, almost as if the house itself worked against her.

She eased her weight onto the step, careful to make sure the step tolerated her. There was no other sound. The next step was better, and she stayed to the outside, hoping they were better supported there. As she neared the bottom, she paused again.

The library door stood closed. It was a strange sort of room to have on the upper level where Marin had promised a different kind of wealth. She wished she'd brought the map, but then she doubted Marin had given her anything more than the basics.

Come to think of it, how *had* Marin known about this place?

Who had she met with to get the information about the location of this supposed valuable item?

Would anyone be in the library at this time of night? She hoped the answers she sought were here. Maybe even in one of the books. That was what Sam counted on. She put her ear to the door to listen, but didn't hear anything, so she reached for the handle.

Locked from the inside, as it had been before.

She pulled out the pick set she carried with her and slowly worked on the lock, twisting it so the tumblers shifted. With a soft click, the lock opened.

Sam breathed out softly, remaining tensed where she was. The sound might be enough to draw attention to her. A minute passed. Another. No one came toward the door.

Feeling relaxed, she pushed open the door.

The room looked much like it had before.

She stepped in, pulling the door closed behind her, and

looked at the shelves lining the walls stuffed with books. She had never seen this many books in one place. Were all highborn homes like this? The few she'd risked sneaking into hadn't seemed the type to have a room such as this, but then she hadn't risked going into all of the rooms, so it was possible that others were just like this. Most of the jobs she took involved merchants rather than highborns, so she didn't break into homes like this all that often.

It was better for her that way. Less of a risk were she caught. Merchants would demand repayment, but there was rarely the risk of execution.

The table at the center of the room, where she'd first found the pages, now had a thick, leather-bound book resting open upon it.

Sam flipped the pages, and saw that they were blank. What a strange book.

As she studied it, she realized the pages were like the sheets she'd taken from the table the last time she'd come. But unlike those sheets, each of these pages bore a single mark in the corner. Sam leaned closer, trying to make it out.

Why would there be a book like this with all the pages unreadable? What purpose would it serve?

Did the other books here have similar pages?

Sam stared at the walls of books. What a strange idea.

She quickly flipped through the pages of the book again before returning it to the page it had been on. Now that she studied it, she noticed that this page was different. Rather than a single mark on the bottom corner, there was a second mark on the top corner.

Maybe that made it more valuable. Maybe there was

some secret written here that she couldn't yet read. She tore the page from the book and stuffed it into her boot before closing it again. At least she could study this page. Maybe she'd find the secret to writing on it that way.

On a whim, she stuffed the entire book into a pocket of her cloak.

The highborns already knew she'd broken into their house. What did it matter if she exposed herself even more?

When she reached the nearest shelf and pulled a book off, light blazed suddenly inside the room.

Sam froze.

She wasn't alone.

The door that led to the stairs of the house had opened, and three men stood just inside, each much larger than any man she'd ever seen. They carried swords and crossbows, likely hired by the highborn who owned this house to protect whatever Marin had *really* been after. Sam glanced behind them, half expecting to see the highborns she'd overheard the first time she'd come, but saw only these brutes.

They all stared at her as she held the book in her hand. Sam smiled a guilty smile and darted toward the door leading back up the stairs to the roof.

She was too slow. Someone grabbed her in a tight grip from behind.

The person holding her searched her pockets, tossing the crossbow onto the floor so it went skittering away from her. She was jerked to the side and pressed against one of the shelves as they searched her more thoroughly. They found the book she'd taken.

Kyza!

"What do you want to do with her?" a rough voice asked.

"Take her downstairs. See what she knows."

Sam didn't see who answered, but there was a strength in the voice, and the way he spoke sent a cold chill through her.

What would the highborns do to her now that they found her with a weapon?

What would happen to Tray?

She'd promised herself that if she were ever caught, she'd remain strong. That she wouldn't scream or cry or do anything like she'd seen others do when they'd been caught. She had promised herself that she would handle it calmly, mostly so she could keep her mind working to figure out a way toward freedom. Panic had a way of making one's mind go in the wrong direction.

As much as she might have wanted to remain calm, she couldn't.

Tears streamed from her eyes as they led her away.

5

CAPTURED AND ESCAPE

Sam was left in a small, windowless room on the first floor. Light from the main hall beyond slipped in under the closed door, giving a soft glow along the floor. Her wrists were bound behind her, and they'd chosen to tie her legs, as well. Escaping from here wouldn't be easy, if it was even possible.

The hard lump of a man who had brought her down to her new-found cell barely regarded her again after tying her to the chair. "Where did you get this book?" He held up the book Sam had found on the table, waving it at her.

Sam stared at it. Could the book be more important than the paper?

When she didn't answer, he stepped toward her, his entire body imposing. "Were you the one who stole the paper from us?"

Sam's mouth went dry. They knew what she'd done.

He glared at her a moment. "Perhaps you need a little

longer to consider your answers. I have ways of making one of your kind answer."

There was no doubting what he meant by her kind. Lowborn.

Turning away, he stood with his back to her, seemingly unconcerned about her presence. And why should he be concerned? Tied as she was, there wasn't a thing she could do to escape.

Kyza!

How stupid had she been rushing in like this? She *knew* there was a risk coming here, and had done it anyway. When she'd been here before, she'd nearly been caught. They would have prepared for her return—and it seemed they were.

Sam steadied her breathing, trying to think through her options. Waiting for what might come next wasn't one of them. The highborns would send her to prison, and seeing as how she carried a crossbow on her, even if she'd only used it to cross the canal, there wouldn't be any way for her to justify having it. The punishment would be severe. Kyza knew they could simply execute her right now and claim they had to because she carried the crossbow on her.

She tried moving her wrists, thinking that she could loosen the bindings, but they didn't budge, not that she expected them to. As she rubbed the ropes against the back of the chair, thinking maybe she could soften them a little, she stared at the man's back.

He was bigger than most men, bigger even than Tray. The cut of his clothing seemed off, not nearly the same display of wealth that the highborns preferred, all flowing silks and ornate embroidery. It was leather, and cut to cling to his body almost too tightly. How would he even get into something like that?

There was something wrong here.

Sam couldn't quite put her finger on what it might be. Maybe it was the fact that he barely looked at her, though what did she expect her captor to do? Mostly it was the sheer size of the man.

She continued sawing the ropes along the back of the chair.

As she did, they began to ease, if only a little.

She pulled on them, working her hands until she could slip them out of the ropes. Skin ripped as she finally freed them, raw and burning from the friction of the rough rope, but at least she was free.

Her hands, at least.

That left her legs.

Keeping an eye on the large man, Sam slowly reached into her boot and withdrew the slender blade her mother had left her long ago. It was something she always kept with her. Not to use as a weapon—with the consequences, Sam had no intention of using a knife as a weapon—but more for the various other ways she could use a blade like this.

Now with her hands free, she sawed at the ropes binding her legs until they fell away.

Now what?

She'd gotten free, but she would have to get past this massive brute of a man. There was no way she could overpower him, which meant she either surprised him, or she found a different way out. She glanced around the room. There was no other way out.

Kyza.

Through the brute. Somehow.

He started turning toward her, and she pushed herself upright in the chair, putting her hands behind her back to feign continued capture. Maybe if he believed she was still bound, he'd eventually leave her.

He had a broad face and deep-set brown eyes. A thin beard covered his chin, nothing like the style favored by the highborns. His hand gripped the hilt of his sword as he studied her.

For a moment, she thought she might get away with hiding that she'd freed herself. His hand seemed to relax on the hilt of his sword, and he started turning away from her before catching himself.

The man turned quickly toward her.

Sam barely had time to react.

She jumped from the chair, flipping her legs in a spiraling kick that struck him in the chest. As she hit him, she twisted, pounding her fists into the sensitive part of his back where she'd get the kidneys.

He grunted, but didn't fall.

She'd fought men larger than her before, but never one quite so big that even her kicks seemed to have no impact. He reached for her, and she dropped, rolling across the floor, kicking out as she did. All she needed was to sweep his feet out from under him, but to do that, she needed to catch him first. The man moved *fast*.

Sam rolled again, this time putting her back against the door. Her breathing quickened, and her heart pounded loudly in her ears as it often did when she fought. There had been a time when she'd found that distracting, but now, the pounding actually seemed to help her focus.

The man eyed her carefully. Rather than unsheathing his sword—what she'd expected and feared—he slid one foot forward, as if readying to attack.

This wasn't any brute. He was a trained fighter.

Sam wouldn't be able to get free if he came at her in a real fighting stance. The way he lowered his shoulder and set his feet told her he knew how to grapple. He would use his much larger size against her. She might be quick, but there were limits to speed.

When she feigned a kick, he took a step back.

As he did, she pulled the door open and darted into the hall.

With the pounding in her head, her eyes seemed to take in the possibilities around her.

There were several doors, but how many led to anyplace from which she could escape? How many would be like the windowless room she'd just managed to get free from?

There was really only one safe option.

The brute stepped from the room as she reached the door on the other side of the hall.

Sam scrambled inside and slammed the door behind her, twisting the lock as quickly as she could.

Only then did she take the time to look around.

She knew what she'd find in the room. It looked no different from when she'd been here last. A lantern gave a soft glow, but that was about it. Relief flooded through her as she realized there wasn't anyone here.

It faded when she saw a body lying motionless on the floor. Blood stained the wood, pooling around the person's head. The stitching along the cloak suggested it was a highborn who had fallen, but what would have happened to the highborn?

There wasn't time to think about it. Hurrying toward the window, she allowed herself a moment to think she might escape. All she had to do was sneak outside the window, grab her staff, and she could cross the canal to safety. She could work out how to help Tray—and how to find what Bastan wanted—later. First, she had to get to safety.

At the window, she ducked behind the curtain as the door splintered.

Kyza, but the brute was strong!

She didn't have to think too much to envision what he'd do to her if he caught her. With those massive hands and the ease with which he crushed the heavy oak door, he'd squash her like an over-ripe tomato.

Feet thundered across the floor, and Sam jumped out the window.

Glass exploded around her, but she ignored it. Something pierced her stomach, and hot pain surged within her, but she refused to acknowledge it. If she did, it would only slow her.

Rolling across the hard stone outside the highborn

home, she found the staff intact. Maybe Kyza hadn't completely abandoned her.

She grabbed it and with a practiced grip checked that the two ends remained twisted together, then used the staff to help herself to her feet. When she reached the canal, she hurriedly lowered one end of the staff into the water.

She felt the brute's presence before she saw him.

Sam spun, kicking out as she did.

Pain surged in her stomach, hot and fresh, and nearly enough to make her pass out.

With a grunt, her grip started to slip on the staff.

If she lost it, there wouldn't be any choice but to jump into the canal. Bleeding as she suspected she was, she didn't like the possibility of one of the giant eels chasing after her, thinking her some sort of treat.

With renewed effort, she squeezed her hands tightly on the staff, clinging to it for safety.

She blinked back tears, and her vision cleared.

As it did, she realized that not one, but two brutes were facing her. The second held his crossbow aimed at her.

She didn't have much choice at this point. Spinning the staff up and out of the water, she caught the nearest man on the side of his head. He staggered but remained standing.

"What in the...?" she muttered.

She flipped her staff around, trying to catch the other man, and it collided with his arm. Somehow, he managed to catch it.

Sam jerked on the staff, but ending up pulling herself toward him.

He brought his fist toward her and she jumped, leaping over her staff, and spinning in the air, kicking as she did.

Her foot collided with his face hard enough to startle him and jar the staff free.

This wasn't a fight she could win. Kyza knew this wasn't a fight she could even survive.

Sam spun toward the edge of the canal and jammed the end of her staff into the water, kicking off.

For a moment, she felt something grab at her, and she twisted. The movement carried her over the water, angled strangely so that instead of landing on the opposite shore, she bounced into a building and slid down.

Sam pulled her staff from the canal and raced away.

The street was dark enough that she could fade into the shadows, but first, she had to find someplace safe. When she did, she could wrap her cloak around her to conceal herself, and hopefully wait out the brutes chasing her.

As she ran, she began thinking about the easiest path back to Bastan's. She couldn't risk exposing him too quickly, so she'd have to take a meandering route—

Something hit her in the shoulder, and she staggered forward. Pain seared through her arm, strong enough that she nearly dropped the staff.

Sam looked at her arm. The pointed tip of a crossbow bolt pierced her shoulder.

She dared a glance back and stared at one of the brutes as he *jumped* over the canal.

He didn't need a staff, and cleared it in a single leap.

What?

No one had the ability to leap the canals. What was that man?

Injured as she now was, she wouldn't be able to fight him off. And if the other brute joined him… there would be no chance. She had to outrun him.

Pain made each step hard. The staff dragged behind her, and she didn't think she'd be able to lift it if she needed to. There was no way she'd be able to jump another canal if it came to that. The only way she'd get to safety was by winding through the streets and hoping they didn't know them as well as she did.

Sam ducked around a corner and hurried forward. She reached the end of the street and turned again, gradually making her way toward Bastan's. It was his request for more information that had sent her back in, so she blamed him for the injury. Would he provide some sort of cover for her if she could reach him?

Her staff continued to bounce off the stone.

It was too loud and would likely only get her caught, but now that she'd gotten it back, she didn't want to lose it again. She stopped in a small doorway and pinched the staff between her knees, twisting the ends apart. In halves, she could store it in the cloak. At least that way, she might be able to move more quietly.

Footsteps hurried along the street.

Sam didn't dare race out from hiding. Instead, she pulled the cloak around her, ducking her head low. Pain throbbed in her shoulder and in her side, sending waves through her that were nearly strong enough to knock her down. How much longer would she be able to keep going?

Whoever chased slowed.

"Where did she go?" The words were hard and accented.

"The last I saw her, she went this way." This was the rough voice of the brute. "I had smelled her, but I no longer do."

Smelled her?

Sam leaned toward the cloak wrapped around her and sniffed. *She* didn't smell anything so how could he?

"You couldn't keep up with her?" the other asked.

"She was skilled. We must be prepared for others like her in the city."

"The others haven't returned. We would have known. It's the reason you wanted—"

"I know the reason I wanted to do this now," the first said.

They moved along the street and their voices grew fainter.

What had she gotten herself into?

Thoughts became more difficult as her vision began to fade.

She didn't have time to figure out what was happening, and it didn't matter, anyway. She needed to find a way to get help. Reaching Bastan was out of the question. The stupid man was too far away. That meant finding someone else.

Sam staggered into the street, keeping her cloak wrapped around her shoulders. The staff weighed down the cloak, but at least it didn't drag along the street, making any more noise.

Blinking through the fog that was masking her vision, she struggled to find the street she needed. She took a turn, and then another. As she did, she realized she was lost.

How could she be lost in the city? Sam *always* knew where she was going in the city.

Strange signs hung over storefronts. A baker. A seamstress. An apothecary.

She stopped. Apothecary.

They were often healers. If nothing else, she could find someone who could pull the bolt from her shoulder and stitch her back up. Maybe even heal her side, removing whatever glass had lodged there.

The door was locked.

Sam debated beating on the door but decided against it. That would make too much noise and might draw the brutes back to her location.

She doubted she could focus well enough to pick the lock, but maybe the knife would be good for something.

She jammed it into the lock as far as she could and twisted.

Long ago, she discovered the blade was strong. Twisting it in some lock couldn't damage it, and she twisted. With a sharp *snap*, the lock broke. Sam pushed on the door and entered the apothecary.

Strange smells assaulted her. Most were those of spices, some she recognized, but most foreign to her nose. Rows of shelves with different jars greeted her, and potted plants lined the window, the earthy scent coming mostly from them. She staggered forward and closed the door behind her.

"Hello?" Her voice barely carried into the shop, fading quickly, as if swallowed by the dark or the strange spices within. Sam staggered forward again, making it another few steps before she started to fall. She grabbed at one of the shelves to catch herself, but managed to do nothing more than pull it down on herself.

"Help!" This came out weakly, barely strong enough for her to be heard in the back of the shop. She tried dragging herself forward, but her arms didn't work like they should, and pain shot through her any time she tried moving them. Breathing became more labored, each breath feeling like someone sat on her chest.

How badly had she been hurt?

Badly enough that she didn't think she'd have made it back to Bastan's had she tried. It was a good thing she'd snuck into the apothecary, even if there wasn't anyone here, but it was too bad she didn't know enough about the different herbs to heal herself.

Now, she'd suffer because of her stupidity. Not only suffer, but given the burning sensation working through her, she wondered if she'd survive.

Tray needed her, and she wouldn't be there for him.

In some ways, that hurt more than anything else. He'd rot in the prison, thinking she hadn't made any attempt to find him.

Sam tried moving forward, deeper into the apothecary shop, but pain prevented her from moving any more than a little bit.

With a frustrated sigh, she rested her head on the cool floor.

She would rest, then she'd try again. Maybe by then, someone would return.

Rest.

Her head settled onto the stone floor, and her eyes fluttered closed. Breathing came raggedly, and she slowly drifted, eventually fading into nothingness.

6

THE HYSTERICAL MONEY LENDER

The bell above the door to his father's apothecary tinkled softly, and Alec turned to see a man with short wiry hair close the door behind him and suppressed a groan. A visit from Hyp could take half a day. Time Alec needed for sorting herbs so vital to their shop, else his father might return and see how little he'd accomplished.

"Anything I can help you with today, Hyp?" he asked, stepping toward him, careful not to trip on the over-flowing stack of his father's notes on the floor next to the desk. The rest of the shop was neatly kept, with row upon row of leaves and grasses and berries all placed in jars meticulously labeled.

Hyp shuffled further into the shop, leaning on a long cane. Always fastidiously dressed, the moneylender wore his coat buttoned to his throat and his dark pants neatly creased. His furrowed brow deepened the closer he came, a pained look narrowing his eyes.

"Alec," he started, glancing around the shop. "Your father has not returned yet?"

"Afraid not, Hyp. I'm not sure when he'll return." Hyp had stopped by the shop almost daily since his father had been away, asking the same question each time. Alec's answers did nothing to dissuade Hyp from coming, and in some ways, the fact that his father wasn't here seemed to empower him.

Hyp swallowed and blinked, nodding slowly. "I thought I should check." He carefully considered the increasingly empty shelves within the shop.

Alec waited, curious what complaint he would have today. "As I said, he's gone collecting medicines." He waved a hand around the shop. "We have to have enough supplies to keep everyone well." He didn't add that he still didn't understand why his father had left this time. Their supplies were still plentiful, though they might be short on a few things. He'd left in a hurry and with fewer supplies than he usually took with him when he went off on his forays around the edges of the city.

Hyp rubbed his eyes. "Yes, yes. I remember."

"How's your vision?" Two days ago, Hyp said everything was suddenly blurry. Before that, it was a throbbing right arm.

Hyp nodded, a serious look coming to his face. "Better," he admitted. "Though less than perfect if I'm being completely honest." He cleared his throat, straightening his coat. "Still, I suppose that comes with age."

Alec sniffed softly. If nothing else, experience with Hyp had taught him patience. Maybe that was the reason his father subjected him to the man every time he entered the shop.

"I suppose if your father still isn't here…" He inhaled deeply, a pained look crossing his face. "I awoke to severe stomach pains and haven't been able to eat anything all day. I've never had anything like it."

Alec looked at him skeptically. "Never?" Stomach pain was one of Hyp's usual complaints.

"Nothing like this." He clutched his hands to his stomach, closing his eyes for effect.

Alec suppressed a sigh and led him to the cot behind the desk at the back of the shop. All around him were the instruments his father would use to examine those coming to the apothecary for help. They were nothing like those used by the physickers at the university, but then apothecaries like his father didn't have the same training or quality of medicines as the physickers. Better than nothing for most, which was the reason his father continued practicing. Alec knew most appreciated everything his father could do, even if it wasn't what the physickers would have managed. At least his father didn't charge the same fees as the physickers.

Hyp lay down, bending his knees to his chest as he did, waiting with an anxious expression on his face.

Alec frowned, biting his lower lip as he considered the best evaluation to satisfy Hyp. Nothing *really* mattered when it came to him. He'd long ago come to that conclusion with Hyp, though it didn't matter. He'd have to examine him, regardless. Otherwise, the man wouldn't be satisfied, and he'd be back the very next day. If Alec took a little extra time now, he might not see

Hyp for a few days, hopefully not until his father returned.

Tilting his head down, he listened first to Hyp's heart, then his chest, before tipping his head to his stomach, hearing nothing unusual. Moving quickly, methodically, he pushed carefully on Hyp's neck, then his chest, before examining his stomach, but the man didn't wince as he palpated. Skin was normal, as well.

Hyp looked up at him, and Alec waved him to stand. "Well?"

Alec shrugged. "Not sure." Nothing he would say could soothe Hyp, anyway. "Maybe it's time you see a physicker."

Many in this part of the city appreciated his father and his medicines, though it was probably just as much that the physickers were selective about who they'd heal. Most, they turned away. Alec wondered if they'd even take on a case like Hyp, or would they send him away, as well? They treated merchants as well as those in the inner sections of the city, so there would be no reason Hyp *couldn't* go to the physickers.

A sour look pinched Hyp's mouth, and he shook his head. "The university?" He grunted and shook his head. "Your father is a better healer than any at the university. Quite a bit cheaper too. Maybe they should call him to help with the princess." He lowered his voice and leaned forward. "You heard the rumors, haven't you? Say she's fallen sick. None have seen her in days, and they say even the physickers can't heal her. Bet your father could do something for her like he's done for me."

Alec didn't want to get into that with Hyp, and instead

helped him to his feet as he handed him his cane. "I'm sorry he's not here for you, Hyp."

Hyp smoothed his coat and nodded, his long face serious. "You tried. I suspect you'll soon be near the healer your father is. And still better than any university healer."

Alec's lips curled in a tight smile. He doubted he would ever rival his father, at least, not without training at the university, and that was now beyond him. As much as he might want to study at the university, he was far too old. "That's nice of you to say." He led him down a side aisle on his way toward the door, grabbing a few supplies as he went. "Try these," he suggested, pressing a few loose leaves and herbs into a small container and handing it to Hyp. "They should soothe your stomach at least."

Hyp nodded and tilted his head before hesitating. "You going to write this down?" He frowned, holding the supplies to his chest, cane now cradled into his arm. "Your father always writes my symptoms down, Alec."

Alec sighed softly, nodding. "Of course, Hyp."

The safest course of action was not to argue with him, but unlike his father, Alec never found value in documenting Hyp's symptoms. Sitting at the desk, he reached for a sheet of paper, suppressing a groan when he realized it was the last. Getting a re-supply of paper was just one more thing on his list of things needing to be done.

He dipped his pen into the open ink bottle and quickly wrote down Hyp's symptoms. *Abdominal pain. Nausea. No physical findings. Suspect hysteria. Given barberry, chamoline, and feverleaf.*

As he wrote, Hyp shuffled toward him, watching. Alec

hurried, shielding his notes from Hyp's eyes as best he could. Then he slid it to the top of the nearest stack.

Hyp nodded as he finished then fished a few coins from his pocket, setting them carefully on the desk. "For supplies."

"Let me know if that helps," Alec said, ignoring the coins. His father rarely cared what people paid, just that they tried.

Hyp tottered toward the door, pausing briefly at the threshold to glance at the clouds and drizzling rain before adjusting his hat and trudging down the street.

Alec quickly closed the door behind him and twisted the lock. A moment of relief at getting Hyp out of the shop washed through him, but faded back into a familiar simmering frustration as he stared at the sky.

Rain again. How much would this delay his father? How much longer before he returned?

He surveyed the shop, thinking he could spend his time organizing—which was what his father would expect of him—or he could go to the market and purchase supplies. At least in the market, he might find some way to bide his time differently. There, he might be able to avoid yet another visit from Hyp. The thought made him remember he'd not updated his notes about Hyp's second visit, same symptoms.

His father wouldn't mind if he closed the shop early for that, would he?

Other than Hyp and his hysteria, there wasn't anyone coming, anyway.

7

THE FALLEN THIEF

When Alec returned from the market, the door to the shop was ajar. He entered carefully, wrinkling his nose. The inside of the shop stank. Normally, there was the scent of the various concoctions his father made, the bite from the various herbs and leaves and oils all mingling together to make a very medicinal odor that hung about everything, but now there was something else to it. The rot was thick, almost enough that he could taste it, and Alec gagged as he headed to the back.

Had he left something out? Something that had turned sour?

He'd only been gone a few hours, not long enough for such a stench to fill the shop.

Even with his father gone, Alec knew what was expected of him. He was to keep the door open, sell to those who knew what they needed, help whoever he felt comfortable helping, and placate any others until he came back. Either that, or send them to the university.

So far, it hadn't been a problem. Most knew his father was gone, leaving the shop empty. A few came and bought various benign herbs, most of them things that wouldn't do any real damage if mixed improperly. The others were like Hyp or had straightforward symptoms.

There was nothing about this odor that was straightforward.

His mind raced through what he might be smelling, but came up with nothing. Leaves dried by the time his father brought them into the shop, leaving nothing more than a hint of what they'd once smelled like. The oils were all stable, and had nothing like this stink. Had some animal snuck into the shop? That was the only other thing he could think of making its way in here, but he'd closed the back door when he'd left… hadn't he?

Alec moved between the shelves, looking for any signs of whatever creature might have managed to sneak in. He expected a rat, maybe a cat. They were unfortunately common enough throughout the city, the canals and the grain that moved along them drawing in the rats, and the rats drawing the cats. He detested both.

As he neared the front of the shop, he almost tripped over the form of a small person lying face down on the ground. Blood pooled around the body, more than he'd ever seen spilled at one time. The sight of blood didn't bother Alec—he'd trained with his father long enough for him to have long ago gotten over his fear of blood—but the stench mixed in with it made him gag.

He'd never smelled anything like it before.

How did this person even get in here?

Using the toe of his boot, he nudged the body. There

wasn't any way he—or she—could still be alive. He'd seen too many injured to think this person would have survived after this much blood loss.

To his surprise, he heard a soft groan.

He tapped his chest twice, making the mark of the Sacred Alms. How could this person still be alive?

Alec leaned toward the body and flipped it over.

As he did, he saw part of the injury. A thick length of wood—like some sort of arrow—pierced the flesh of the shoulder. The tip had congealed, the blood thicker than it should be, and the stench came from that.

He jerked back the hand that had started reaching for the wound. A stink like that, with the blood thickened as it was, meant it was likely poison of some sort. Some poisons could soak through the flesh.

If he did nothing, this person—a young woman, he realized as he saw her dark hair spilling beneath the hood of her cloak—wouldn't survive.

His father wouldn't approve if he did nothing.

Alec lifted the woman carefully, scooping under her back, and carried her to the cot. Blood stained his shirt, and would stain the cot, as well. One more thing he'd have to clean. He searched for something with which to grasp the arrow and found a pair of heavy tongs. They would give enough grip.

When he touched the tongs to the arrow, the woman moaned.

She didn't move otherwise. He wondered if she *could* move as injured as she was. It might be that nothing he would do would even matter, but he had to try.

The arrow came out slowly. There was resistance,

more than he would have expected, but he wondered if the congealed blood prevented it from sliding out more easily.

Alec carefully put the arrow in an empty jar before turning his attention back to the wound. Now that the arrow was gone, blood oozed, but it wasn't the oozing of a normal wound.

Poison. It had to be.

What would have happened for her to have been shot like this? And why with a poisoned arrow?

Alec shook the thought away. Now wasn't the time for those questions. Healing first, then questions.

He grabbed a roll of cloth, tore off a thick wad, and pressed it against the wound. Blood quickly soaked through the cloth. It wouldn't be enough. He'd have to stitch the wound to give this woman any sort of chance.

Tearing off a longer strip of cloth, he wrapped it around her shoulder and tied it off over the wound, then stepped away to find the supplies he needed. His father kept a sharp needle and thread for such situations, but his father preferred not to use them. Most of the people who came to his shop searched for medicine rather than surgical healing. Those who needed more ended up at the university.

The first few places he looked didn't have what he needed. By the time he reached the bottom draw of the desk, he'd almost begun to wonder if his father had gotten rid of the suturing supplies, but he found a spool of a thick black thread with a jar of needles at the back of the drawer.

Pulling off a length of thread long enough to make a

few stitches, Alec ran it quickly through the needle. The steadiness of his hands surprised him. He carried it back to the woman and unraveled the already saturated cloth covering her wound.

He shifted her cloak out of the way. Had he more time, he would have preferred to take it off, but he didn't want to aggravate the wound any further and risk more bleeding. To fully examine the extent of her injury, he had to gently tear some of the fabric away to expose the area around the wound.

The flesh around her shoulder had blackened.

Could the poisoning have caused that?

Alec wished his father were here. He knew as much about medicines as anyone, and he'd likely know which poison had been used, and what could counter it. As it was, Alec would be on his own to come up with something that would work.

After the stitching was done.

He made quick work of sewing up the injury, tying the last stitch and cutting the remaining thread with a knife. He watched the wound and noted it still seeped even after he was done, but less than before.

Tearing off another strip of cloth from the roll, he started to wrap her shoulder again before deciding against it. First, she needed some sort of salve to cover it, then he could wrap it.

What should he use?

He hurried along the row of shelves, carrying a ceramic bowl with him. He grabbed two erass leaves—best to stimulate healing—and added a joxberry. That would stave off infection. What he needed was something that would counter the potential effect of the poison. What would work?

Without knowing what he countered, he needed to find something nonspecific. More leaves to stimulate healing. Erass again? It might work, but two leaves would be potent enough. Felth root? Alec shook his head. Felth would work with healing, but would likely counter the effect of the erass.

He had made it to a row of oils. Most were obtained from plants, though his father had collected a few stranger oils. There was the oil from wolf fat, said to lead to increased virility. Roach oil—something he couldn't believe his father could collect—would promote health, but it didn't seem right. What else would work?

The only other thing he could think of was terash oil. Terash were strange aquatic creatures found along the edges of the city, and his father said their oil would augment the healing effect of other substances in a mixture. In this case, he hoped the oil would work with the erass leaves and the joxberry. Together, they might be enough to help this woman.

Using the thick pestle, he ground the leaves and berry together, and then added a few drops of the terash oil. The exact combination wasn't too important—he didn't think. When adequately combined, he smeared it onto the skin around her shoulder.

The woman gasped.

Alec worked quickly and wrapped up her shoulder, using more strips of cloth. Would the oozing continue? The blackness he'd seen around her shoulder had seemed to spread, now working along her arm. It might already be too late for her with what had been done.

He stepped back and leaned on the table. There was nothing to do now but wait.

With healing, that was often the hardest part.

The woman moaned and tried to move.

Alec grabbed her and held her. She continued writhing, moaning as he touched her side to hold her down, making his hand sticky.

Why sticky?

He jerked his hand back. Blood stained it.

This wasn't the thick, congealed kind of blood she'd had around her shoulder, this was a more normal sort of bleeding.

Sacred Alms, but he should have remembered to examine her more closely. He'd been so caught up with her shoulder wound that he hadn't paid any attention to the fact that there might be another wound he had to deal with.

Alec settled into his training, focusing as his father had taught him. He started at her head and worked down, looking for signs of other injuries. There wasn't anything on her head. He searched through her hair, using a comb to separate the strands so he could take a better look at her scalp, but found nothing. He tilted her jaw from side to side, and found nothing.

Alec hesitated as he did this. The woman was lovely.

Shaking the thought away, he moved down to her chest. She would have to forgive his intrusion if she lived. Peeling apart her shirt, he looked for other injuries there, and found none. He continued on to her abdomen and stopped to suck in a sharp breath.

Two massive punctures bled steadily.

A thick piece of glass protruded from one. Alec grabbed it and pulled it free, placing pressure on the wound as he did. She moaned again, but settled somewhat, looking more comfortable than she had before.

How had she survived both the shoulder injury *and* the glass in her side?

This woman was incredibly strong. Alec couldn't help but be impressed.

The glass wounds were more typical injuries. He grabbed the roll of cloth and tore off a length to apply pressure, slowing the bleeding. They'd have to be stitched like the other.

When he felt comfortable that the bleeding slowed, he hurried to gather more thread and made quick work of sewing up these additional wounds. After finishing, he smeared more of the salve he'd made onto them before binding her with even more cloth. Healing her had required he use almost all of the cloth they had in the shop, so he'd have to purchase more before his father returned, possibly even more before he was finished with this woman.

Deciding not to make the same mistake as before, he continued his survey looking for injuries, working his way down her legs and then her arms. Other than a few scrapes, he found nothing else.

He set her belongings on the floor next to the cot. Other than a knife he'd found, there was really only her boots. He hadn't wanted to move her too much to remove her cloak, not wanting to disrupt the stitches.

As he set the boots on the floor, a scrap of folded paper fell from inside one of them.

Alec picked it up and carefully unfolded it. For her to hide paper in her boot meant it would be important. At least, that had been his expectation, but the page was blank.

Alec took a seat in his father's heavy wooden chair, angling it to watch her as he studied the blank page. There was a mark in the bottom corner, and another in the top corner, but he didn't recognize the symbol.

All the strangeness around her continued to build. What had happened to her? How could a woman like this have ended up as injured as she was?

The answer was obvious, even if unlikely. She was from one of the outer sections where crime was more common.

With the shop several streets away from the nearest canal, they didn't get the same level of traffic through here as they did in the busier sections of the city, which meant they didn't see the same amount of crime, but that didn't mean crime didn't exist here. Alec had seen plenty of people come to his father's shop with injuries, most often nothing more than a knife wound, or a broken bone from a fall, nothing quite like what this woman had presented with. Many came from the outer sections of the city, his father's reputation drawing them in. Maybe that was why she had come here.

For now, she lived. If she awoke—and given the severity of her injuries, including the glass to the abdomen that possibly meant a bowel injury—he could ask what happened. Until then... he waited.

Alec surveyed the shop. Blood trailed toward the front door, leaving a long, dark streak along the floorboards. Some of the shelves toward the front of the shop were knocked down and the front door stood ajar.

With a sigh, he stood. Waiting for her to heal didn't mean he could let the shop remain in this shape.

8

A DEEPER COLORANT

Alec returned to the shop with a new bundle of cloth and a few other supplies. Mostly, he'd bought some bread and dried beef along with a few vegetables. If the woman did wake, he'd need to feed her. One of the many things his father had taught him was that injuries required energy to heal, and the body needed to eat to make energy.

He found her still lying on the cot, sleeping peacefully.

She hadn't fully woken since he'd found her a few hours ago, though Alec hadn't really expected her to. He'd given her poppy milk—only a few drops, but enough for her to rest comfortably. Maybe when she *did* wake, the pain wouldn't overwhelm her. Otherwise, with the extent of her injuries, it was possible she'd come around screaming.

It appeared she *had* turned over, and now rested on her good shoulder. Dark hair hung around her face, pooling into the hood of the strange cloak she wore that seemed to collect the light from the single lantern he'd left burning. He hadn't wanted her to awaken disoriented and scared.

Alec set his supplies down on the desk and decided to examine his patient. The shoulder injury in particular worried him, especially with the black streaks he'd seen running down her arm by the time he'd managed to get the arrow out.

With her cloak covering her, he couldn't examine her as well as he wanted. Alec worked carefully to slip the cloak from her shoulders and set it off to the side before returning his attention to her injuries.

The wound remained closed, the stitches holding. Blood no longer oozed from it as it had before. The blackness around the wound remained, but Alec couldn't tell if it had gotten worse or not.

He tentatively touched the wound, running the back of his finger along the sides to test for warmth. He detected none. No infection—at least, none he could pick up that way. Without any drainage, it made it even less likely.

Alec wrapped her shoulder again. When finished, he remembered that the arrow he'd pulled from her arm remained in a jar by the wall. Rather than discarding it, he placed a top on it and moved it to a protected shelf. When his father returned, he could ask whether he knew anything about the kind of poison used on the arrow.

There was still nothing for him to do other than wait. Alec covered her with a blanket and tucked it around her, wanting her to at least be comfortable.

He sat at the desk, glancing at the woman every so often. She didn't move, though her breathing was regular and soft. Alec couldn't help but wonder about her. What was her name? Where had she come from? Why had she been shot? And why this strange blank sheet of paper hidden in her boot?

Alec kept the page smoothed out on top of the desk, running his finger along the edges. The paper was thick, almost a parchment, but the surface appeared incredibly smooth. He rubbed the surface, but felt none of the usual grain to the page.

Setting it aside, he turned to the stack of papers near the corner of the desk. On the top was the one with Hyp's symptoms, all spelled out as he had been taught. His father kept a log of symptoms and treatments, a journal of sorts, and could track what had worked and what hadn't. This record more than anything probably made him a better healer than most.

Alec should add the woman's injuries and her symptoms to it, but as he searched the top of the desk, he didn't find anything to write on. Had he used the last of the paper too? Then he remembered he had, and should have picked some up while out earlier. More than any of the other supplies, his father would be angriest to learn he'd not left him any paper.

He'd be sure to procure a new supply before his father returned.

He eyed the blank sheet the woman had brought. She wouldn't mind if he used it, would she? He could jot a few notes and keep that as record—and payment—for his healing. Besides, the page was blank anyway.

Alec reached for the quill and dipped it carefully into the jar of black ink his father kept near the corner of the desk, and started writing. With the smoothness to the paper, he wasn't sure how well the ink would take. Maybe it'd blob up and smear.

The ink adhered for a moment, then faded completely, leaving no trace of his writing. He tried again, and again the same thing happened. And again.

Alec sat back and considered the parchment before glancing over to the woman. Was *this* the reason she'd kept it in her boot? What kind of strange paper had she hidden?

Perhaps different ink?

Grabbing another bottle, this one dyed a deep blue, he cleaned his pen before dipping it into the ink. The blue barely colored the parchment before disappearing, fading away as if it was never there. He tried another, a thick brown ink his father preferred but Alec detested. The ink lingered a moment longer than the others before fading.

The sound of the bell above the door startled him and he looked up. He'd meant to repair the lock when he returned but had forgotten. He felt a moment of panic that Hyp had returned.

Mrs. Rubbles, a thin, older woman who ran the stationery store, approached the desk and looked from him to the parchment and bottles of ink. "Beautiful parchment. It'll need a deeper colorant."

Alec nodded as he looked up at her. "I think you're right, Mrs. Rubbles."

"Your father still not in?" she asked.

"Not yet. He went for supplies about a week ago but isn't back yet."

Alec stood and walked toward Mrs. Rubbles, and as he

did, his father's training set in. *Faint sheen of sweat. Eyes slightly pronounced. Visible mass on neck. Likely glandular problem.*

"I might be able to help you until he returns," he offered, but he wasn't certain whether he really could. Hyp was one thing—his illnesses weren't real—but Mrs. Rubbles clearly needed the help of someone like his father, maybe a physicker.

She eyed him a moment and then nodded. "I'm sure you can, Alec."

He smiled and moved to stand in front of her. "What symptoms have you noticed?"

"At my age?" she asked with a laugh. "What haven't I noticed? Achy joints. Hair is too thin. Skin too loose! Bowels don't work one day and then work too well." She threw her arms up. "I can deal with the symptoms, but not having to close my shop! Is there anything you can do?"

Alec glanced at the woman on the cot before pulling out the chair and waving for Mrs. Rubbles to sit. It would have to do. Calling Mrs. Rubbles eccentric was often an understatement, but also did her a disservice. A proud woman, and one of the few female shop owners, she cared a great deal about her business, and he knew she would not be slowed by any minor symptoms.

A brief exam revealed a racing heart along with the other signs he'd noted upon her arrival. Alec considered the symptoms. No doubt glandular. There was little curative he could do until his father returned, but he just might be able to help. Leaving her in the chair, he walked toward the shelves and grabbed methimanine seeds, buglebalm leaves, and motherwort. Compounding them carefully, he placed the mixture into a small container and handed it to Mrs. Rubbles.

"Mix a spoonful with hot water once daily," Alec said. "I'll have father stop by when he returns, but this should help until then."

She stood shakily and nodded. "I'm sure it will." Hobbling around the desk, she set a half-silver mark near the paper he'd been writing on. "You're much like your father, you know. Keep at it, and you might make it to the university."

"I'm too old now. Besides, what would my father do without me?"

She smiled at him and tapped her temple. "What indeed?" Her eyes protruded slightly, making her look a bit excitable. Pausing as she turned toward the front of the shop, she said, "I like coffee grounds, but sometimes soot is needed."

He frowned, worried for a moment that her mind was finally slipping. But she simply snorted, laughing as she pointed toward the page and then slowly ambled out of the shop.

Alec looked back at the desk. Darker colorant. If any would know about ink and parchment, it would be Mrs. Rubbles. He could have followed her to her store and bought more paper with the coins she'd paid him, but he was determined to figure out why he couldn't write on the page. At least until the woman woke. Then he'd have different questions.

Starting with coffee grounds, he gathered a few potential colorants off the shelves, shoveling a bit of soot out of the small stove at the back of the shop last.

He tried the coffee grounds first, mixing them into the thick brown ink his father preferred. That had seemed to linger the longest. Taking a deep breath, he started writing on the page. The ink lingered—possibly even a little longer than before—but ultimately absorbed into the page.

The soot was next, but did little to make the ink work any better. Then he mixed his own base. Years of working with his father and taking notes had taught him how to mix simple inks. Separating this into several smaller bottles, he added various colorants. The violet leaves of brackberry. Crushed oak gall mixed with a few drops of limseed. Shavings from a walnut. None worked.

He managed to cut his finger on the walnut in the process of preparing it. As he sucked his finger, he stared at the page, wondering at its secret. A drop of blood dripped from his cut finger onto the parchment. Alec grunted and grabbed a rag, smearing it across his blood on the page. Too late, he realized it was the rag he'd used on the woman when cleaning her wound and covered with her blood, and now stained his hand.

He thought the parchment might absorb the blood, but to his surprise, it remained, a crimson stain.

Alec held his breath, waiting. The smear of blood stayed, slowly congealing.

Moments passed as he realized the blood wouldn't fade.

A morbid sense of excitement filled him as an idea came to him. Squeezing his cut finger into one of the remaining unaltered ink bases, he wondered just how much blood was necessary to work. Some of the woman's blood remained on his hand and probably mixed in with what he dripped into the jar. Would that matter?

When he dipped his pen into the ink, his arm ached, as if he'd strained something carrying the bundle of supplies back to the shop. Without giving it any more thought, he started writing.

Alec wrote down the woman's symptoms.

Unlike before, the ink and the words he wrote remained, and were not absorbed into the parchment. Though the bottled ink looked light red, the ink upon the paper took on a deep maroon, almost black. He touched it hesitantly, fearful that it might smear, but he needn't have worried. It dried almost immediately.

Alec started with a description of the arrow wound to the shoulder, and the way the blood congealed, thick around the arrow's shaft, documenting how he'd removed it and then sutured the wound. He added a comment about the salve he'd created, writing it in a tight script, the format different from what his father preferred, trying to keep it neater. He moved on to describe the injury to her side, including his concern about whether the glass shard had penetrated her abdomen. Lastly, he added his thoughts about the blackening along her shoulder.

Poison? Has the tissue already begun necrosing or is this from the congealing of her blood?

Tingling in his arm persisted as he wrote, an annoying ache that eventually increased to something more, a warmth that spread through him.

The small ink bottle was nearly empty when he finished. Alec frowned, wondering how he had used the ink so quickly, before gathering a few more supplies to mix additional base. Only then did he realize how dark the shop had become.

Had he really spent the rest of the day trying to determine how to write on the paper?

What a waste. He could have better used the time going to Mrs. Rubbles' shop and getting more paper. He might have discovered a way to write on the page, but what value did that bring, other than to satisfy his curiosity?

Alec looked over to the woman. She rested comfortably beneath the blanket.

He pulled it back and unwrapped the dressing around her shoulder, looking at the wound. At least the salve seemed to be working. The injury seemed less blackened than before, though Alec didn't know if what he saw was real, or the effect of the shadows.

After replacing the dressing, he covered her back up and returned to the desk, determined to at least organize his father's stack of papers while waiting on her to awaken. His gaze kept drifting toward the page where he'd documented the woman's injuries, and he realized he hadn't noted what he'd done for Mrs. Rubbles. More than the injury to the woman, his father would want that documented. He could use the page for now, and later transcribe it into his journal.

Alec reached for more of the base and pricked his finger as he prepared another bottle of the blood ink before starting to write once more.

9

THE THIEF AWAKENS

Alec startled awake, practically falling off of his chair. Someone coughed near him, and his mind immediately took to processing it, categorizing the cough as *dry, no sign of phlegm, likely irritant.* Even half-awake, his mind worked as his father had trained.

Who coughed?

He rubbed sleep from his eyes and felt the aching of his back from the way he'd been sitting in the chair. Had he really fallen asleep sitting up? The last thing he remembered doing was documenting Mrs. Rubbles' symptoms, then he'd begun to drift away.

There came another cough, and he spun in his seat.

The woman was awake.

She sat on the edge of the cot, her injured arm held against her stomach, the other propped up behind her on the cot, almost as if to hold her upright. The woman looked over to him, her dark eyes seeming to take him in quickly.

"Where am I?" she asked in a soft voice.

"You're in Aelus's Apothecary," Alec answered.

She blinked, and it seemed as if she remembered. With her good arm, she touched her shoulder. "How bad was it?"

"You've been out for the better part of two days. Maybe longer," he added, realizing he didn't know exactly how long he'd been sleeping. It was possible it was much longer than he expected. She arched a brow at him. Alec leaned forward and took a deep breath. "Plenty bad. I wasn't sure you'd survive the injury. What happened?"

She shook her head. "I got shot, that's what happened."

"I took the arrow out," he said, motioning toward the jar where he'd kept it.

"Not an arrow. A crossbow bolt. Shorter. Thicker."

Thicker certainly described what he'd pulled from her arm. "It was poisoned." He stood and walked over to the cot. "May I?" he asked, motioning toward the bandage.

She watched him a moment before shrugging.

Alec removed the dressing as quickly as he could, wanting to see the skin beneath. The sutures still held, and her movement hadn't caused additional bleeding. Some blackness remained, but not as there had been. He reached for the salve and smeared a little more across the wound before replacing the dressing.

"I'll have to do your stomach too."

She touched her stomach with her good hand and her eyes widened slightly. "The window," she muttered.

"A window?"

"Had to jump through it. There was no other way."

Alec waited, thinking she'd offer something more, but she didn't. "What's your name?"

She looked around the shop before her gaze settled on him. "Samara Elseth."

"Samara, I'm—"

"Please. Just Sam."

Alec smiled. Sam didn't fit her any more than the idea of her as some sort of thief. "Sam," he repeated. "I'm Alec Stross."

"You're the apothecary?" She gave him an appraising stare.

Alec flushed. "I'm his son."

She nodded and tried to stand but shook her head. "What do I owe you for healing me?"

"Whatever you can pay."

With a frown, she laughed but stopped abruptly, grabbing her stomach. Her face twisted in a grimace. "What kind of business is that?"

"It's what my father does. He charges only what people can afford to pay."

"I don't have anything on me now, but I can get some coin to you. I imagine I made enough of a mess. You shouldn't have to clean up after me."

Alec glanced toward the now clean floor. It had taken quite a bit of scrubbing for him to get the stains removed, and even after everything he'd tried, he couldn't get it all.

"It's fine. Besides, it gave me a chance to experiment on the paper you had with you. I hope you don't mind me using it, but I'd run out and... well, you were out."

She started forward before catching herself. "You were able to write on it?"

Alec shrugged. "Not at first. I don't know what kind of paper you have there, but most inks didn't work. I even tried a few different colorants, but without success."

"What worked?"

Alec flushed. "It was an accident really. I was trying to use walnut shell, but I cut my finger and the oil in the shell didn't seem to work but the—"

"Alec. What worked?"

"Blood. When my blood dripped onto the page, it didn't absorb." Well, hers too. When he'd wiped the rag across the page, her blood had stained the page along with his.

Sam leaned back, wincing as she did. He still couldn't believe she managed to sit up as easily as she did, given the extent of her injuries, but the fact that she'd survived at all told him how strong she must be.

"Blood? Why would they need blood to write on their page?"

"Who?"

She blinked and looked over, finally shaking her head. "Can I see it?"

He hesitated, but took the page off the desk and handed it to her. The ink had absorbed into the page, soaking in so it appeared strangely faded, lessened somewhat, almost as if it had been written a long time ago. The paper remained smooth, almost slick.

Sam scrunched up her face as she studied it. "You wrote this?"

He nodded.

"You have neat handwriting."

He shrugged. "My father needs to be able to read this."

"Why?"

He flushed again under the intensity of her gaze. "We make a record of everyone who comes into the apothecary. My father documents what he gives, how it works, that sort of thing."

"Your father sounds like a physicker."

He shrugged. "Just a healer, but one who takes his role seriously."

Sam scooted forward on the cot until she reached the end. She teetered there for a moment before managing to stand. She let out a little whoop, like a cry or grunt of victory, and Alec couldn't help but smile.

"Where are you going?"

She looked at the floor, staring at her boots for a long moment. "I need to get back, but I think I need your help with my boots. And my cloak." She squeezed her eyes closed. "The damn rope is gone though. I doubt Marin will get me more."

"You need to rest a little longer," he said. He tried slipping his arm around her shoulders, looking to guide her back to the cot, but she pushed away from him with her good arm. Alec was surprised at the strength she still showed. Even after the extent of injuries she had, she still had a feistiness to her. He held his hands up. "Fine. I'll help you with your boots. I don't think you should risk yourself yet. Whoever hurt you might still be out there."

Her eyes narrowed. "Kyza." She whispered it under her breath.

Many thought using a god's name in that way would only draw unwanted attention, but Alec didn't believe in that sort of thing. He didn't really believe in those gods.

His father had taught him a different set of beliefs, and he'd seen firsthand how effective they could be.

"Has anyone come looking for me?"

"The only people who've come here have come for my father." When her brow furrowed in a frown, he hurriedly added, "They want his healing. He's pretty well known around here. He might not be a physicker, but he's a skilled enough healer and doesn't charge nearly as much as the physickers."

"They only care for the highborns, anyway."

Alec blinked. "There's no difference between highborns and lowborns. It's only a matter of where you live."

She shook her head with a frown. "That's the kind of thing only someone… wait a minute. Where am I?"

"You're in the Arrend section," he said.

Sam tried taking a step forward but staggered back. "Kyza. Arrend? Isn't that a merchant section?" Alec nodded, and she frowned. "How would I have made it this far?"

"Far? Where are you from?"

She looked past him, toward the door. "Caster."

"Caster? That's got to be a half-dozen sections from here. How did you…"

She ignored him and stepped into her boots, wincing as she did. When she managed to get them on without his help, she turned to him, a hard glare pinching her face. "Are you going to stand there and watch me, call for the guards, or give me my cloak?"

In spite of her small stature, she managed to make herself look much more intimidating.

Alec hurriedly grabbed her cloak and handed it to her.

"I'm not going to call the guard." After finding her injured and bleeding out in the shop, that was what he *should* have done, but there was something about Sam that made him not want to.

She took a step forward and staggered.

Alec took hold of her by her good arm, propping her up. She shot him a glare, but he ignored it, holding her steady. "You're in no condition to walk." He tried to give her a firm glare of his own. "Rest. I have food, and I can start a fire, and you can get a little more sleep."

She shook her head. "I can't. There's someone waiting for me."

She slipped her hand inside her cloak and grabbed a long, slender stick that she tucked between her legs. Then she reached in again and grabbed another one and screwed them together. How had he not noticed that in the cloak when he'd moved it off her?

Sam tapped the staff on the ground, leaning on it for support as she made her way to the door. Alec followed her, staying only a step or two behind her, but she seemed to get stronger with each step. When she reached the door, she thrust the page toward him.

"You keep this for your records."

"I can help you back," he offered.

She shook her head. "Not from Arrend, you can't. Besides, I'm not sure you want to be seen helping a lowborn like me."

"I told you that didn't matter."

"Of course it matters. It's all that matters." She stared at him a moment and then spun and pushed the door open, letting in some of the cool night air. He watched as she disappeared into the darkness.

He considered following her, but she was right. He really *couldn't* help her, not if she intended to go back to Caster.

Alec closed the door with a sigh, leaning on it, wondering if he'd ever find out how well she healed.

10

A RETURN TO CASTER

S am staggered through the streets, leaning on the canal staff as she went. Each step was painful—but far less painful than she would have expected. Kyza knew she was lucky to even be alive! That Alec had managed to save her... She didn't want to think about what would have happened to Tray had she died. Even surviving, she still didn't know what happened to him. That was why she needed to get back to Bastan and see what he'd heard. At least she had an answer for him about the pages, though she didn't know if it was an answer he'd want.

She struggled to stay upright as she made her way along the street. The buildings along here were all newer, most two stories high with some higher, and better kept than those in the outer sections of the city. Most were painted in bright colors, leaving her feeling out of place. Warehouses ran along the canals like they did in most of the merchant sections.

How had she managed to get to this part of the city?

Arrend was in the opposite direction of where she'd been going, at least where she *thought* she was going. The pain had made it difficult to know anything with much clarity. All she wanted to do now was rest, but she didn't dare relax, not until she had returned to more familiar streets.

When Sam wasn't leaning on the staff for support, she dragged it, hating how helpless she felt. When she *did* reach Bastan, there was no way she'd let him know how she was doing. She needed to put forward a strong face for him. Otherwise, he'd likely take advantage of her injury.

One of the canals loomed in front of her.

Sam paused, staring at the water. In the faint moonlight, the water of the canal practically glittered, making it look like dozens of gems scattered across the surface. In some ways, it was actually beautiful. Except for the eels she knew were swimming beneath the surface, just waiting for her exposed flesh so they could bite.

With her injury, she couldn't jump the canal. That left her walking back.

As she followed its edge, she wondered if maybe she should have taken Alec up on his offer and let him walk her back. At least he could have walked her toward her part of the city. If she collapsed now, she doubted she'd be able to get back up.

Turning slowly, the canal changed course here, circling around the section of the city. Each section was an island, and some were larger than others, all interconnected by bridges, but often by a single bridge. No barges moved tonight, though if she waited long enough, she didn't doubt that she'd eventually come across some.

In the distance, a bridge arched over the canal. That was where she'd need to head. First across the canal, then back to Caster and Bastan. Once there, she could even risk asking for help. Maybe she could reach her small apartment and take a nap before finding Bastan.

The bridge seemed to take forever to reach. When she did, she climbed the stairs slowly, each step causing pain to shoot through her stomach, which then caused pain to race up her shoulder. At the top of the stairs, she paused and looked around.

There was movement behind her, she was certain of it.

Her heart fluttered.

She wouldn't be able to outrun the brutes if they chased her again. She didn't think she could outrun a child if one chased her. All she wanted to do was drag herself home.

Hurrying forward, she paused again to glance back.

Was there movement in the shadows?

She wasn't sure. Maybe.

The uncertainty was worse than knowing.

Leaning on her staff even more, she climbed down the steps on the other side of the canal and hurried into the darkness, and into the shadows, trying to ignore the pain in her side, and the pain in her shoulder, and trying to ignore the sense that someone followed her.

Sam stopped in the entrance of the tavern before making her way through the front room and into the back where she'd find Bastan.

She took in his massive table and the rows of shelves, but he was not here. She thought about rifling through the papers he had there before deciding against it. If he found out, he'd be more than angry. He'd likely take it out on her in some way.

She turned away from the room and made her way back to the tavern and threw herself into a booth near the wall where she rested her staff. She kept it assembled in case she had to dash away quickly, but in her current condition, she didn't see herself dashing anywhere.

Kevin approached. He was a few years older than she, had a long face and the faint beginning of a beard. His mop of dirty brown hair covered his eyes. In spite of that, he had a wide smile that made him almost cute.

"Sam, you look like shit."

She shook her head with a laugh. "I feel like it too."

"What happened? You've been gone for a few days. You've even got Bastan worried about you."

"Aw. You really think he's worried?" He didn't really care about anyone other than himself. Bastan was an ass in that way, but he'd also watch after her if he promised to do so. That was why she believed him when he claimed he'd help Tray.

"He left here this morning searching for you again. Came back in a mood. Then he left again tonight. Haven't seen him in a while."

She frowned. It wasn't like Bastan to be gone that much. He liked to keep close tabs on the tavern, and worried about his precious paintings, making it even more unusual for him to sneak away. Maybe he really *was* worried about her.

More likely, he was worried about some artwork he'd discovered, though maybe he *was* worried about the thief he always used to acquire it. She'd make sure he *did* worry about her. After all, she'd nearly died.

Could he have heard what happened?

If he had, what would he do? She didn't think Bastan would try to help her, not with her breaking into a high-born house. Likely, he'd be more concerned that she'd revealed one of his secrets. She knew too much about him, and about his entire operation, for him to completely leave her alone.

"You can tell him I didn't say anything," she said to Kevin.

"That's not what I was getting at."

"No? Well you can let Bastan know I'm fine."

"You don't look fine," Bastan said.

She swiveled in the booth until she could see him. He stood in shadows near the door, his hard eyes weighing her. Sam resisted the urge to shrink away from his gaze. That would only draw more of his focus, and she wanted nothing more to do with him than to tell him what she'd learned about the paper and find a place to curl up like a dog.

"Bastan. Did you hear I came back?"

"I didn't need to. I see that you're back." He waved Kevin away, and the younger man offered a beseeching look to Sam before hurrying back toward the kitchen. She hadn't even had the chance to tell him what she wanted to eat yet. Her stomach rumbled, and she knew she should have stayed with Alec long enough for the food he promised. Now Bastan would have her wait even longer.

He took a seat on the bench across from her, resting his muscled forearms on the table. A thick blue opal ring on his middle finger drew her eye. "Tell me, Sam, what happened to you?"

She shook her head. "I went back like you asked and almost got caught."

"Almost?"

"I got away."

He touched his chin, a frown furrowing his brow. "You got away, or they let you get away?"

She peeled back her cloak to show him the stitched wound. The strange blackness around it looked better already. Lucky she'd ended up with Alec. Had she wandered into any other place, she wouldn't have survived.

"If they were going to let me get away, do you think they'd have sunk a bolt into my arm?"

"The highborns used a crossbow on you?"

"Them, or their brutes. Pretty much the same as far as my shoulder is concerned."

Bastan shook his head. "They wouldn't do that. They prefer more elegant weapons. Highborns feel the sword is the only weapon that can be used. If someone used a crossbow on you, it wasn't a highborn."

She shrugged. "They might not have been highborn, but they were *with* highborns."

Who else but highborns would have been in that house? They had been almost waiting for her there. Maybe the brutes weren't highborn, but there was no doubt in her mind the men she'd overheard the first time she'd gone had been. He was the reason she'd been nabbed.

"You're smarter than this, Sam. You've evaded the highborn guards before. Why would they use crossbows when they have other weapons of choice?"

She sat back, pondering his comment. "Then who else would it have been?"

"Did you tell anyone else about the paper?"

"That's what you think this is about? That paper is useless, Bastan. It takes *blood* to write on it, and the blood doesn't fade! There are no secret messages to be found on it."

"It's not useless, and I *can* believe this would be all about the paper. I need to know if there are others working in the city…" His voice had continued to rise in intensity and he paused, leaning forward once again, his gaze intent. "What do you mean it takes blood? Is that what you found when you went back?"

"Not there. When I went back, I found a book. I took a page from it to examine and see if we could find the secret, but then I got grabbed. The healer who helped nurse me back took that sheet from me and figured out that it took blood to mark on the page."

Bastan stood suddenly and hurried toward his back room, pausing at the door and waiting for her. "Are you coming?"

"Where?"

"To prove this. Come on."

She grabbed her staff and used it to push herself up from the bench. Without it, she didn't know if she would have managed standing. The pain in her side seemed to flare as she stood, getting worse than it had been before. Her shoulder still ached, but that was less than it had been. If the pain persisted, she might have to return to Alec and see if there was anything he could do to help. She wasn't sure she'd be able to put up with it for too long. She might be tough, but there were limits to what she could tolerate.

When she reached Bastan's room, she paused, leaning on the staff. "How is Tray?"

Bastan waved his hand. "I don't know anything more than what I told you before. He's alive. They have him locked up, but they're not harming him."

"What are they doing then?"

Bastan flicked his eyes up to her almost as if he didn't want to answer. "They're questioning him, but the royals are preoccupied, so I doubt anything will happen with Tray too quickly."

From the way he said it, she knew it was more than just questioning. Bastan meant they were *questioning* him. There was a difference when it came to the highborns and those who worked for them.

In some ways, that was worse than sentencing him. She could tell it from Bastan's face too. Either he worried for her—unlikely—or he worried about what Tray might say under interrogation—which was much *more* likely.

"Why are they preoccupied?"

"Something has happened in the palace. I haven't been able to find out what quite yet."

"And you intend to?"

"They're distracted. Knowing that gives me an advantage. You, too, especially when it comes to Tray."

"Bastan—"

"I'll do what's necessary, Sam. If I can get him free, you know I will. If he speaks too much…"

"You're not going to be the reason Tray is killed. I won't help you if you do."

"You're too dramatic. They'll let him out, but I don't know when. And didn't you just tell me how to write on the paper?" He took a seat behind his table and motioned her toward the long, plush chair. "Sit. I'll call Kevin to get you some food. Maybe that will stop your stomach from rumbling like an avalanche every few minutes." He laughed softly to himself. "For a girl as small as you are, you sure do have to eat a lot."

"Don't call me a girl." She hated that, especially since she knew she looked young, but there was nothing she could do about that other than use it to her advantage when someone thought to use her presumed youth against her.

"That's no insult, Sam. You're a girl to me. Besides, you're half my age, so that makes you a girl."

It was the first time she had any idea about how old Bastan actually was. Most assumed he was nearly forty, but no one had confirmation. Now, he'd told her without her needing to ask.

Bastan opened a drawer on his table and pulled out one of the sheets of parchment she'd first brought him, setting it on the desk and smoothing it. "I haven't sold any of these. Yet. They'll be more valuable once their secret is known."

"There's nothing valuable in paper you can only write on in blood."

Bastan stared at the page. "I'm not so sure. There are rumors of something like this within the university."

"The physickers?"

He barely nodded. "Most of the physickers use their science to heal, but there's long been a rumor that they have another way of healing when that fails. It's probably why they're able to charge so much," he finished with a smile.

"You think they have magic paper?" For some reason, hearing that made the physickers' ability sound so much less exciting. She'd always had visions of sterile walls, of the physickers moving from room to room, using medicines much like what Alec had concocted to heal others, and having knowledge that no one else could even understand. If it was all about magic... that would be disappointing.

"Who's to say? They're far more advanced than any healer you'll find in Caster."

He reached into his drawer and pulled out a small vial of blue ink and set it on the table. Dipping his quill into the ink, he started writing. The ink faded the same as it had when he'd tried that before.

"You already know what will happen with that."

"I have to prove that it will," he said. "So I know what is different when I add this." He pulled a knife from a sheath at his belt and pricked his thumb with a wince. When he was finished, he dropped the blood into the ink bottle and stirred it with the quill. Taking the quill out, he started writing across the surface in a neat and flowing script.

Sam watched, her breath held as she did. Would it work for him the same way it had worked for Alec?

The ink had a reddish tint to it and clung to the page for a moment before fading away much like it had before. Bastan swore softly under his breath and dipped the quill into the ink again before scrawling across the page. The ink almost appeared to float atop the surface of the page before being absorbed.

"You saw this work?" he asked.

"I saw what he wrote. It worked, Bastan." She thought about getting up and joining him at the table, but the pain in her side was too much. "Try a little more blood."

Bastan looked up at her then, his lips pressed together in a frown. It seemed as if he needed to make a decision, and when he did, he squeezed the end of the thumb he'd pricked, drawing out a wheel of blood. He smeared this onto the page, writing in a looping script that was nothing like when he wrote with the pen.

The blood smeared across the page.

"See?" she said to him.

Even as she spoke, the blood began to darken, becoming brown, and then slowly disappeared.

With a wince, she climbed out of her chair and hobbled to the table. "What's different?"

Bastan stared at the page. "You said blood was the key."

"Because that's what he told me. He showed me the page that he'd written on using blood."

"The one you stole from the book?"

She nodded.

"It's possible, then, that this is a different type of paper. Maybe it's one that will not react with blood."

Sam wondered if that might be true. The paper seemed the same as what she'd taken from the highborn house before, but why would it work for Alec and not for Bastan? Was it the kind of ink he used? Alec had seemed to know something about inks, and she remembered him mentioning something about walnut...

"Maybe it's the base," she said. "I think he had other things mixed into the ink as well as the blood."

Only, hadn't the page had a bloody smear along the top of it, one that would have only come from when he said he'd accidentally cut himself on the walnut shell? That hadn't required the ink or the other things in the base.

Bastan continued staring at the page. Sam had seen that kind of expression from him before, and it had her slightly worried. "What are you planning?"

"I might pay a visit to this healer friend of yours and see what he figured out with the paper. Maybe there's more to it than only the blood. If there is, and if that's how the highborns can communicate with each other, then I'll do everything I need to understand."

Sam was too tired to care what he intended, other than worrying about Alec. He'd helped her, and she didn't want Bastan doing anything that would harm him.

"Only questions, Bastan. Don't hurt him."

"You care about a healer you just met?"

"I wouldn't be alive if it weren't for him. I owe him."

"I need to know the secret to this paper, Sam."

"That doesn't mean you have to torture him. You can ask him questions."

Bastan's mouth twisted in a look of almost distaste.

"I'll do whatever I need to get the answers," he said. "There are men working in my city that I need to know about. I *will* have answers, even if that means going to your apothecary friend."

"And if he's highborn?"

Bastan laughed. "Highborns don't work as apothecaries. Physickers, yes, but apothecaries are merchants. I *can* question a merchant without fear of reprisal."

"Just... don't."

"You'll owe me."

She stuck her tongue out at him. She didn't have the energy for much else.

"I promise to be circumspect in my questioning."

He stared at the page, ignoring her. Sam had enough experience with Bastan to know he wouldn't say anything more unless he wanted to. Once he got into a mindset like this, he was bound to remain focused.

She could wait for him to finish, but she preferred to leave instead. She needed to sleep, then she had to start planning how to get Tray out of the highborn cells before their questioners harmed him.

"Can I have a sheet?" she asked.

Bastan didn't answer.

Sam sniffed and used her staff like a cane as she stomped around to the other side of his table and pulled one of the remaining sheets from the drawer, folding it and stuffing it into the pocket of her cloak. Through it all, Bastan didn't look up, so she left him alone so she could go rest.

11

SEARCHING FOR SUPPLIES

A lec sat at the desk, the quill resting lightly in his hand, the nib still coated in the thick blood ink he'd mixed. He didn't know why he continued using this ink, but that he'd used the pen in the blood ink as long as he had, he probably needed to pick up another quill, as well. Otherwise, his father would be upset.

He looked at the words he'd added to Sam's piece of paper describing Hyp's symptoms. They were really no different from when he'd visited earlier. He pulled the sheet of his father's paper and looked at the notes he'd written after that visit.

Mild abdominal discomfort. Shortness of breath. Sweaty palms. Likely hysteria. Given prolac leaves and loral berries.

The same. But on this visit, Hyp had seemed even more miserable than he had before, though Alec didn't know how that was possible. With Hyp, he always seemed miserable.

Sighing once more, he set the page on top of the stack

with the others. He stoppered the ink and used a section of torn-off cloth to wipe down the quill. Another length of cloth covered his thumb, keeping the fresh cut he'd used to mix the blood ink dry.

He kept waiting for his father to return, but with each passing day, he began to suspect this was one of his longer harvests. Every so often, his father would disappear for weeks at a time.

Alec left the shop, twisting the lock behind him. It had taken a little working to repair the lock, but he'd managed to fix the damage Sam had caused. He didn't really blame her for breaking in. With the injuries she'd sustained, she needed any sort of healing she could find, regardless of whether it came from an apothecary or one of the physickers, though if she really *was* lowborn, the physickers wouldn't take her on. It was often hard enough to get them to take on those from Arrend, especially since they were so far removed from the wealthier sections of the city. Arrend wasn't near the edge of the city—not lowborn as Sam would have said—but situated where they were, they weren't highborn. They were merchants, a middle class in the city.

It was one of the reasons why Alec didn't think he'd ever be able to study at the university, even if age weren't an issue. He trained with his father, and he had come to terms with the fact that he would never be anything more than an apothecary, but part of him *did* want to go and study. How much more could he learn if he went? How many more could he help?

The street was busy. In the distance, he heard the sounds of gulls swooping over the canals, and the loud hollers from the barge drivers stopping to deliver grain, or textiles, or other supplies to the merchants. A few people made their way along the street, and most nodded at him as he passed. Alec weaved through the street on his way toward Mrs. Rubbles' shop and paused outside.

She had a well-kept shop that was the envy of many of the other shop owners in the area. Clean glass windows displayed her recent acquisitions, with prices neatly written on them. Most wouldn't dare waste paper on something like that, but as she was a stationery seller, it seemed only fitting that she would.

Through the window, he didn't see anyone inside, and when he pushed open the door—hearing a tinkling bell much like the one his father used above their door—he didn't see her behind the counter, either.

Alec wandered the rows of supplies. Stacks of paper were neatly arranged toward the front of the shop, most of high quality. He traced his fingers along the pages, realizing that even these of high quality didn't really compete with the fine paper Sam possessed. Where had she gotten paper like that?

One wall had various inks, all of different colors. A few powdered inks were there, letting those with particular artistic flair have the ability to mix whatever colors they wanted. His father would occasionally mix specific colors, mostly because he liked to add diagrams to his journal, but Alec had never really found the need to draw the same way his father did. That was as much because he had no artistic skill as because he didn't find the same value.

She had pencils and paints and other kinds of paper

throughout the store. Lumps of wax and various seals could be found also.

"Alec," she said, sweeping out from the back of the store, a wide smile plastered on her face. "I'm grateful to see you! Whatever you gave me worked. I'm feeling *much* better than I was before."

He appraised her with a clinical eye and noted the swelling of her neck seemed to have gone down, and she no longer had the sheen of sweat he'd seen the last time. Would her heart rate have slowed too? She'd had an obvious glandular issue, one the medicines he'd given her should only have suppressed, but she looked as she claimed she felt—better than when he'd last seen her.

"I'm glad to hear it. I'd still like you to see my father when he gets back."

She waved a hand dismissively. "Only if I start feeling poorly again. Why bother Aelus when I'm well?"

"I think I only masked it, Mrs. Rubbles. You'll need to see my father to get a more definitive solution."

"Alec, you shouldn't doubt your skills. You're nearly the healer your father is. I think in a few more years, he might even succeed in getting you into the university."

Alec forced a smile. As much as he wanted that opportunity, he would take over the apothecary when his father decided it was time to retire and continue to help others in this part of the city.

"That's nice of you to say," he said. "When you have some free time, you should stop down to the shop so I can do a more thorough assessment. You know how my father likes to have everything documented."

"I know. That's why he's my best customer. You know

he's the only one I order specific paper for? He has particular needs for the stock, wanting to ensure it holds up over time, as if the other paper I could sell him wouldn't." She shrugged. "But for Aelus, I'd do anything."

Alec nodded. Most felt the same way about his father. This part of the city was close in ways other parts were not, but his father's willingness to care for others—regardless of their ability to pay—endeared him to others. Alec didn't always agree with his father and the fact that he was willing to give away his services.

"Do you have any of his preferred paper?"

Mrs. Rubbles tapped the side of her nose. "I always keep a little in stock. Nothing like that paper you had. I would *love* to have a chance to learn more about it." Alec smiled as she hurried around to the back of the store, moving with a swifter pace than he'd seen her manage in quite a while, before popping back out and handing a large stack of paper to him. "I'll bill your father as I always do."

Alec nodded, looking at the quills on one of the shelves. Most were standard quills, but there was one that looked as if it had an ink reservoir within it. He picked it up and turned it over. "This is new, isn't it?"

Mrs. Rubbles smiled. "This style comes from Lycithan."

"Lycithan?"

"They're far down the coast. A hard sail, from what I hear, but they have such artisans there who can turn the wood."

"It's amazing."

"If you like this, you should see the jewelry they

produce. It's equally impressive, and equally expensive, but a Lycithan jewel is said to steal any woman's heart," she added with a laugh. "Did you ever figure out the right mixture of ink?"

Alec frowned. For some reason, he felt uncomfortable sharing with Mrs. Rubbles what he'd needed to do to write on the page. There was a part of him that felt uncomfortable admitting that he'd used his own blood to write on the paper, but it was the only thing that had worked. Nothing else, even with all the different colorants he could try, made a difference.

"Have you ever known any paper not to accept ink?" he asked.

Mrs. Rubbles frowned. "Not take ink? That wouldn't be common, or of much use, unless there was only a particular kind of ink that worked. I could see that having some value."

"Why?"

She shrugged. "There are plenty of reasons to want to communicate covertly, Alec."

"But once it's written, there's nothing covert about it."

Mrs. Rubbles grinned at him and winked. Alec was taken aback. Normally, she was a reserved woman, and the arthritis in her hips made her move slowly. There was something almost playful about her today. Had he given her something that would make her like this?

"Watch this," she said. She went behind her counter and pulled out a sheet of parchment. It had yellowed edges that curled slightly as if it had been rolled up for a long time. She took a bottle out from underneath her table and dipped a narrow pen into the ink, then wrote her name in a flowing script: *Marcella Rubbles.*

She set her pen down and reached for another bottle beneath the table. She dipped a brush into the bottle and brushed it across the ink. Alec watched, fascinated. As he did, the ink began to fade then disappeared completely. It looked much like what the other paper had done, almost as if it were coated in the liquid Mrs. Rubbles used.

"What is that?" he asked.

She winked at him again. "That, my boy, is the secret most in my position would not share. Since you have me feeling better than I have in years, I figured I owed you at least a demonstration. Now watch." She took the page over to a lantern and held it above to catch the heat. As she did, the paper began to glow softly, and the writing became clearer, revealing her name once more.

Mrs. Rubbles set the page down on the counter with a flourish.

"What's to keep people from just holding any page up to heat to reveal the writing?"

She nodded. "That's a good question. There's always a mark on the page, usually in the corner, that tells you what reagent to use to reveal the writing. Some will be revealed by heat, though that's too common to be of much use. There are a few that are combustible, so that when heat is applied, the page blackens and burns. A few require a specific chemical, but those are only useful if you can guarantee the recipient will have the right chemical."

Had the page Sam stole—he had to believe the page was stolen, and not one she'd come across by any other means—had such a mark? He didn't remember. He'd been so focused on trying to write on the page that he hadn't considered looking to see if there was anything else.

"And you know the different marks?" he asked.

"Not all. Many are kept secret, only shared between those who will need to know. Those within the palace have a specific treatment they use on all their pages, making intercepting them almost impossible."

With the quality of the page, he wondered if maybe that was what Sam had acquired. If that were the case, what was hidden beneath his writing? What secret did he mask?

"Ah, this isn't really a topic I should be sharing with you, anyway, Alec. You'll be more likely to document the medicines you use and the way treatments succeed, especially when you get to the university, so I shouldn't fill your mind with worry about things like this. If you're interested in inks today, I can show you the collection I have, and see if there's anything there that might interest you?"

"That's all right, Mrs. Rubbles. I should be getting back to the shop."

She tapped her hand on the counter. "You tell your father when he returns that he needs to come speak to me. Now that I know you're such a skilled healer, I think he might be able to hand over more of the responsibility of the day-to-day activity to you, and I have ways I can use him!"

Alec bobbed his head in a nod. "I'll tell him."

He left the stationery store, holding on to the bundle of paper from Mrs. Rubbles. Heavy clouds darkened the sky, and he worried about coming rain. Alec had hopes of being able to wander in the city a little longer, thinking maybe he could find his way toward the Caster section —*not* because of Sam, but to see where she would have gotten hurt—but with rain coming, he decided against it. Better not to risk damaging the paper.

When he returned to the shop, he noted the door ajar.

Hadn't he repaired the lock?

Alec was certain he had, but maybe he hadn't managed to completely fix it. It was one more problem to deal with. A gust of wind met him at the door, and he hurriedly closed it behind him. He'd need something to hold it closed until he could fix it properly. For now, the simple barricade would have to do.

Turning back to face the inside of the shop, he realized he wasn't alone.

A hulking man stood near the back of the shop. With the coming storm, the inside of the shop was dimly lit, though a lantern remained glowing. The man held papers out toward the lantern, his thick brow furrowed as it appeared he attempted to read them. A sword hung from his waist, but that wasn't what drew Alec's attention. It was the crossbow slung over his shoulder.

The man pulled his eyes off the page and glared at Alec.

"Can I help you?" Alec asked. He noticed that one of the pages the man held was the one he'd written Sam's symptoms on.

"Is this your place?" He had a thick accent. Was that from one of the outer sections? Alec hadn't traveled across the entirety of the city—the extensive canals made that difficult—but his father had. He'd probably recognize the accent.

"This is my father's apothecary," he answered. Alec stayed toward the front of the shop, not wanting to risk the crossbow. If this was the man who attacked Sam, then he wanted to be as careful as possible. That meant having a way out.

"Apothecary. With notes like these, it appears you would be one of the famed physickers."

Alec swallowed. That was always the risk of his father's notes. Some within the university didn't take all that kindly to having others do many of the same things they did, especially when they had as much skill as his father did.

"Not a physicker. An apothecary. We keep notes of what works, and nothing more. We're not trying to infringe on the physickers."

The man's glower deepened. "Do you think I care about the physickers?"

Alec didn't know. As he took a slow step backward, moving toward the door, the massive man pulled the crossbow from his shoulder and casually aimed it at him.

"I thought you said this was your shop?"

Alec nodded.

"Then where are you slinking off to?"

His heart started pounding, and his mind began working through all the symptoms he experienced. *Rapid heart rate. Sweating. Breathing becoming erratic.* They could be Hyp's symptoms just as well as they were his.

"I don't want any trouble. Take whatever you need."

The man snorted. "No trouble?" He took a step forward, the crossbow still aimed at his chest.

Alec didn't dare move. If he did, and if the man triggered the crossbow, who would be there to heal him? He'd seen the effect the poison used on the bolt would have, and without his father or access to the university, he doubted he'd survive.

"What I *need* is to find out where she is."

Sam.

"I don't know where she went," he said quickly. Lying to this man would only end up with him hurt. Telling the truth might lead to the same place, but at least he might survive.

"You helped her?"

Alec nodded. "She broke in and was bleeding. She nearly died from a crossbow…"

The man smiled grimly. "Nearly. That's what I needed to hear." He shook the pages in his other hand, hovering them slightly above the lantern. "And which of these is your notes on her?"

Something about this man told Alec that he didn't want him to have the page describing Sam's injuries, so Alec took a chance. "The one on the bottom," he said, pointing to the page on which he'd first written Hyp's symptoms. If the man couldn't read—and there were many who could not—maybe he'd leave Alec alone and only take the sheet.

The man crumpled the sheet and stuffed it in his pocket. The rest he set on the desk. He pulled a small flask from inside his pocket and poured it on the pages. Even from where Alec stood, he could smell the kerosene.

"Don't—"

He didn't have a chance to finish.

The man tipped the lantern on its side. Flames begin licking the pages, racing across the surface, and working down the desk. Within moments, the entirety of the desk was engulfed in flames and thick smoke.

Alec spun and raced for the door.

He heard the first bolt whiz past him, sinking into the doorframe, but pulled the door open and ran, not waiting for another.

In the street, rain pelted him. The sky was a black and purple bruise, and thunder rolled. Most of the time when it rained like this, he hated it, but with the fire in the shop, he couldn't help but feel relief. Even if the shop went completely up in flames, the damage would be limited by the rain.

That wouldn't restore everything his father had harvested over the years. All those leaves, berries, grasses, and even the oils. Everything would burn.

He hurried to an overhang across the street and ducked around the corner.

Once hidden, Alec peeked his head out long enough to see the huge man come racing from inside the shop. Flames followed, hissing from the rain. Plumes of bitter smoke, scented by the different leaves and herbs his father had within the shop, came with it.

Another man joined the first, almost as large.

What had Sam gotten him into?

He crouched, afraid to move, forced to watch as the shop began to burn. The apothecary was far enough away from other buildings that it didn't risk them coming down unless the flames leaped out of control. With the rain, there should be no way that would happen.

A loud explosion thundered from within the shop.

Flames exploded outward, first catching on the front of the shop, then climbing to the roof, quickly engulfing the building. The rain seemed to have no effect, sizzling away and leaving a thick blanket of steam hanging like fog over the street. The heat from the fire pushed him back, making it hard for him to even breath.

Alec couldn't move.

His father's shop was a complete loss. The brick walls managed to stay standing, but he was certain nothing was salvageable. The fire seemed to weaken. It didn't happen gradually, but all of a sudden, and with a massive gust of heated air, like some angry god sucking in the heat and flame and swallowing it.

Alec could do nothing but stare. Sweat mixed with rain and possibly tears, all of it running down his face.

Where would he go now?

What would his father do?

What would *he* do?

THE VALUE OF PAPER

When Sam awoke, her head throbbed. It was a pulsing sort of pain that ran from her scalp, almost through the ends of her dark hair, and went in waves down her body before stopping at her toes.

She sat up in her bed and stared at the window for long moments, trying to focus her mind on where she was and what had happened to her. Bright light streamed through her window, and she wondered how she'd managed to sleep at all with as bright as it was. Normally, she needed the dark, but she'd obviously forgotten to throw the blanket over the window like she normally did.

How long had she slept?

Long enough that she began to think what she'd experienced had been some sort of dream. Maybe not a dream. A nightmare.

But had it been a dream, would she remember the pain she knew now? Would she remember the searing heat from the crossbow shooting through her shoulder, or the way the glass had punctured her side, leaving her almost gasping for air? Would she remember the brutes chasing her, and her feeling helpless, unable to do anything to get away, feeling like she'd get caught by another bolt in the back, or have one sink through her chest as she turned down the wrong street.

Her shoulder throbbed, but less than her head. Her stomach ached, as well, but it was a hunger-type pain, nothing more. That didn't seem right.

Sam reached for the bandage on her right shoulder, and unraveled it slowly. When Alec had shown her the wound the first time, she'd almost gagged. Not only had the wound looked angry and possibly infected, and not only had the strange blackening to her flesh made her nervous, but there was an odor to it, almost like her flesh had already started to rot.

When she unrolled the cloth, she looked at her shoulder. The long cut appeared healed beneath the stitches. The blackness that had consumed her shoulder wasn't there anymore.

Either she'd been asleep *much* longer than she realized, or Alec's healing was incredible.

She pulled up her shirt and looked at her stomach. The cut there had healed, the skin smooth and pink, but otherwise much better than before. She touched the stitches, and they crumbled, falling free from her skin as if they weren't meant to be there.

What in the world?

Sam took a tentative breath.

What had pained her before was now gone. All she felt now was the soft ache where the wounds *had* been.

Her stomach rumbled again.

She must have been asleep longer than she knew. Otherwise, she wouldn't be this hungry. Before leaving Bastan, she'd convinced Kevin to serve her a heaping bowl of stew along with two hunks of bread. There was no way she should still be this hungry unless she'd been out for a few days.

If that were the case, *why* had she slept so long?

Sam stood. The wobble to her legs was gone, as was the need to cling to the staff. She stood in front of the window and pulled it open, taking a deep breath of air. It had a crispness to it, and she sighed, letting it fill her lungs.

Whatever had healed her—either time or the concoction Alec used—she would take advantage of it.

Dressing quickly, she threw her cloak back over her shoulders and stuffed the staff into one of the interior pockets. To this, she added the folded-up page of paper she'd taken from Bastan. Maybe she'd try to see if it would work for her later. There were other things she had to worry about first. Like Tray.

Outside the room, she hurried down the hall and reached the outside. There was a bustle of people in the street, enough for her to know it was late in the day. Maybe she'd only slept all night, waking in the middle of the day. That would explain why her stomach rumbled as it did.

She needed to get to Tray, but Bastan claimed he was trying to help. She wasn't convinced that he was, which made her feel the need to discover on her own whether he really *was* helping, and whether what he'd told her was true.

There was only one person she knew she could go to for that kind of information, but she wasn't sure she wanted to trust Marin again, especially after she'd misled her when it came to the gems before.

Sam moved quickly through the streets, weaving around others, the pain in her side fading to nothing the farther she went. As she walked, even the throbbing in her head started to fade. Other than the hunger, she felt refreshed.

The buildings in the Caster section were nothing like those in other sections. Most thought Caster one of the oldest sections of the city. It was certainly the most run down. Stone crumbled from the faces of many of them, and boards were often used to prevent additional deterioration, but left the fronts of the buildings looking even worse. Had they only been painted, it might be better, but they were left raw. It was unfortunate. Most of these buildings, while old, had been well made once. Now they were dirty and broken, like the people of Caster.

In some places, the buildings had fallen, leaving piles of stone. Eventually, someone cleared the rubble and rebuilt, often squeezing two buildings into the same space, but it made it look worse.

When she reached Marin's building—one of the better kept buildings in this section of the city—she paused outside, staring up at the window. The woman wouldn't likely be there. She was never in when Sam stopped by. Most of the time, Marin found her rather than the other way around.

Sam decided to try anyway.

She went through the main door and up the hall before she reached Marin's rooms, pausing to give a respectful knock. There was no answer.

Figures.

Sam tried again, giving her another minute to answer, but none came.

She slipped her lock-pick set out of a cloak pocket and wiggled it in the door until the lock sprung open. As it did, she let out a soft cry of success, cutting it off as she worried she'd been too loud. Tray always warned her about that.

The inside of Marin's home was dark. Sam stood in the doorway until her eyes adjusted, and then closed the door behind her. There was an herbal scent to the room that reminded her in some ways of how Alec's shop had smelled. A narrow bed was shoved against one wall, and there was a table and chair next to it, much like what she'd seen in Bastan's room. They were more alike than either of them would ever admit, not that she'd tell them that. Neither would appreciate the comparison.

A stack of papers on the desk drew her attention.

Sam stepped over and thumbed through it. She found a few diagrams much like the one she'd been given for the home she'd invaded. Were these other places that Marin intended to break into? What else would she find in these homes? Nothing valuable. Maybe only more paper.

Sam put the papers back down, ensuring they were the way she'd found them. A row of ink reminded her of Bastan again, as did the quill resting in front of it. All she needed was to find a drawer full of paper she couldn't write on and she'd feel like she was in Bastan's office.

There was a small chest resting along the wall and Sam flipped it open. She found another cloak like the one she wore along with a coil of rope. That might be useful for her.

Sam left the table and went to the window, peeking out from behind the curtain to peer at the street.

Marin headed toward her home.

Kyza!

She needed to be more careful. If Marin caught her here, it'd be almost as bad as Bastan finding her in his office alone, and she *never* risked breaking into his office.

Sam hurried toward the door and ducked behind it just as she heard steps along the floorboards. There wasn't any way she could get out, not without Marin knowing she'd been here.

Kyza!

She took a quick survey of the room, but there was no place for her to hide here, either.

Sam twisted the lock, thankful that it fell into place quietly, and hurried to the window. Ducking behind the curtain, she pulled open the window and climbed out. It reminded her of what she'd had to do with the highborn house.

Hanging from the ledge, she reached with one hand and pulled the window almost completely closed, and dangled where she was. From here, the drop was too high for her to survive. She started uncoiling the rope, readying to climb down, when she heard the distinctive note of the woman's voice.

"She wasn't supposed to get caught," Marin said. "There shouldn't have been anyone there. We had word she was in the—"

"Does it matter? She escaped." This came from another, deeper voice in a coarse whisper.

"And nearly died, from what I hear."

"But she didn't."

"She's far too valuable alive for us to risk her."

Sam didn't understand what she had overheard. Why would she be valuable to Marin? And did Marin know more about what happened to her?

Her arms began to ache, and she had started to slide down the rope, not wanting to get caught, when Marin appeared at the window and grabbed Sam's arm before she could move.

Sam was tossed into the room and came to her feet scanning for the other voice. There was no sign of the other person who had been with Marin. Flowers were situated around the room, almost strategically, that she hadn't noticed when she'd first entered. Marin didn't seem the type for such frivolity. The scents of herbs filled her nose again, and the air had a charge to it, an energy, that Sam couldn't fully understand.

Marin watched her intently. Was it amusement or annoyance in her glare? "How long have you been listening?"

"Long enough," Sam said.

Marin tipped her head, and a hint of a smile played along her lips. "Your mother would have been proud."

That was the last thing Sam had expected to hear. "My mother? What does she have to do with anything?"

Marin sighed deeply and motioned toward her door. "She has to do with everything. Sit down. We need to talk."

"I don't want to sit down. I want to help Tray. I want answers."

Marin stood by her window. "We'll see what we can do about the first, and I'll do what I can to provide the second."

"I need your help with Tray," Sam said, pushing out the words in a hurry. She needed to get Marin on her side as quickly as possible, and if nothing else, the woman had an affection for her brother.

"Others are working on it," Marin said.

"Others? Like Bastan? He said he had a man inside the prison but that he didn't want to use him unless he had to. I don't think he really wants to do anything to help him, but I know you at least care for him. Or you seem to. I'll do whatever you need, Marin. I'll work for you. Take whatever job you require. Just help me get my brother back."

Marin turned away from the window and met Sam's eyes. "I want your brother back as much as you do."

Sam doubted that, but she wasn't about to argue with Marin, especially not when she needed her help. "Bastan won't be able to help. He'll want to, but Bastan is only out for himself."

"How is that any different from the rest of us?" Marin asked.

"I've not been only out for myself. I've wanted to do anything I could to help Tray. That's why I've done what I have. I want to keep him safe."

"For you. You wanted to keep your family safe, not that anyone would ever blame you. But that was as much for you as it was for Tray, don't you think?"

Sam stood uncertain how to answer. She never felt like she'd done anything for herself. Hadn't she always done what she had to help Tray for his sake? With their family gone, who else would look after him? Who else but Sam cared about him the way that she did?

"Will you help him?" she asked. What else was there to say?

Marin studied her for a moment. "I'll do what I can."

Sam clasped her hands together nervously. "Thank you." When Marin said nothing more, Sam went on. "Why did you say my mother would have been proud of me?"

Marin's expression changed. Was it sadness or something else that caused her eyes to glitter softly? "Because she would have been. Your mother wanted you to know where you came from, but it wasn't safe to share."

"And you know?"

"I know better than anyone."

"Why?"

Marin watched her for a moment before turning to one of the shelves and pulling a tall book from it, opening it in her palms and holding it out to Sam. "Do you recognize this?"

Sam studied the page. There was nothing on it other than a single symbol in the bottom corner. The page reminded her of the one she'd stolen from the book in the highborn house, the one that she'd stuffed in her boot and left behind when Alec had healed her.

Did Marin have more of those pages?

Could the paper really have been what she'd sought?

Sam hadn't thought that likely, but when Bastan had discussed ways the paper could be used, she realized there might be more to it than she'd considered. Certainly, Bastan had seen plenty of ways for the paper to be useful, why wouldn't Marin be the same?

"From your expression and lack of response, I take it that you've seen this before."

"It's the same as what you sent me into the highborn house after," Sam accused.

"Yes. The same type of paper, only this is different. This has been written on, unlike what you were to acquire."

"You knew it was paper in the highborn house? Why didn't you tell me!"

"Would you have gone after it if you had thought it was paper? Would you have taken the same risk?"

"Of course not. For paper? What's the point of going after paper? I know Bastan thinks there's value in it—"

"Because Bastan recognizes the uses, even if he's not sure *why* he recognizes them."

"You expect me to believe that this paper is worth more than the palace gems?"

Marin leaned toward her, fixing her with an intense stare. "Why do you think the palace *has* the gems?"

"To control the wealth. They have the lowborns mine them, and then they hoard them, controlling the wealth we have available to us."

Marin smiled. "You sound as if you've been listening to Bastan."

Sam didn't answer. She might have heard him say

something similar once before. "If not to control the lowborns, then why would they hoard it?"

"For something far more valuable."

Marin looked at the paper, and Sam frowned. "You can't really believe they use them to buy this paper."

"There are other reasons, but the simple answer is that they're connected far more than most realize. And yes, this paper is much more valuable than the gems." Marin closed the book and tapped the page. "How much do you think a single page costs?"

"In gems?"

Marin nodded.

"I suppose you could probably get quite a few pages for one of the gems." It was nice paper, but there was no way it was worth anything more than that, was there?

Marin held up her hand, palm facing upward.

"What is that?" Sam asked.

"This size of gem," Marin said.

"What, your hand?"

"That's the size required to purchase a single sheet of paper, and that's *if* you can find the source."

Sam's breath caught. "But I grabbed"—she paused to think about how many pages she'd taken from the high-born house—"probably two dozen sheets!"

Marin tipped her head in a nod. "That is what I hear."

"Does Bastan know?"

Marin shook her head. "No. He only knows the pages have some value, not the extent of it. Bastan understands quality though. I have diverted as many of my resources as I can to obtain the pages from him."

"I don't understand. Why are these pages so valuable? Why can't you write on them?"

"Ah, but that's the very thing that *makes* them valuable."

"Because you can't write on them? That doesn't make any sense."

"It's not that they can't be written on, but that only a certain few have the ability to do so."

Sam had tried, but had not been able to do anything. Bastan had tried but failed. Alec... He had managed to write on the page, even if it was one that had already been marked. Did that make it *more* likely that he'd be able to write on it, or less?

"Who has the ability?"

"Samara, these are complicated questions you're asking. I am willing to share with you that the paper itself is valuable, and I'm willing to help you understand that it's important to reclaim what Bastan now possesses, but the rest..."

"Please. If it has something to do with what happened to Tray, I deserve to know."

"Deserve?"

"You sent me there. It's *your* fault he was captured."

Marin sighed. "It has to do with a battle older than you know. One few in the city know about, and the reason we are isolated as we are."

"What kind of battle?"

Marin looked past Sam, staring at the door. Her brow furrowed in a crease. "Ah, it seems we have even less time than I realized." She went to the trunk at the end of her bed and flipped open the top, pulling a crossbow and sword from it. She stood on one side of her door, her back to the doorway. "Go. I think you've attempted to escape through the window once before?"

Sam glanced over at the window. "Who's coming?"

"Thelns, from the sound of it. They're heavy footed, but you can probably hear that, can't you?"

There was a steady and deep sound of footsteps across the floorboards. There was a rhythm to the sound that she had heard before. She could almost close her eyes and imagine the steady thudding sound as it chased her, the pain throbbing in her shoulder... her stomach on fire from the glass that had punctured it.

"The brutes?" she asked.

Marin raised a finger to her lips. "Brutes. As good a name as any, and fitting." She tipped her head to the door, listening for a moment. Her hand tensed on the crossbow, holding it against the frame of the door. "Thelns are dangerous, for us especially. They have a way of following those like us, tracking us through our scent, and their poison affects us more than others."

Sam tried to parse through everything she'd said but could only come up with one question. "Poison?"

She thought about what Alec had told her about the crossbow bolt that had pierced her shoulder. There had been a poison on it, one that he didn't recognize. He'd still managed to heal her, though.

Marin nodded, focusing on the door. "If it reaches our bloodstream, we die. There's no cure for it." Marin slipped the sword into a sheath Sam hadn't seen and grabbed the door. "You should move, Samara. It's dangerous for you to remain. I'll hold them off as long as possible."

Sam crossed the room and pulled the window open, looking down into the street. She didn't see any movement, but she'd learned that didn't always matter.

"You can be healed from the poison, though."

"There's no cure," Marin said. "It's how your mother died."

Sam was pulling the window open when Marin's words sank in. "It's *what?*"

Marin considered her for a moment. "This isn't how you should find out, but it's how your mother died. Theln bolt to the stomach. There was no cure. She knew she was going to die. Told me I had to make sure you were safe."

The floor outside Marin's room creaked.

"You have to go, Samara. There will be time for answers later."

Marin looked over to her, her eyes urging Sam on.

She climbed over the window sill and stood motionless for a moment.

Marin took a step back as the door splintered open.

Sam ducked down, barely managing to do so in time before a bolt shot across the room, sinking into the wall near where she'd been standing.

Marin fired her crossbow, and it caught the man in the neck.

"Go!" she urged Sam without looking over again.

There was the sound of more steps along the floor.

Sam dropped from the window, hanging as she had when she'd broken just a short time ago. Then, she'd feared only Marin catching her. This time, she feared the brutes reaching her, and what they would do if they did.

In spite of the fear running through her, a different emotion consumed her.

Marin didn't just know of her mother, she knew her well.

She'd always believed that Marin knew of her. The things that she said about her mother had always had a ring of truth to them, but this was more that she *knew* her. More than that, there was a secret to her mother that Sam would never have suspected.

How had her mother kept a secret from her? More importantly, *why* had she hidden a secret from her?

There was a shout from inside Marin's home just as Sam was busy tying the rope outside the window again. She waited, hoping she'd hear Marin come after her, but she didn't. Instead, Marin spoke calmly.

"You shouldn't have risked the city, Ralun."

"You were hiding her?"

Sam shivered. She'd heard that voice before.

Before Sam could think about how he'd found her, her hands slipped, and she slid down the rope, reaching the street. She hesitated a moment before jerking the rope free.

What was she to do now? Marin involved her in something much bigger than a simple theft, and now Tray was missing. Bastan *could* help, but she doubted that he would. Why would he risk himself unnecessarily?

That left only Sam, but how was she supposed to get to Tray? What could she do?

Nothing.

Which meant that Tray would remain trapped, held in the cells while the royals dealt with... whatever it was taking place in the palace. He hadn't done anything, and she had to believe that he'd eventually be freed, but what if he wasn't? What if the royals decided it would be simpler to get rid of a threat?

Being lowborn, living on the streets, thieving to keep them alive. All she and Tray had was each other. She had to help him.

As she ran, she hazarded a glance back and saw the face of the brute who had shot her staring down at her. How had he found her?

And why did it seem Marin knew him?

13

BEGINNING TO PLAN

S am raced through the streets, keeping her ears and eyes open and prepared for the possibility that the brutes chased her. She didn't hear them, but Sam wasn't sure whether she would hear them now.

Was Marin still alive? Why did it seem Marin had known one of them?

There was a time when she wouldn't have cared, but that was before she thought Marin had the answers she'd been searching for.

Sam needed help, and knew she had no option other than Bastan.

That wasn't an option she cared for, but what else could she do? The man was connected, and maybe he didn't care for Tray the way she did or even the way Marin did, but he was the only one she thought could help.

The sound of footsteps behind her turned her away from Caster, and as she ran, jumping from section to section, she realized where she was headed, even if unintentionally.

This section of the city was so much different from hers, with buildings that were well maintained rising on either side of a wide street. The people here were better dressed, and they glanced at her as she passed, though there was little she could do to hide from their notice. She hoped to avoid too much detection, but doing so wasn't completely possible here. But she had needed—well, *wanted*—to come.

Where was the apothecary?

She had been injured when she'd come along here before, but not so injured that she should have lost track of where it was in this section of the city. When she'd left Alec, she had been mostly restored—at least enough that she shouldn't have lost her way during the journey.

A few lights glowed in windows, and the air of this part of the city had less of the stink from the canals than in Caster. She passed what had to have been a bakery, and her mouth immediately began watering, but Sam tore herself away, refusing to succumb to her growling stomach. It wouldn't do for her to be caught in this section. Likely, someone would identify her as a thief—correctly—and might send the city guard after her. If that happened, there would be nothing she could do to help Tray.

She wandered past an empty spot, likely a place where a new building was going up, and continued onward. In these sections of the city, there were many buildings that were torn down and replaced by something new, always by some rich merchant with more money than sense. At least in the Caster section, they knew well enough to simply reuse buildings. That was what Bastan would have done and had done.

Sam made a circle of the streets before coming back to that empty area. She was sure it was where Alec's apothecary had been. When she took a closer look, she realized it had not be torn down, but burned. She now caught whiff of fresh ash.

Whatever had happened here, she was sure it had not been accidental. Could it have been because he had helped her?

Rage began to simmer within her.

Could Bastan be responsible for what had happened here? She'd made a point of telling him about the apothecary, but only because she was sick and had been healed, not because she had wanted to put Alec in any kind of danger.

He had told her he intended to acquire more of the paper that he thought was so valuable, confident he would uncover some secret of the highborns.

Sam spun and raced to the canal. When she reached it, she barely paused before planting her canal staff and leaping over the water. She hurried through the nearby sections before reaching Caster. Once there, she separated the ends of her canal staff and stuffed them into hiding beneath her cloak. She stalked toward the tavern, her rage quickening her pace. Once inside, she barreled through to Bastan's office.

"Did you do it?" Sam asked, before realizing that Bastan wasn't alone. There was another man in the room, and it was someone she didn't recognize. He had the delicate embroidery that signified someone from the palace, but he didn't have the look of a highborn. Maybe he wasn't a highborn but only served them.

Bastan looked up at her, his flat expression taking her in for a long moment. "Sam, I will be with you in a moment."

He turned his attention back to the man and lowered his voice, saying something in a tight whisper that Sam couldn't make out. After a moment, the man laughed, leveling a long stare at Sam before leaving the room and pulling the door closed behind him.

Bastan clasped his hands on the table. "Now, Sam, would you care to tell me why you raced into my office and disrupted a meeting. What could be so important that you stormed in here the way you did?"

Sam approached the table. Her rage surging through her once again. "Did you do it?"

"Do what, Sam?"

"I told you about the apothecary because he helped me. Why would you have gone and destroyed his shop?"

Bastan blinked. "Destroy? I destroyed nothing. I haven't even had a chance to go find this apothecary. It's not as if you gave me enough information to locate it. Gods, Sam, I don't even know which section of the city it's in."

Sam steadied her breathing. Maybe Bastan hadn't been responsible, but if it wasn't him, then who? What had happened?

"Why did you return to this apothecary?" Bastan asked.

Sam didn't have a good answer. After getting away from Marin's home, she had wanted nothing more than to try to understand why the brutes had chased her. How would they have even found her?

"I was trying…" She shook the thought away. "Who were you meeting with?"

Bastan smiled at her. "That's not how this works."

"No? How does it work?"

"You work for me, remember?"

Sam shook her head. "I don't work for you. You agreed to help me with my brother—which you haven't even done—in exchange for more information about the paper. Which I provided. I think that our arrangement is incomplete, mostly because you haven't done what you promised."

Bastan sighed, and his gaze drifted past her to the door. "I've been trying to do what I promised. Truly I have. Finding out anything these days is difficult."

"What do you mean by these days?"

"I mean that information out of the palace is difficult to obtain. It wasn't easy even during the best of times, but now…" Bastan shook his head. "Now there is nothing that's getting out of the palace."

"What happened? What changed?"

"What changed is the princess and her damned illness. The palace is in a bit of an uproar, and nothing's moving in or out." He looked up at her with a bright intensity in his eyes. "Including out of the prisons. I'm sorry, Sam, I really am, but whatever is happening has made it difficult to find out anything about your brother. Until this whole business with the princess is over, your brother isn't going anywhere, I'm afraid."

Sam shook her head. "That's not acceptable."

"Acceptable or not, it is what it is. If I had more money—"

"You *do* have more money."

"Fine. Then perhaps I should say if I were *willing* to spend more money, I might be able to discover more about what was taking place, but as I said, I'm not willing to risk it. Not even for Tray."

"What does that mean?"

"It means that I can't do anything to help your brother."

"And I can?"

Bastan chuckled. "Only if you want to end up with him. No. I was trying to say that I don't think anything can be done for him until this business with the princess is over. There's no point in risking yourself."

"This is my brother we're talking about, Bastan."

"And this is what's happening during a highly sensitive time, Sam. We've done what we can, and I don't know that anything more can be done until it's all concluded."

"I refuse to believe that," she said and started to leave.

"Sam," Bastan called after her. She paused a moment then turned back to face him.

"I trust your skill. You're one of the best thieves I can hire, Sam, but I can see in your eyes what you're intending. This is beyond even you."

"What am I intending?"

"You think you can break your brother out of prison. Even if you could get in, using the tunnels between the palace and the prison, there's no way you could get back out. Don't risk it."

Sam glared at him and bit back the response she

wanted to say, choosing to say nothing at all. She turned away and left him. As she pulled his office door closed behind her, she wondered why he had even bothered to tell her that there were tunnels between the palace and the prison.

Unless he had wanted her to know.

Why tell her so obliquely? Why not tell her more directly?

As her gaze spun around the tavern, she spied the man who had been in the office when she'd arrived, and she wondered if perhaps Bastan feared he was being observed. Could someone from the palace have come to spy on him?

Sam stormed out of the tavern.

Without meaning to, her feet, and her canal staff, brought her across the outer sections of the city and toward the prison rising up in the distance. It was hard to miss. It was designed to draw the eye, a remote and isolated section of the city, situated alone on its own island, ringed by the canals, most of them much wider than found anywhere else in the city other than around the palace itself.

It would be difficult to reach, if not impossible. She thought she might be able to jump to that section, but if she tried, she risked landing in the water, and not being able to get herself free. A swim across the canal of that size would be dangerous, especially if the eels *were* real, and she was convinced that they were.

And then, if she did reach the other side, it would be nearly impossible to penetrate the prison. Kyza knew that she wouldn't be quick enough, or strong enough, to scale the massive wall rising around it, topped by sharp wire. Even the stone itself had razor sharp metal worked into it, as if the highborns feared those inside might escape the prison even though they were probably not only inside cells, but bound, as well. Even then, she would need to escape detection by any one of the dozen or so guards on the grounds.

Her imagination created the scene on the other side of the wall. There would likely be more of the same sharp metal worked into the stone, a way to keep the lowborns from even walking along them. Anything to keep them confined. Did they even allow light? She could imagine the highborn jailors keeping the cells dark, nothing but constant night as some sort of torture to those they confined. Tray wouldn't do well in the dark, not if forced to stay there long term.

She had no idea if they'd already questioned him. Had he given them what they needed? Had they punished him if not? Maybe she was already too late.

If something had happened to the princess as Bastan claimed—and as Sam herself had begun to hear rumored —why would Tray's jailers even care what happened to him? How long would he remain captured, unable to do anything, and unable to free himself? How long would Tray hold out hope that she might find a way to him? How long would it be before he gave up and thought that she wasn't coming for him? That was her job as the older sister.

Though she was the one to execute the jobs, Tray had always been the one who had watched over her, making sure nothing happened to her on all of the missions she agreed to take. What did it matter that she took the missions for both of their sakes, wanting nothing more than to find a way to buy them out of Caster.

It wasn't as if Sam thought they could ever be highborns. Finding enough money to buy their way into those inner sections of the city was impossible, even for a skilled thief like herself. No, what she wanted was simply a moderate level of safety, like the kind she could find somewhere like Alec's section of the city.

She chided herself for thinking that way.

Even with money from Marin, that was beyond her.

She needed to be content with what she could do, and that was finding some way to help her brother. She *would* rescue him.

Somehow.

Sam made a slow circuit around the sections outside the prison. The far wall ended in a massive drop-off, practically a cliff, overlooking the bay. Anyone thinking to escape that way wouldn't survive.

She paused, watching the bay. Faint starlight twinkled off the water, and she could see the ends of a few of the canals as they fed into the bay. Two barges started into the canals, both likely coming from the massive ship at anchor in the middle of the bay. Dozens of other ships just like it were also anchored just off shore.

Was this to be her fate if she couldn't get to him and if this business with the princess never ended? Always wondering what happened to Tray? Never to know what the highborns did to him? Sam wasn't sure she would be able to live not knowing, and she didn't want to keep getting deeper and deeper in debt with Bastan, and she wasn't completely convinced he was doing everything he could to help, anyway.

Sam stared at the walls, her eyes drawn to the razor-sharp metal along the top, thinking of Tray inside the prison, with nothing but *these* walls, perhaps stuck in the dark, not able to find his way free. She knew what she had to do. She just didn't like it.

Somehow, she would have to use the information that Bastan had given her.

The thought stayed with her as she crept away from the prison section of the city and deeper into the city itself. Find Tray, then get him free. She didn't know *how*.

She was drawn, the sight of the palace gleaming in the moonlight seeming to pull her in. This section of the city was much nicer than the others, and mostly that was because the palace sat in the heart of it. She rarely risked coming too close, partly afraid that she would get caught, and partly because she didn't have the right clothing to blend in, not like she did in Caster. There, at least, her cloak blended in somewhat, even if the rest of the clothing she preferred to wear did not.

The streets had a somber air to them that she could practically feel. Was that because of what was happening with the princess? Maybe it was more than simply a rumor. If that were the case, and whatever had happened to her influenced the section of the city this far out, then maybe Bastan's information was reliable.

If a tunnel did run between the palace and the prison, the first challenge was getting into the palace. How in the world would she reach it undetected, with palace guards all around? And then, how would she locate this mystery tunnel?

It was more than the security, which she expected to be significant inside the palace. It was her paralyzing fear of being found inside. She was lowborn. She had no business being where there were royals. How could she risk this?

But, for Tray, how could she not?

Something that she'd overheard, a rumor about the palace, came to mind. There had always been rumors of a connection between the palace and the university. Maybe if she could access the tunnels from there, she could find her way under the palace to reach the prison. Having to roam through the university to locate them, she didn't think she'd feel quite as out of place as she would in the palace, though perhaps she should. Even Alec hadn't felt as though he belonged in the university, and he was a skilled healer, more skilled than any she'd ever met. If he wasn't willing to go to the university, should she risk it?

For Tray, she would.

14

A JOB FOR TRAY

S am tightened her cloak and checked the crossbow, feeling a little nervous about the fact that she carried real bolts with her this time rather than the kind meant for scaling walls. The return to Caster for her supplies had done nothing other than steel her resolve. What did it matter if this went wrong, and she was caught? There would be no hiding the fact that she had weapons on her. She intended to break into the prison and get Tray out. Either it worked and she escaped, or she was caught and punished.

The dark only concealed so much, and she hoped the cloak covered the rest. Would it conceal her as she attempted the most foolish break-in she'd ever attempted?

Sam pushed those thoughts out of her mind. They did her no good, and only made her feel less confident in what needed to happen.

Circling back to Marin's home before risking this had revealed what Sam had feared. The other woman was gone. There hadn't been any blood, so Sam hoped she had managed to escape, but even if she had, where would she have gone?

Her absence left no one but Sam to help Tray. The longer he remained trapped, the more she worried about him. And if the royals were distracted by whatever had happened to the princess, Sam might have an opportunity to sneak in and rescue him, but that opportunity wouldn't last for long.

She had to hurry.

The streets were empty at this time of night. Quiet. A stillness hung over everything, and Sam imagined the city itself held its breath, waiting to see what she would do as she approached the university.

This jump was the easiest, but put her in the most danger. As soon as she made this crossing, she entered a part of the city where she could be easily noticed. Not that the risk lessened anywhere else, but across this canal, her very presence would be questioned. The outer sections of the city were easy enough to move through— and not well guarded. The farther toward the center of the city she went, the more likely it was that she'd encounter guards—and attract attention.

When she reached the canal, she pulled her staff free from her cloak and threaded the two ends together. Taking a running leap, she stabbed the staff deep into the canal and flipped, soaring across the water. Something splashed as she did. Sam refused to look down, refused to even consider what might be lurking beneath the surface.

Then she landed on the other side.

She pulled her staff free and shook water from it,

ducking against the nearest building. After taking a moment to take in her unfamiliar surroundings, she skulked along the street, trying to remain concealed as much as possible. She kept her eyes locked on her distant target. Reach the university. Break in. Use the tunnels to hopefully bypass the palace and reach the prison. If the rumored access through the university was there, that would be the easy part.

The buildings in this part of the city were neater, cleaner. Most rose three or more stories above her. Many were wood, though still solid, nothing like the old stone buildings in the outer sections of the city. Even the paint on the storefronts looked fresh, bright, and vibrant even in the darkness. Sam noted seamstresses, fletchers, bakers, ink makers, and even an apothecary that made her think of Alec.

The next canal appeared.

She jumped, racing through the streets, going across canal after canal until she neared the center sections of the city. Sam tried to ignore the fatigue already threatening her. She had to for Tray.

This canal would be wider. The moonless night made it difficult to fully appreciate the width of the canal, but she'd seen the maps Bastan had of the canal system. If they were to scale—and knowing Bastan, they would be—they would be an accurate representation of what she faced.

The timing of the jump would matter this time, but she wouldn't be able to get set the same way that she normally did. It was possible the staff would slip, or she'd lose her grip, or she mistimed the jump, or...

She could spend an hour thinking through what *could* go wrong. She had to trust it wouldn't, or she'd never make it across. These were the jumps when she missed Tray the most. With his size—and his strength—she had never feared the width of canals. Though she was the older sister, if something happened, she appreciated that he was always there watching over her.

Sam closed her eyes, took a breath, and jumped.

While in the air, she flipped the staff down, catching the bottom of the canal. In that moment, she prayed, hoping the staff held.

Through the length of the wood, she felt the way it tried to slide, but then caught.

Sam suppressed a cry of victory as she kicked, trying to make it the rest of the way across. She angled down, and her feet touched the other side, but only barely. Leaning forward, she tumbled onto the hard rock on the other side, pulling the staff free as she did.

Her heart raced, and she took a moment to settle it.

When she dared stand, she looked back. A faint glow to the night gave her light enough to see. The canal here was *much* wider than she had expected, much wider than Bastan's drawings had reflected. She was lucky to have cleared it.

That wasn't what bothered her.

If the map was wrong about *this* canal, what about the next? Would she even be able to cross?

She was still near enough that she could turn back. Going back meant hoping Bastan would be able to reach the inside of the prison, even though he had already told her that he was unwilling to do so. Bastan had connections, but he wouldn't use them. Had it been Marin, Sam believed she'd do more for Tray, but Bastan... She knew what motivated him: money. And she didn't have enough to influence him.

The answer was simple. If she turned back now, Tray would remain in prison. And maybe die. All because of her.

There was no one else. She was on her own.

Sam pulled her gaze away from the water and started forward.

She remained along the edge of the buildings, holding close to the walls, letting the shadows catch on her cloak, trusting that it would keep her hidden.

A dark figure moved in the distance.

Sam froze, ducking against the wall and wrapping her cloak around her.

She waited, and the shape moved past.

Sighing softly, she counted to ten before starting off again. This time, she moved more cautiously. Each step was a test of how silently she could walk. She listened to the way the wind blew, paying attention to the caress of it across her exposed face, the way it tugged at her cloak, and the scents it carried with it. The wind would carry *her* scent along with others, but there was no getting around that.

The final canal was near. She could smell it, but more than that, she could hear the way the water lapped softly at the edges of the canal. Sam approached cautiously, remaining close to a low building for long moments before determining it was safe to go any further, and studied the canal.

Her heart sank as she did.

The last canal had been wide. This one was wider. Much wider.

Sam stood at the canal's edge, letting the sound of the water flowing through it wash over her. Normally, she found peace in the sound, a gentleness that she wouldn't get anywhere else, a sense of quiet that let her simply *be*. But not today. Today, her heart raced, leaving her with a lingering sense of anxiety, and perspiration beaded on her brow. She was unaccustomed to feeling nervous moving around the city. This was a new sensation for her, and one she didn't care for.

Would the staff allow her to even reach the other side?

Placing her feet as close to the edge as she dared, she stretched the staff across the canal, straining to see how far it would reach. If she more than passed the midpoint of the canal, she thought she might have a chance of crossing it.

The staff reached *maybe* to the middle of the canal.

That didn't take into consideration the depth of the water, which would shorten her reach by another six or seven feet. There would be no flying over the canal this time.

Swimming was an option, but recalling the sound of whatever splashed beneath her when she crossed the last canal left her not wanting to risk it. The eels might *not* be found here, but then again, they *might*. She didn't want to risk getting nibbled at by a hungry eel. Or worse.

Could she find one of the barges? If she could find one tied up, she could borrow it... only that risked raising the alarm before she was ready. Stealth and silence were required. Once she reached the university, she was confident she could slip undetected through the building. Reach the tunnels. That was her mission. Once there… then she'd have to figure out how to get to the prison.

One step at a time. She tried not to get too far ahead of herself.

The other option would be to risk a jump, but with the width of the canal, she wasn't sure she liked that idea. If she got a running start, she could jump, get enough distance under her, and thrust the staff into the bottom of the canal while in the air. The timing would be even more difficult than what she was accustomed to, but it might give her a chance to reach farther than she could otherwise.

Sam looked along the street. She liked this idea less than she liked the idea of finding a barge to steal. At least with that, there wasn't the risk of splashing down in the water. This close to the palace, the damn eels were even more prevalent than they were farther out, as if they were drawn in from the sea to spread throughout the city.

Tray. This was for Tray.

Wouldn't he do the same for her?

Could she be fast enough here? Could she be strong enough with her jump to reach the other side?

Sam swore under her breath, and, after taking a deep breath and settling her nerves, she ran.

At the edge of the water, she jumped.

Sam didn't have the strength or speed that her brother possessed, but she'd always been a pretty good jumper, and years of sneaking and climbing had made her strong enough. The jump carried her over the water, and as she reached the peak of her arc, she jabbed the spear with as much force as she could generate.

It struck the bottom of the canal, but sank in *much* further than she had expected.

The surface of the water was barely four feet below her.

Her hands slipped. Sam gripped it tightly, desperately, and kicked her legs. The movement sent her gliding slowly, as if the water intended to hold her upright, before allowing her to sink toward the opposite shore.

It was still too far away.

Sam braced herself for the frigid water, but even that didn't prepare her for the cold she experienced.

When she'd ended up in the canal the last time, the water had been cold. Flowing from the sea never left the water warm enough for comfort, but this was even worse. It felt like icy fingers gripped her chest, and her breath burst from her lungs.

Sam didn't risk coming to the surface for a breath. When she'd splashed down, she immediately kicked, diving below the surface, all too aware of the noise that she made by splashing into the water. She was as afraid of what might be *in* the water with her as she was of who might find her if and when she reached the other side.

Something pinched at her cloak.

Sam jerked, trying to spin. Images of eels biting at her made her panic.

There came another bite. This time, she felt the teeth.

She'd never seen one of the canal eels, and didn't want to see one now. They were rumored to get big enough that they could tear flesh from her easily. At least she was wrapped in the cloak, but it had flapped open somewhat during the jump, and it didn't protect her completely. If one of the eels swam up the arm or under the bottom of the cloak...

Sam kicked again, straining to reach the other side.

Her heart raced. She gripped the staff tightly, but met resistance. Something held on to the staff.

She yanked on it. This had been her one constant companion in all the time she'd been sneaking through the city. The staff been left behind by her mother, something of hers that she could call her own. Had she sunk it too deeply into the muck at the bottom of the canal?

The staff wouldn't move.

Not only that, but it felt like something grabbed the other end. Sam had a mental image of an icy hand pulling it away from her. If she held on, she wouldn't be able to get any farther, but letting go meant losing the last connection to her mother.

There was another nibble on her arm.

Sam flapped her arm to keep from becoming an eel treat, and jerked the staff to no avail. It remained stuck and she had to let go.

With a few more kicks, she reached the rocky edge of the canal and scrambled free. At that moment, she didn't care how much noise she made, only that she managed to get free.

Sam flopped onto the ground and stared at the water. It swirled where she'd been and where she thought the staff remained. Was that a fin breaking the water?

She rolled away, trying not to think of what she'd lost.

If she reached Tray, it would be worth it. Her mother would have agreed.

Water dripped off the cloak as Sam made her way toward the university. Now that she was on this side of the canal, there was no going back. She wasn't about to attempt to swim, not after seeing the clear indentations on her cloak, with the line of teeth. Without the cloak, she would have been eel food. Even with it, she had almost been.

The university loomed in the distance, a great smudge of darkness in the night. As she approached, she contemplated how she'd enter. Thankfully, she still had the crossbow, and she thought she could fire one of the bolts and use the rope to climb, but she'd have to choose her entry point well.

The wide street here ran from the canal toward the university, growing wider the closer it came to the palace. This late at night, she was the only one in the street, but she still made an effort to remain hidden, keeping herself protected by the shadows between buildings and the cloak concealing her.

A wide lawn, an open expanse of green dotted with trees, opened before her.

She'd never seen so much green. The air smelled of flowers and leaves and the scent of wet earth. Sam imagined it looked lovely in the daylight. At night, it was nothing more than shades of darkness, though even then, she could tell there had been artistry in the garden.

Hiding would be more difficult here.

There were a few copses of trees she could hide within, but nothing that would give her that much cover, especially if one of the guards happened to be making rounds when she attempted it. Toward the back side of the university, she found a cluster of trees nearer the street and decided that would have to be where she made her attempt.

She let the silence surround her as she considered the approach. The cloak would shield her from quite a bit, but wouldn't conceal her completely, especially as she moved.

Then again, getting caught might actually help. Then she could get into the prison and find out what had happened with Tray.

But that would not be ideal. If she were caught, they'd confiscate her cloak and her rope and the crossbow, all the things she needed. Better to find a way in carefully. Quietly.

Sam pulled the cloak over her shoulder, tucking the hood down around her face to keep her pale skin from catching any stray moonlight, and started across the street. When she reached the edge of the garden, she thought she saw distant movement, but wasn't certain. Now wasn't the time to back out. She carefully made her way to the trees, and stopped.

Smooth bark pressed against her face, and she almost sneezed. Sam took a step back but stayed within the shadows cast by the others around her, and searched for her next move.

The closer to the university she got, the more trees there would be, but they were planted in singles, spaced apart so that she would either have to run to them, or risk moving slowly and getting caught in the open. But she wasn't there yet. Sam waited for a gust of wind to pick up and hurried to the next cluster of trees. There were only a few here, but they cast dark enough shadows that she didn't fear getting caught. Roots arched out of the ground, and one of them tugged at her feet as she started toward the next cluster of trees, sending Sam sprawling onto the ground.

She suppressed the swear that came to her lips as she froze, knowing that to be the better strategy than rushing forward. Sudden movement would only draw the eye. Her falling would do that enough as it was.

When she heard nothing, she crawled forward, staying low as she did. As she neared the next cluster of trees, she heard footsteps.

Sam fought against sudden panic and fought the urge to hurry toward the trees. They wouldn't hide her any better than flattening herself out on the ground, but at least they'd provide her with a sense of protection, real or not.

The footsteps passed.

Now she knew someone else was out here. Likely patrolling, but she hadn't been able to see to know for certain. She would have to be extra careful, but then, she thought she had been when she'd tripped.

At the trees, she slowly raised herself up, wrapping her arms around the trunk of the tree, hoping that it looked only as if the tree had widened and not so obvious that there was someone here. Sam peered into the darkness, searching for the source of the footsteps she'd heard, but there was no evidence of anyone there.

That made her uncomfortable.

She could move, but what if she encountered the

patrol again? This time, if she was standing, they'd likely see her. The other option involved crawling along the ground, but she wouldn't be able to move very fast that way.

What choice was there? To escape notice, she had to stay low.

The university was still a hundred yards or more away.

Creeping forward on elbows and knees, she slid forward. Had she not still been soaked from her dip into the canal, she would have become soaked by dew collected on the grass. She heard a shuffling sound and paused, but it didn't repeat, and she continued onward.

The wall of the university loomed in front of her.

Sam finally allowed herself to feel relief. This was the first hurdle to saving her brother, and one of the biggest. Reaching the university, even if she wasn't in it yet, felt like victory.

As she started to stand, something grabbed the back of her cloak.

Sam kicked, but it did no good. The grip was too strong.

Her hood pulled back from her face, and she stared into the flat gray eyes of one of a soldier. Was it one of the brutes? It didn't look like the one that had shot her.

A dark grin spread across his face. "Sneaking in to reclaim it?"

"I'm not—"

"A dangerous plan. You Theln sympathizers should return to your home."

Theln sympathizer? That made no sense to her.
"You've got it wrong."

"I don't think so," he hissed, his voice pitched low and gravely. "And now you'll tell us what you did with the rest."

"You can let me go. I'll return to my section, and no one will have to know."

"I'll know."

He lifted her diminutive form with one arm and slammed her into the wall. Sam didn't even have a chance to object before she passed out.

15

A FATHER'S SECRET

The stink of ash and the mixture of burned leaves and oils filled Alec's nostrils. He doubted too many others would understand what they smelled, but Alec recognized it. The smell was that of his failure, that of loss. The apothecary was gone, burned to the ground, and he didn't understand *why*.

Dusk approached as he meandered along the streets. He passed shops with owners he knew, men and women who would offer their help, especially with as often as his father had helped them, but he didn't want to do anything other than keep wandering. The more distance he could put between him and the shop, the easier it was for him to imagine it never happened.

But all he had to do was turn around, and he could still see the way the ash and smoke swirled into the sky. Alec tried not to think about the questions that came to mind, such as why they'd been targeted, or why the man had seemed so interested in his notes about Sam's injuries, or why was it theirs was the only business that had burned? Those were questions without answers. Or maybe they had answers, but they weren't the kind he wanted.

Someone touched his arm, and he spun, jerking his arm free in a panic.

Mrs. Rubbles stared at him, her sharp eyes seeming to take in soot covering his face and clothes, and she nodded. "Come with me, then."

She tugged on his shirt, not giving him any chance to object.

Alec went along with her willingly. Mrs. Rubbles had always been kind to him, and right now, he needed some kindness because he didn't know what he would do otherwise.

She pulled him onto a side street leading behind her shop and then up a narrow flight of stairs to the top where she pushed open the door revealing a tidy home neatly decorated. A small fire burned softly in a corner hearth, sending waves of warmth into the room. A pair of formal chairs angled toward a lacquered table in the middle of the room. A tray of steaming meat rested on the table, with two plates set on either side.

"Sit. Eat."

"Mrs. Rubbles—"

She shook her head and forced him into one of the chairs. "Sit, I said." She waited until he did, and he found the chair surprisingly comfortable. Then she disappeared behind another doorway before reappearing with two finely painted ceramic cups. Mrs. Rubbles took a seat opposite him and handed him one of the cups. "What happened?"

Alec rubbed his eyes. How could he answer that question when he didn't really know himself? "The shop burned," he said. It was the only thing he could think of telling her.

"I saw that. I even went through there to see if there was anything I could help you save. There were a few items..." She shook her head. "It doesn't matter now. What I don't understand is *how?*"

Alec brought the cup of tea to his nose and inhaled. It smelled bitter and strong, the kind of tea that would wake him up, if that was what he wanted. Alec wasn't sure he did.

"A man came into the shop. He was looking for something I didn't have. When I told him, he poured"—he tried to think of what the man had poured around the apothecary. Oil? Kerosene? Something that had been highly flammable, but also limited in its effect, not burning the neighboring stores—"something around the inside of the shop and then ignited it."

Mrs. Rubbles sat with her hands clasped on her lap, watching him. She nodded once toward the tray of meat. "Eat, Alec. You'll need your strength."

"I'm fine, Mrs. Rubbles."

"Eat," she said again.

She sat back with her arms crossed while waiting for him. From the set of her jaw and the hard expression she wore, Alec could tell she wouldn't say anything more until he did as she instructed.

He took a deep breath and took a bite of the meat. It was smoky and warm, but more than that, it was delicious. The taste of the meat washed away the remaining ash in his throat. For that, he was thankful.

Alec made quick work of the meat, taking sips of tea in between bites, with Mrs. Rubbles watching him the entire time. When he finished, she carried the tray away before returning and sitting across from him again.

"What can you tell me about the man who did this?" she asked.

"Mrs. Rubbles—"

She raised her hand, cutting him off. "If anyone is willing to intentionally burn down one of our stores, others need to know. Describe him for me."

Alec closed his eyes, thinking back to what the man had looked like. The memory of him was vivid. "He had flat gray eyes," he started. They were the feature he remembered best. "Tall, and incredibly muscular. He had short hair and there was something about his face." He tried to remember the scar but couldn't picture it clearly. "He'd either been burned or branded."

When he opened his eyes, he saw Mrs. Rubbles pressing her hands together. Her brow was furrowed in a troubled expression.

A fleeting thought hit him. How was this the same woman he'd seen at the shop only a few days ago? That woman had been frail and failing, whatever glandular issue she suffered from making her sickly. This woman had a strength to her, and a sharpness to her eyes that he hadn't seen before.

After watching him for a moment more, Mrs. Rubbles stood and went to a cupboard in the back of the room before returning and sitting. She carried a stack of fine paper and a thick piece of charcoal. Settling herself into the chair, she started drawing.

Alec couldn't take his eyes off her as she worked. Her hand moved in a steady fashion, each stroke controlled and intentional. As she worked, the face of the man who had burned his father's shop appeared on the page, the detail so vivid that he knew she'd seen him before.

Mrs. Rubbles finished and set the charcoal down. "Is this him?"

He swallowed. Even as a drawing, there was something about his stare that unsettled him. "That's him. You've seen him before."

Mrs. Rubbles dusted her hands off and held the page down on her lap. "I've seen him," she agreed. "And wish I hadn't."

"When?"

"He came into my store a few days ago. He was looking for a specific type of paper, but I didn't have what he wanted. He said it had been stolen and thought someone might have tried selling it off. He was pleasant enough," she said, scratching at her chin and leaving a smudge of charcoal, "but there was a darkness about him I could almost feel." She stared at her drawing. "I was happy when he left and thought that was the end of it."

"He came into my father's shop looking for a woman I'd healed," Alec admitted. Mrs. Rubbles' eyes widened slightly. "She came to the shop, well... she broke into it. She was bleeding everywhere, and had an injury to her shoulder." He didn't think Mrs. Rubbles needed to know that Sam had a crossbow bolt lodged in her arm. That would only bring up different questions.

"You healed this woman?"

Alec shrugged. "I stitched her up and applied a salve. It wasn't much more than that."

She scratched her chin again. "I wonder what he wanted with her?"

"He never said. When he saw the notes I made—"

"You took notes on her injury?"

He nodded. "My father would be disappointed if I didn't. You've seen the way he documents. Everyone who comes to the shop has their symptoms noted, even if there's nothing we can do."

Mrs. Rubbles frowned. "Did you document *my* symptoms?"

"Of course."

"I thought you were out of paper?"

Alec flushed. "I am. Was. The woman had a scrap of strange paper with her. That's what you saw me working on when you came in."

"That's what you needed the darker pigment for," she said. Alec nodded. "Do you still have this page?"

He shook his head. "It burned with the shop."

Mrs. Rubbles sat silently for a while, staring at her drawing of the man on the page. "This is dangerous, Alec."

"I know it's dangerous. My father's shop—"

She looked up from the page, her eyes practically glowing with intensity. "Not only your father's shop. This man," she said, patting the page, "has a dangerous look to him."

Dangerous didn't describe him well enough. The man had attacked Sam and then burned down the apothecary. How could he be anything other than dangerous?

"I intend to stay away from him." But where? Now that the shop was gone—his home—where would he go? He sighed. "I wish I knew how to find my father."

She stared at the drawing and then sighed. "I agree you must find your father, Alec. This is beyond my ability to help."

"He's gone harvesting. I don't know when he'll return."

She met his eyes. "You can send word to him through the university."

Alec blinked, and then laughed. "He left a note. He went to the Narvin Plains to harvest." The plains were to the east of the city on a thin stretch of land and known to have dozens of types of healing plants, most that couldn't be found anywhere else. Alec had gone with his father when he was much younger, back when his mother still lived and could run the shop, but since she'd been gone, his father had taken the harvesting trips on his own, more and more often leaving Alec in charge of the shop while he was away. Most of the time, that involved keeping the door open and allowing others to purchase what they needed. This had been the first time he'd risked attempting to heal without his father around.

Mrs. Rubbles reached into a pocket, pulled out a folded sheet of paper, and handed it over to him.

She nodded to the paper and sat back, waiting.

Alec carefully unfolded the paper. He recognized it as one of Mrs. Rubbles' finer stock, the paper thick, with smooth edges. As he opened it, he saw the writing on the inside in a hand he recognized.

There was no doubt in Alec's mind that this had come from his father's hand. There was a neatness to it that reminded him of Mrs. Rubbles' home. The angle to the lettering matched his father's left handedness, and the way Alec crossed his letters matched his father's writing. The paper was wrinkled and appeared to have been written long ago.

But the content... how could his father have written what Alec saw on the page?

"He gave this to me a long time ago. He said if anything ever happened to him..." She shook her head. "I hope he'll forgive me for revealing this to you. It really should have been him, but as your shop has burned, there really isn't anywhere else for you to go."

"He wants me to go to the university?" he asked after reading through the note. It was directed to Mrs. Rubbles, a request if anything were to happen to him and guidance on what she should do with Alec, but more than that, it gave details about his father that Alec had never known.

Could his father have studied at the university and he'd not known?

She nodded. "He would have preferred to share with you himself, but there wasn't a good time."

"Not a good time? How about before he left, he tells me that he planned to go to the one place I didn't think he'd ever go? Why couldn't he share that with me?"

"Alec—"

He stood, gripping the note, but the anger he felt faded quickly. It wasn't Mrs. Rubbles' fault his father had hidden from him where he'd gone—that was entirely on his father—but she had known, and she hadn't shared with him.

"Why would he hide this from me?"

She sat for a moment, watching him with the same hard expression she'd worn since he first came in. "There are things you don't understand, Alec, that you can't understand."

He held on to the piece of paper, the note that held information his father had entrusted Mrs. Rubbles with but hadn't felt him capable of understanding.

What else had his father hidden from him? Why would he hide the fact that he'd studied at the university? Shouldn't he be willing to share that, especially knowing what he did about what Alec wanted?

She sighed, as if reading his thoughts. "Go to the main entrance, tell them his name, and ask for help. There is really nothing more to it than that."

Alec stood and looked once more at the paper. There was no doubting that it was his father's writing, but *why*? Why would he hide that from him?

"Alec?"

He paused at the door and looked back to Mrs. Rubbles.

"I really am sorry about what happened to the apothecary. If you need anything…"

He considered various answers, before deciding only to nod. What more could he say?

16

A VISIT TO THE UNIVERSITY

The massive gate to the university rose in front of Alec, its arched iron gates left open. Guards stood on either side of the gate, questioning each who approached. There was a line nearly one-hundred deep, and few had the clean clothing of those from the more central sections of the city.

Alec fingered the note in his pocket as he shuffled forward. An older woman stood in front of him, every so often clutching at a necklace she wore, likely some token of one of the gods, such as Kyza or Yisl. A young girl holding on to her mother's hand stood behind him. The smells around him were that of sweat and filth, but he noted the stink of rot, like that of a wound that had festered far too long. In his time working with his father, he had come to know that odor all too well.

Mrs. Rubbles hadn't mentioned the line at the gate.

Alec had never attempted to gain entry to the university. Given the cost, few did. Most couldn't afford their healing, even if they were allowed entry. But there seemed plenty willing to attempt it, and from what he could tell just looking around, those he saw had various illnesses.

Some, like the young girl five places in front of him, had growths needing to be removed. The university surgeons wouldn't struggle with such techniques. Now that he knew his father spent time in the university, he wondered if he had learned under some of the senior surgeons found here. Alec had always believed his father had studied and learned the art of healing from books and others with knowledge of medicines and herbs. Knowing his father came to the university, that he might work *with* the university physickers, felt a betrayal of sorts, though Alec knew it shouldn't.

Other illnesses were subtler. He saw a man so thin that he might as well be bones. A wasting disease, and one Alec had seen before. His mind started racing through different herbs he could try to heal the man, though he knew none of them would likely be as effective as what the university could offer. There was a woman with no hair, and a thick liniment rubbed onto her scalp. There were few solutions known for that, but rogan root mixed with a touch of linseed might work. Alec had seen that be effective before.

The longer he stood in line, the more he began to diagnose those around him. There were a few with glandular issues, much like what he'd seen from Mrs. Rubbles. There were others with splints on arms or legs, some with bandages covering festering wounds Alec could smell. A few others with the same wasting illness.

By the time he'd reached the front of the line, he had

an inventory of ailments from all of those around him. Had he brought paper, he might even have taken the time to document what he'd seen, but what would the point have been without any way to test the effectiveness of his solutions. Many were turned away as they approached the guards near the gate. Was that because their illnesses were determined to be untreatable or because they weren't sick enough? He imagined the physickers only wanted to treat the sickest of the sick, and even then, they could be selective.

He shuffled forward without paying attention to where he was going when a firm grip pulled on his arm.

"Where do you think you're going?"

Alec pulled his attention off the old woman who had been in front of him. She disappeared now behind the gate, escorted by a young woman in a short gray jacket with dark hair rolled into a bun. The man standing next to him smelled of feverleaf, a heady aroma that filled his nostrils. The dark leaves stained the man's lower teeth and he chewed silently while watching Alec. He wore a longer jacket that matched the one worn by the young woman he'd just seen.

Alec had assumed they were guards, but realized they were students. Did the length of the jacket signify rank? As much time as he'd spent healing others over the years, and learning from his father, he'd never spent any time thinking about the university or the students within. It was a place he'd dreamed of coming, but knew was beyond him.

Now that he *was* here, he didn't know what they expected of him. Was he to pass the note his father had written to Mrs. Rubbles? What would that get him other than more stares like the ones he got from them now?

Alec decided the simplest answer was best. "I'm looking for Aelus Stross," he said, and immediately wished he would have said something else. It wasn't that he expected his father to be here, but that he wanted to send word to him. "I was told I could get word to him here."

The student glanced over his shoulder, and Alec noted another student, similarly dressed, shrugged. "And that would be?"

"He's an apothecary."

The student grinned, and the feverleaf protruded from between a pair of teeth. "There are no apothecaries here. If that's what you seek, you'll need to go back into the outer sections. We are physickers here."

"He's my father. As I said, I was told I could get word to him—"

The nearest student twisted him by the arm, spinning him away from the gate so that he faced the line of people. There had to be several hundred here now. All of them seeking healing. Alec couldn't imagine being able to accommodate that many patients, and he couldn't imagine the income they would bring in, especially if rumors about what the physickers charged were true.

"Stop wasting our time. There are countless others who have come for actual healing, and they have money to pay. Do you have money for healing?"

Alec touched his pocket. He had some coins, but doubted they would be enough. "I'm not here for healing. I'm here for my father."

"If you can't pay, then you shouldn't be here," the student said.

Physicker or healer, his father had never cared whether those who came to him were able to pay. He made certain they paid what they could, and nothing more.

For so long, all he'd wanted was to learn to heal like those in the university, but was this what he wanted for himself?

Alec looked at the others in line and realized that there would be no way for him to get through and get word to his father. Even if he managed to enter the university— and that was not a given, especially considering how long the line was—he doubted he would even find his father.

If he couldn't find his father and get word to him, how would he know about the shop? Alec didn't want his father to return only to find a pile of ash and debris where his shop had once been.

When his father returned from his collection, Alec would need to be there.

Besides, maybe there was something he could find in the remains of the shop. He could sort through it.

He turned away, ignoring the glares shooting in his direction, and elbowed his way back across the bridge and over to his section. The walk back took much longer than the walk over, and his heart was heavy. It felt strange returning but not having a place to return to. He knew enough people in the section that he thought he would have a place to stay, but that wasn't what he wanted, either.

He wanted his shop back.

When he reached it, the sun was shining, and he wandered through the piles of debris. Everything was burned, at least, almost everything was burned. There were still a few things here. A couple of jars had survived mostly intact, though the high heat would likely have destroyed the contents making them unstable and essentially unusable. There were other items here, like the broken end of a bench, and the remnants of shelves, but not enough for him to find anything that was even familiar to him.

There was nothing for him here.

Where was he going to go? Now that everything he cared about was gone, what was there for him to do?

17

A PURPOSE FOR THE PAPER

Pain throbbed in her head as Sam came around. Lights flashed behind her eyes, and at first, she thought they were real before realizing that she saw only flashes from the pain throbbing in her skull. That pain prevented her from detecting anything else. There was nothing other than the splitting headache and a steady drumming noise that added to her misery.

Where was she?

Alive. There was that much, at least.

When she tried to move, she discovered her arms were bound, trapped in cold chains. Her legs were, as well, confining her. Sam rolled her head to the side, trying to see the chains, but all she knew was the steady flashing of light.

"Why did you come here?"

It wasn't one of the brutes' voice, but who was it?

"Where am I?"

The man laughed, and she heard him move. There was

nothing stealthy about the way he moved. "You approached the university and don't know what it is?"

Could she really still be in the university rather than in one of the prison cells? And how did she get here? How would the brute who caught her have access to the university?

"I know what the university is."

"You didn't expect us to leave you here." There came a scraping, like stone across stone, and he loomed closer to her. "It would have been a mistake to send you anywhere else before I had a chance to question you."

"What do you want with me?"

"I would ask you the same. You lowborns wouldn't normally risk sneaking into the university. What is worth the risk for you to try?" He glared at her. "Are *you* the one responsible for her illness?"

Sam frowned. "What? I don't know what you're talking about."

His glare softened. "Maybe you don't. Did you come because you thought you can find more of the easar? Did *they* send you after it?"

Sam wished stars didn't flicker in her vision the way they did. She struggled to understand what he was saying. "Easar?"

"Like too many of the fools here, you probably think it paper and nothing more."

"I know there's something more to it. I know it's valuable."

The man laughed. "Valuable would be an understatement. You can't understand how valuable the easar is. You don't understand the power the paper concentrates."

Power?

Could there be more to the paper than she had realized? It had required blood to write on, but Bastan's blood hadn't worked.

"What kind of power?" she asked.

"The kind that allows those with the necessary knowledge to accomplish great things. The kind of power that keeps the city safe from the outside."

Was *that* why she had recovered as quickly as she had? Not only had she stolen paper from highborns, but it had been *magic* paper.

Kyza.

The man watched her and she knew she needed to say something. Anything.

"Each page is worth a gem," Sam said.

The man's laughter died off. "Perhaps you *can* understand." He leaned closer to her. She smelled... perfume. That wasn't what she expected from one of the brutes. "Where is the rest of what you stole from us?"

"I sold it," she said.

"The only market for easar paper is the palace, and they wouldn't have stolen it. Did you plan to return it to *them*?"

There was something about the way he said it that caught her attention. "Who are you talking about?"

The man grunted a dark laugh. "As if you don't know. The Thelns. I know you're a sympathizer. You have to be for you to risk coming here for the paper. Now. Where is the rest of it?"

"There was market enough. I managed three silver eagles."

The man laughed. "Silvers? You traded easar for silvers?"

Sam tried to shrug, but her chained arms prevented her. Instead, she nodded. "When you need to eat, you'll take what's offered."

"Why were you here?"

Sam tried to think quickly. "I thought I could find more of the paper here. I have a contact in the university."

The man's laughter cut her off. "Who did you sell it to?"

"Ten silvers, and I'll tell you."

"You'll tell me, or you die," he said as Sam caught sight of the glint off a blade as it came close to her face.

Sam licked her lips and swallowed. There was a fine line between foolishness and bravery. She knew she was stepping awfully close to it, but didn't on which side she'd land. "If you kill me, you won't find out."

"I have ways of finding the easar."

"Then you don't need me."

The man fell into silence, and for a moment, Sam thought she'd made a mistake. She let the silence linger for a while, and then offered, "I can get the paper back, if that's all you want. I don't need the silver."

The man laughed. "No? What would you need?"

Sam blinked. There was a fuzziness to the edge of her vision now, and she managed to make out the man's outline. He was tall and thin, and had flat eyes that watched her with a dark intensity.

She had seen him before.

He was in the highborn house she'd broken into. Why would he be in the university?

Because he was a highborn.

Was he working with the Thelns or against them? He accused her of being a Theln sympathizer, so it didn't seem as if he were working *with* them.

What was going on here?

Somehow, she had gotten herself involved in something *way* beyond thieving, especially if it involved the university and brutes like the Thelns. And all she wanted was to get away. Help Tray.

Maybe this man could help. Could she turn this to her advantage? "My brother. That's the only thing I've been after."

The man pulled the knife back and studied her. "You have a brother?"

She nodded. "He was captured and imprisoned. I've been trying to find a way to rescue him..."

"And you thought breaking into the university would be the best way to rescue him?"

Sam swallowed. How much did she tell the truth and how much did she deceive him? She had a sense that he'd know if she attempted to deceive him too much. "I didn't think to rescue him. I came to plead for his release."

That *could* have been the truth, if only she hadn't come in the middle of the night and covered with a cloak designed to conceal her. That, and the crossbow. How would she explain that?

"You chose an interesting time to attempt your plea."

"I would never have made it during the daytime." That much was true. Had she attempted to cross the canals earlier, she would have been stopped on the outer ring long before she ever came close to reaching the palace.

"Where is he?"

"The prison, I think."

The man grunted. "You were a fool to attempt coming here. You were even more of a fool to tell me about your brother."

Before Sam could say anything, he struck her on the side of the head with the handle of his knife.

Sam came around slowly, her head throbbing just as much as it had the last time she'd awoken, but there were no stars distorting her vision. No longer were her wrists cuffed or her legs chained. She moved them freely, feeling a little release.

Her mouth was dry, and she worked her tongue around the inside and across her lips, tasting dry blood that she tried to swallow.

How long had she been out this time?

She'd told the highborn about her brother. That had been a mistake. But he hadn't killed her. That much was a surprise. Either he needed her, or he wanted to torment her. More likely than not, he needed her to find the paper.

Hopefully, Bastan hadn't done anything stupid like attempting to sell it. Doing that would only draw more attention.

Magic paper.

If they could understand the secret to it, maybe she wouldn't have to stay a lowborn. Maybe she could use it to save Tray.

First, she had to escape.

Sam sat up.

She was in a plain room. Walls were a smooth white, and there was no window, only a single barred door blocking her exit. When the throbbing in her head managed to settle, she went to the door and unsurprisingly found it locked. What was surprising was the fact that her cloak was folded neatly and set in one corner. Her clothing was untouched, and she still had her boots on. Sam resisted the urge to pull off her right one to see if the paper remained hidden within... and her mother's knife.

Where was she now?

When she'd awoken before, the highborn claimed she was in the university. Sam doubted she was still there, but the smooth walls and flooring made it unlikely that she was in the prison. Where had she been brought?

Sam searched her cloak, but the crossbow and rope were gone.

Kyza. Now what would she do?

Unwilling to await a fate she was sure would not be in her favor, she needed a way out. Leaning against the wall nearest the door, she slipped her hand along the leather folds of her boot. She smiled when she discovered the knife was still where she'd hidden it.

When she picked the lock, she didn't know what she'd find on the other side of the door. Where would they have taken her?

Sam slipped the cloak around her shoulders. If nothing else, wearing it gave her a certain comfort. She worked the tip of the knife into the lock on the door, levering it from side to side, feeling for the tumblers. It would be easier with a proper pick set, but then she hadn't thought about hiding one in her boots to go along with the knife.

It didn't work.

She sank to the ground and stared around the room. Was there anything in here she could use to help her get free?

The bed was the only item in here. It was made of stout wood, and a thin mattress was set on it, but that was it. No other furniture. Sam figured herself fortunate to have even that much.

Could she carve off a section of wood and use it?

She glanced at the door. There wasn't anything else for her to do other than wait. But she wasn't about to simply sit here and do nothing. That just wasn't her.

Kneeling in front of the bed, she started working on the post, gliding the knife along the surface as she tried to pry a section free. If she could carve a few narrow slivers, maybe she could use them like a pick set.

Sam tried not to think about the fact that she was getting her hopes up again. What choice did she have if she wanted to get Tray out of prison?

As she managed to get sections free, she carved them into a set that would be similar to her other lock pick. These might not be strong enough, but she had to try, and right now, she had nothing but time.

If she failed…

Sam didn't want to think about what would happen if she failed. She'd be stuck here, but worse, Tray would be stuck in prison, likely awaiting execution with no one willing to do anything to help him.

Voices drifted from outside the door.

"Why is she here, Larenth?"

"She's after easar paper. She's the one who stole it from—"

Someone made a hushing sound. "This isn't the place to discuss that so openly." It sounded like the man who'd smelled of perfume.

"No? There are no others here."

"We still need to be careful. *They* are responsible for what happened to the princess."

"Word of that cannot get out. We don't need to raise fear of attack."

"Then what do you intend?"

"We have someone we can blame. A thief *and* a sympathizer. It would believable enough." There was a pause. "She has a brother. He was captured watching the house the night she broke in. He's probably with them too."

"Can there really be so many in the city after all this time?"

"Where else would they have gone?"

"We need to keep this quiet. If the Anders know what has been done to the Thelns…"

The Anders. That meant the ruling family.

"That's why we must place the blame on them."

The voices faded, disappearing.

Sam picked the lock of her cell and poked her head out the door. She did it cautiously, not certain whether she would draw attention to herself, and saw no one. The hall was empty.

Though it was empty, there was a horrible smell. It

was awful; nothing like anything she'd ever encountered before.

Sam wanted only to get away from the stench, but she was confused. Why was she here?

She crept slowly along the bright marble hallway, more wealth in the floor around her than she would ever see, and came upon a door. The stench seemed to come from whatever lay behind the door.

Curiosity made her push the door open.

She almost gagged as she did. On the other side, she found a person lying in a massive bed.

Sam blinked. Even from a distance, she recognized who it was.

The princess.

That was who they had been talking about. The rumored illness was real.

Sam had never seen her before, but there were stories of her beauty. She was sick, as sickly as what Bastan had believed, and lay motionless. Her breathing was slow and steady, and if it was she who the men she'd overheard were talking about, she didn't have much longer to live.

And then what?

Then they would pin the blame on her and Tray. That was what they had been talking about. They thought she was *with* the Thelns.

Kyza.

What had she gotten herself into? And what did this have to do with the easar paper? Not just the paper, but the *power* of the paper. The *magic* of the paper.

That was the part that Sam didn't understand.

Sam glanced into the room one more time before

pulling the door closed. If she did nothing, they would blame her and Tray for the princess's illness, but if she could get the princess help... maybe they could get out of this.

Only, how was she ever to find Alec, especially with his shop destroyed? Even if she *did* find him, would he know enough about the paper to help?

THE THELNS ATTACK

The Caster section of the city welcomed her back with the familiar smells and sounds greeting her.

Escaping from the university had been easier than she had expected. The bridge was unguarded, and once she'd thrown herself out a window, she had been able to wind her way around the outside of the building before reaching the bridge leading across the canal so that she didn't have to try to jump it.

She would return to Alec's section of the city, but only after she grabbed more of the paper. She needed to gather herself, check in with Bastan to grab more of the easar paper, and warn him that she might have been pinched. There might not be anything that he could do, but she felt she needed to share what she'd learned. Maybe there was something Bastan and his connections could do to help.

Sam was fairly close to the tavern. In Caster, everything was sort of close. She wound her way through the streets, ignoring the glares as she pushed her way through crowds of people, until she saw Bastan's tavern in the distance.

As she neared, the tavern exploded.

Sam was thrown back by the force of the explosion. Heat burned across her face, and she shielded it with her cloak. Her ears rang and her head throbbed.

Long moments passed before she was able to make sense of what was happening around her. People ran away from her, some screaming as they passed her. The sound was muted.

Sam went the opposite direction, heading toward the explosion. Had the brutes discovered her? Had they followed her back to Bastan's tavern before?

That one brute *had* said that he could smell her, whatever that meant. If he could, maybe they had known where she had gone. Maybe they had known about Bastan.

Was Bastan there?

What of the other people who worked for him?

It wasn't that Bastan worked with bad people. There were plenty he worked with that she cared about, especially Kevin, a cook who had always ensured she had food when she stopped into the tavern. Had anyone been inside when the tavern exploded?

Flames roared from the building, the heat of it nearly pressing her back. She fought against it, hurrying forward, in spite of knowing that she shouldn't.

Someone caught her arm and she spun, fearing one of the brutes.

"Not that way, Sam."

It was Bastan. Soot stained his face, and his eyes were

wide and wild. Blood soaked his shirt, but Sam couldn't tell where he'd been hurt. He held the hilt of a sword, the blade almost black, unmindful of the rules of lowborns carrying weapons.

His personal guards, Stepan and Hilam, stood on either side of him, either guarding him or keeping watch. They were enormous—almost as large as the brutes—and she often wondered if they had some special abilities. There were rumors that some of the people coming to Verdholm for safety had power, though they kept it concealed. It wouldn't surprise her to discover that Bastan collected people with power much the same way he collected paintings.

"What happened?" she asked.

"Looks like we got hit," Bastan said. He took her by the elbow and guided her away from the street, ducking into an alleyway between a butcher and a candle maker. Both shops looked empty.

"Was it Thelns?" she asked.

Bastan's grip on her elbow squeezed harder. "What?"

Sam shook her head. It didn't do any good to hide what she knew from Bastan, not when he could help her understand. "They attacked Marin. I think they were the same ones who attacked me. And… they chased me when I was trying to break into the university."

"Why were you breaking into the university?"

"Because you told me the palace and the prison were connected by tunnels, and I already knew there was some connection between the university in the palace."

Bastan breathed out a heavy sigh, shaking his head, and then he nodded to Stepan. The man turned and hurried from the alley, his hand under his long wool cloak.

"Were these Thelns the same ones who attacked you before?"

Sam nodded. She wouldn't be able to shake the terror she'd felt. Living in Caster, she had often experienced strange people. Many were rumored to have power of their own, though she had never seen it. But the Thelns had been unlike anything she'd ever encountered.

"I should have moved sooner," Bastan said, frustration seething in his voice. "If someone thinks to move into *my* territory—"

"I think this is about more than your territory. It's about the paper."

"Are you sure?" Bastan asked.

Sam wasn't sure about anything anymore. "That's what Marin said."

"Where is she... You were with her when she was attacked?"

"I was there. She's the one who told me it's about the paper." That, and what she'd learned at the university. She still needed to keep that from Bastan, at least for now.

"The damn *paper*? We can barely write on it. Why would they care about it?"

She hadn't gotten the opportunity to get the answers before the brutes got to Marin's. Sam didn't think it possible that Marin had gotten away. She might have had a weapon, but how likely was it that she could have fought off two brutes and escaped?

"I don't know. Marin seemed to know something about it. She doesn't think you should sell it." She didn't want to tell Bastan that the paper might have magical qualities—not yet. If she did, he'd never give her access to it.

"I shouldn't? What does she want me to do with it?"

"She says each sheet is worth as much as a single gem." She held her hand out, much like Marin had done for her.

"To who?"

"I don't know. The highborns, I suppose." Or the palace, if what the highborn had told her was true.

In the distance, there came another explosion, this one muted. Sam felt it as it thundered through her.

"We need to get moving," Bastan said. "There's a place we can go. I can keep us safe there."

He motioned to Hilam and started off through the alley, emerging on the street on the other side. People ran quickly along the street here, as well, but there wasn't the same sense of purpose and fear as there was on the other street.

Bastan moved toward the tavern, though it was a street away now. When they were nearing the tavern, he stopped and entered a storefront without any signage.

Hilam locked the door behind them.

The room was empty. A couple of tall, dusty tables were scattered throughout the room, the stools tipped toward them, resting so the back legs were in the air. A wide stone hearth along the back wall looked as if it hadn't seen any logs for years, but the inside of the hearth was heavily charred. A long counter ran along the opposite wall, a thick layer of dust coating everything.

Another tavern?

"How many places do you own?" she asked Bastan.

He glanced back at her. "Enough to keep my interests safe."

Bastan stood in front of the hearth and tapped on the stones in what seemed a pattern. As he did, the back of the hearth slid to the side, revealing a dark opening.

Sam looked at it and started laughing. "A hidden entrance? How very Bastan-like of you."

"I think I'll take that as a compliment," he said.

"You should."

He motioned her through, and she entered an empty room. Sam turned to face Bastan, and he carried a lantern in with him.

"Bastan, I don't think I have much time."

"Why do you say that? We got hit, Sam. Those bastards are after you, and if they're now after me, we need to keep us both safe."

"If you keep me safe, if you keep me here, then I won't be able to help Tray."

"You won't be able to help him if you're dead, either. I'm going to sweep through Caster and make sure none of these bastards are here."

"I don't know that it's safe. You haven't faced them. They're dangerous."

"*I'm* dangerous."

The way he said it made her believe that he was. For some reason, the idea of something happening to Bastan bothered her. "Don't risk yourself like this."

"I'm not going to sit back while Caster is attacked. They already hit Marin?"

Sam nodded slowly. "There's more, Bastan. A lot more. I think... I think it's how I can get Tray released." She told him about what she saw with the princess, and Bastan watched her for a long moment, his face unreadable.

"You found the princess at the university. And you say that these highborns intended for you to take the fall for what happened with her. And they will blame you for being some sort of Theln sympathizer."

"That's what it sounded like."

"First of all, I can spread the word that you aren't. Tray too."

"Will that even do any good? If highborns already have it in their head to blame us, there's nothing you can do. But maybe—*maybe*—if I can get to the princess, we can fix this."

Bastan laughed and glanced behind him again, as if worried someone might be coming through the dark tavern and after him.

"What's so funny?"

"Only you talking about helping one of the highborn. And the princess, at that. If nothing else, you've always been consistent with your hatred for the highborns."

"That hasn't changed, but if she dies, they'll blame Tray for what happened."

Bastan watched her for a moment. "Even if that were possible, why would you think that you have some way of healing her that they don't in the university? Why would you believe that you were somehow more capable than all of the physickers?"

Sam shook her head. She couldn't answer that without betraying the secret of the paper to Bastan, and if he knew that, he wouldn't let her leave his sight. "Do you have any more of the paper left? Did it all burn up in your tavern?"

She hadn't thought of that, but maybe it was all gone. With what she now knew about how valuable it was, she needed to get the other dozen pages.

"Sam—"

Sam shook her head. "No, Bastan. Do you have any or not?"

Bastan studied her for a moment before reaching into his pocket. He pulled out a folded slip of paper and handed it over to her. "I doubt this will do you any good."

She shrugged and started past him, pushing back out into the dusty tavern.

Bastan grabbed for her shoulder, and she shrugged him off.

"Do you think you can buy your way through this?" Bastan asked.

"Not buy my way, but there might be something that can be done. I just have to find the person who can help me."

"Don't get hurt doing this, Sam. I can protect you in Caster, but outside of our section you'll be on your own."

Sam arched a brow at him. "Why, Bastan. I would almost believe that you were concerned about me."

"If you knew anything about me, then you'd know I am always concerned about you. When have I ever shown you otherwise?"

She left the tavern, making her way back out into the night. In the distance, she could smell the fires still burning, but there were no more explosions, nothing thundering and disrupting the quiet of the night. For that, Sam was thankful. Could the Thelns have attacked other places she had been? That was the only connection she had...

which made it likely that they had attacked Alec's apothecary, as well.

Kyza!

Was it her fault that his shop had been destroyed?

Now there was even more reason for her to find him.

She raced through the Caster section, and jumped over the canals, eventually reaching his section. She hurried along until she found his shop. At least, the remains of it.

She crawled through the ash and leaned against the neighboring wall. She would wait. Eventually, Alec would return. He would have to. She knew how much this place meant to him. And when he did, she would get his help.

He *had* figured out the secret to the paper. And the paper was power. Now it would be the key to getting her brother out of prison.

19

REUNION

The noise caught his attention and Alec spun, sending ash into the air.

He'd been looking through the remains of the shop, trying to salvage what he could, when he noticed something in the corner. As he approached, there was movement. Memories of the attack—and the destruction of the shop that followed—sent him staggering back a step where he almost fell over.

He tried spinning to the side, but fell, tripping over his feet and landing on his back. When he looked up—half expecting one of the same large attackers—he instead saw a face he hadn't thought he'd see again.

Sam stared at him, her mouth pinched in a strange line as if she struggled to make sense of what she saw. She wore the same strange cloak he'd seen when she'd snuck into the apothecary, with its odd ability to practically draw light, concealing her in shadows. Bruises along her cheeks left him wondering what had happened to her, but otherwise, she looked well. She leaned against her staff, though she tried to conceal it.

As before, he couldn't shake the attraction he felt when looking at her. She had a rounded jaw and eyes that seemed to take in everything, and wavy black hair that hung beyond her shoulders. She was lovely.

"Sam?" he asked, trying to get back to his feet. He tripped on a damaged bookcase and tried to make it look graceful when he knew it was anything *but* graceful.

She breathed out a sharp sigh. "Alec. Kyza knows it seems like I've been waiting for you forever."

"What do you mean?" He wiped his hands on his jacket, trying to ignore the fluttering in his chest. It did not do for him to allow himself any sort of attraction to her. "Are you still sick? I thought the healing worked for you. Had the poison set, you would have been dead by now."

He didn't mean to be so blunt, but his surprise at finding her here overwhelmed his ability to speak more tactfully.

"I'm fine. Your healing worked well. Maybe too well," she added.

"Then why did you come here?"

She looked around at everything, and he could tell by the lack of expression in her eyes that she had seen the destruction of the shop well enough before now. How long had she been waiting for him? "What happened here?"

"I... I don't know. It exploded. I was lucky I got out."

"I know the feeling."

"You do?"

She shook her head. "Listen, Alec. I'm glad to see you. I think you might be the only person who can help me."

"Help you? You said you weren't still sick."

"I'm not, but there is someone who is. And I need your help to get my brother out of prison, even if it means breaking into prison."

"What? Why would you ever think about doing that?"

Sam sighed. "My brother is there. I need to do whatever I can to rescue him."

Alec couldn't imagine anyone wanting to break *in* to the prison. It was said to be impossible to escape, and held only the most dangerous. But Sam didn't strike him as dangerous, and he suspected her brother wasn't dangerous, either.

"What... what did he do?" He hated asking, especially if it was something dangerous. Alec hadn't ever done anything dangerous and didn't think that he even *could*. But Sam *was* dangerous—or at least was involved with dangerous people.

Sam sighed, wondering how much she should share. "The night I... borrowed... some paper from the highborns, he was grabbed. He wasn't doing anything but watching over me, but with his size, they probably thought he was up to no good—"

"While you were the one up to no good?"

Sam smiled, making her even more attractive, if that were possible. "It's usually me. Most of the time, Tray just watches out for me, trying to keep me from getting in trouble. I can't carry weapons, so he's my protection."

"No weapons? What about the knife you had when you first came to me?"

"That's different. It's barely more than a sliver of metal. Anyway, he's my protection, and without him there... I got captured," she said. "Kyza knows I was lucky to get out, and I need to do what I can to get *him* out. Even if it means helping a highborn."

A dozen questions came to mind, but the one he asked was, "Who—or what—are the brutes?" If they were the ones who had attacked her, one of them was likely the same man who had destroyed the shop. After seeing what they were capable of doing, he didn't think he wanted anything to do with them.

Sam squeezed her eyes shut and shook her head. "I don't know much about them. They're not from the city, I know that much at least. Someone I know called them Thelns, but I don't know if that even means anything. All I know is that they've attempted to kill me twice. And I believe they've poisoned the princess which the highborns intend to pin on me to hide the fact that Thelns are in the city."

"They *what?*"

Sam breathed out heavily, and she looked around her. A pained look crossed her face. "They poisoned the princess. I saw her. She's... I don't know how to describe what she is. Sick. Wasting away. Dying. And they are hoping to blame Tray and me for what happened."

"Why would they want to do that?" That didn't make any sense to him. Why would Sam matter to them at all?

"Because I stole that paper. Nearly died in the process. There is much we don't know about this paper, but with my brother in prison, I think the only way I *might* be able to save him would be to help the princess get better, so we can't take the blame for what happened. That's why I want your help. The healers in the university aren't able to heal her."

"Physickers." When she frowned at him, he said, "Physickers. That's what they're called. They're not healers or apothecaries."

"Call them what you want, but that's why I need you."

"Sam… I don't think I can help."

"You don't even know what I'm asking," she said.

"It seems like you're asking me to help you do something inside the university." He arched a brow at her, waiting to see how she would respond, and Sam only met his gaze. "Is that it? Is that what you're intending? To break into the university?"

"I don't know what I'm intending, only that I have no way of helping Tray otherwise. If we can somehow help the princess, then I have to believe there's something she can do for him."

Alec shook his head. "When you were here with me the last time," he said, waving around what was once his father's shop, "you were pretty clear that you had no interest in helping the highborns."

"I will if it helps me. Most of us lowborns don't really care what happens in the palace, so long as it doesn't affect us. Well, *this* affects me."

"You think those of us in the Arrend section are so different?"

"You're not lowborn."

Alec shook his head. "You speak of sections as if they matter. I've not seen that it matters which section you come from."

"Because you're from a closer section to the high-borns." She shook herself, looking around at the remains of his shop.

Alec followed her gaze. In the growing daylight, it was hard not to take in all the destruction that had happened here. The shop was in ruins. And, if what Sam told him was true, it was because of some plot against the princess.

"Sam—"

Sam grabbed him on the arm. Alec was surprised by the strength in her grip. She wasn't very tall, but she was strong. "Don't say it like that. Didn't you say you would help heal others regardless of their ability to pay?"

"That was my father. I'm not my father."

Sam smiled. "I don't know your father, but I know what you were able to do for me. If you could help heal me, there has to be something you can do for the princess."

Alec sighed. It seemed it would do no good to argue with Sam. How could he prove to her that there was nothing he could do? That if the physickers at the university were unable to help the princess, he would be unlikely to offer anything more? Even were his father here, it might not matter.

"At least come. See if there's anything you can do. Do it for my brother."

"I don't know your brother, and if what you said is true, then he's a guest of the palace prison."

"A guest?"

Alec flushed. "I didn't know how else to phrase it."

"You could have just said prisoner. Because that's what he is."

"And I don't know him." He shook his head, looking around. There wasn't anything in the shop for him, not anymore. There was no shop.

And as much as he wanted to say no, his father's training kicked in, telling him that he needed to help, even if he did nothing more than look to see what he might be able to offer. He doubted he would be able to offer anything, but maybe he could gather information that he could provide to his father when he returned. And maybe he could find some way to get word to his father from within the university.

But doing so would require breaking in.

That wasn't something he was willing to do, even for Sam.

"They won't release him, Alec," she said, her voice now in a whisper. She swallowed back what seemed to be a lump in her throat. "With what happened to the princess, they will blame me. They will blame Tray. Do you know what that means? Do you know what those in the palace do to those of us who are lowborn?"

Alec studied her face, wishing there was something he could say, but she was right. He had no idea what it was like to live in her section, where she had to learn to sneak and thieve to make a living. It was nothing like his section with the cozy shops he'd known as home. The Arrend section was large enough that he'd barely ever left, staying mostly within the confines of the canal borders. Other than when he had gone looking for his father at the university, there had only been a few times he'd ventured beyond his section and never out of the city.

"You don't know that they will do anything to him."

"I know. I've known too many to get lost to highborns with power. Alec…" She swallowed again, and licked her lips, looking down at the ground. Alec wished that he could reassure her that everything would be fine, somehow provide comfort to her, but what was there for him to say? "I can't lose someone else from my family. He's all I have left."

Alec thought about it for a long moment then shook his head. He shouldn't even be considering it, but he was. Doing it risked any chance he had for a future of studying at the university. It risked any chance of him ever becoming a physicker himself. "Do you have any money?"

"Money?"

He nodded. "That's how were going to get you back into the university."

20

SMOKE INHALATION

They walked toward the university section of the city, and Alec glanced over at Sam. She fidgeted with the edge of her cloak and looked around as if trying to think of some way to run, but he kept his arm looped through hers, feeling the heat of her body as it radiated against him. As they approached the university, she tensed.

"What are you concerned about?" he whispered.

"I'm concerned about what happened the last time I was here."

She rubbed her jaw, and he glanced at the fading bruise on her cheek. It angered him that anyone associated with the university would do something like that. And they had to be associated with the university, didn't they? Otherwise they shouldn't be allowed access to it.

"We're taking a different way. Once we're inside…"

"Once we're inside, I can find the way."

"I still don't know what you expect me to do."

She looked up at him and his heart fluttered. "I'll explain when we're inside."

"You know I'm only an apothecary, and an apprentice at that."

Sam patted him on the arm. "You're more than that."

They joined the line leading up to the entrance. Alec fingered the coins in his pocket that Sam had grabbed, trying not to think about how she had grabbed them. Had she stolen them from someone, or was it money she had?

The line was as long as it had been the day before, and he hoped that different students would be screening people at the entrance. If it was the same ones, would they recognize him? Likely they wouldn't. There were hundreds of people in line, all waiting for healing, and likely only a few with the ability to pay.

"Let me lead when we get up there," Alec said.

Sam patted the long staff that she had tucked under her cloak before nodding to him, and said nothing.

They approached the pair of students, and Alec was pleased to note that they were not the same. He breathed out, preparing his story. What would it take to get through and gain entrance to the university? Now that they were here, he worried that they didn't even have enough money. He hadn't given that much thought. When he'd been here before, he hadn't tried to figure out how much it cost to gain entrance.

"Do you have the necessary fee?" The student who asked was young, possibly as young as Alec, and he had dark eyes that looked at him with boredom. Obviously, they didn't expect Alec to have the money.

"Please. My sister..."

Alec feigned an attempt to push past. He had seen others doing the same, and thought it would show a sense of urgency. Having that urgency would make his request more believable… At least he hoped so.

"Your sister?" He frowned as he studied Sam. Would it not be believable for them to be siblings? They didn't look terribly similar, though he'd rubbed some soot on Sam's face, using that to add to the presenting complaint.

"Please," Alec started again. "My sister needs help." He fished the coins from his pocket. "This is what I have. It's not much, but it's all I have." Others who had come had not brought coins out. Alec took a chance, thinking that it might be the key difference between them, a way for him to differentiate him from the others seeking help.

The student glanced at the flash of coins before nodding and making a single motion over his head. As he did, a young man emerged from a hidden doorway behind the gate and scooped the coins from Alec's hands before leading them through the gate.

Sam held tightly to his arm, squeezing it as they were escorted away.

Alec stared at the student who'd granted him access. The next person in line was holding out empty palms, and the student was pointing away from the gate. There was a part of him that had hoped that healing at the university wasn't only about how much someone was able to pay, but he'd seen enough evidence from those in line to know otherwise.

"What would have happened if he hadn't been able to pay?" Sam asked the man leading him into a narrow entrance.

The man glanced back. He had a soft and clean-shaven face, and wore his hair parted down the middle, longer than Alec would have felt comfortable. "You wouldn't have been given entrance if you couldn't pay."

"What about those with severe illnesses?" Alec asked, knowing that he shouldn't. Anything that drew attention to them put them in danger. They were trying to gain entrance to the university, not challenge the protocol within the university.

"The physickers are limited on who they can heal. We must save our talents for those who need them most."

"And they're the ones who can pay?" Sam asked, glancing over to Alec.

He knew what she was thinking. Highborns would have the ability to pay, where lowborns would not. At least his father wouldn't have cared.

Or would he?

He thought he had known his father, but then he had never known that he had spent any time here. Had he come away with the same philosophy, hiding it behind healing others?

No. His father was genuine in his desire to help others.

The student nodded. "Healing bears a burden for all."

He said it as if he'd said the words before.

"But it's a burden only those with the ability to pay can reach," Sam said.

Alec took her hand and squeezed, trying to silence her. Now wasn't the time for a debate about the differences between highborns and lowborns. Then again, he had never really seen a difference. There were poorer sections of the city, where people like Sam and others who lived in them referred to themselves as lowborns, and there were those with wealth. How is that different from any other city?

As they made their way inside, he thought of all those in the line, those who didn't and wouldn't have the ability to pay. Had he access to the apothecary, he would have tried to help them. He would have attempted *something* rather than simply turning them away. The idea ate at him. Maybe it had done the same to his father.

"Where are you taking us?" Sam asked.

The young man didn't even look back. "The intake room."

He led them through a series of connecting chambers, each growing narrower and narrower. Lanterns hanging on the walls gave enough light to see, and there were a few windows cut into the walls, as well, though less light spilled through them.

Finally, they stopped at a doorway. The student pulled a keyring from his pocket and inserted a large key into the lock before pushing the door open. Dozens of benches lined the room, each occupied by several people. Alec noted the quality of dress was higher here, and those within the room looked less sick than those he'd seen outside.

"This is the intake room?" Alec asked, glancing over at Sam. She shook her head. She hadn't been in a place like this when she'd been here.

"This is where you'll be assessed and assigned the correct physicker. From there, they will decide what additional cost will be incurred."

Additional cost. He'd thought what he'd paid to gain

admittance in the first place was exorbitant. What would have happened had his father asked for that much money to heal others?

"How much additional cost would we be looking at?" Sam asked. She looked at Alec as she did.

The man frowned at him. "You should wait to see the physicker before asking these questions."

He led them to the nearest bench, which was occupied by five others, each of whom sat silently and stared straight ahead. As Alec looked around the room, he realized that no one really spoke, there was a somberness to the room, a stillness that he wouldn't have expected. Almost as if everyone waiting here held their breath while the physickers determined what would happen to them.

Alec and Sam took a seat and looked up to the student, but he disappeared before Alec had a chance to ask him any more questions. Sitting down, he was acutely aware of the soot on their clothing and likely on his face, feeling so out of place here in the sterile environment of those with the money to pay for healing.

"See?" Sam said.

"I see," Alec whispered.

Every so often, the door to the room opened, and a man or woman in a long jacket entered. Alec decided they must be the physickers. Their jackets hung past their knees, and they were older, unlike the students who'd brought them here. They chose people from along the benches to speak to before guiding them off. There didn't seem to be any order to it.

After they'd waited for a while, a thin woman approached. She had a severe expression, and her black hair was pulled back from her brow and tied behind her head. "You will come with me," she said.

The others on the bench with them looked over, and Alec couldn't help but note the expression of longing on the face of each. What ailments did they suffer from that they would come here and be willing to pay the rates the physickers charged? As he looked at them, he mentally began assessing their symptoms, trying to determine what they might suffer from, but was pulled away before he had a chance to come up with a diagnosis for most of them.

The woman led them away and into a small alcove off the main room. She left them there, alone, without saying another word.

There was no place to sit.

"This is so different from the way you do your healing," Sam whispered.

Alec was thankful that she whispered. There were small vents on the wall, and he worried that sound would travel. He leaned toward one, letting the fresh air blow through and fill his nostrils. "My father trained here," he said.

"I thought you said your father was an apothecary, not a physicker."

Alec sighed and pulled the note from his pocket, unfolding it and handing it over to Sam. She scanned it quickly before handing it back.

"That's why you came here?" When he didn't answer, she shrugged. "You were familiar with what it would take to gain entry, so I suspected you've been here before. You came after you were given that note, didn't you?"

"I came before I thought through what I was going to

do when I got here. It's not like they would even recognize my father. To them, he's only an apothecary. The physickers don't view them the same—"

Soft whispering came through the vent from the other side of the wall. Alec raised his finger to his lips to quiet Sam so he could listen.

"What do you have?" he overheard a man speaking in hushed tones.

"From the look of the clothing, a burn."

This was a woman's voice, and he suspected it came from the one who'd brought them back here.

"Clothing?"

"They're covered in filth. No burns on their faces or hands."

"And they were able to afford entry?"

"I guess they had at least three silvers," someone said.

"Maybe he's here because she burned something off," the man suggested.

The woman laughed softly. "You should talk. What do you have?"

"Who knows? A few more silvers, and I'll give them a salve. They'll probably believe it helps."

"You'll never be raised to full physicker with that mindset," the woman said.

"You don't think so? It's more about what you bring in than what you do…"

Alec didn't hear the rest. He pulled back from the wall and stood staring at the door.

The conversation disgusted him, but there had to be real healers here, otherwise why would people continue coming for healing? Where would his father have learned what he had?

What would happen were he to actually *need* healing? How would he manage to get that? If these weren't even the full healers, how would he get in front of those with the ability to actually do something to help others?

The door opened, and the thin woman returned. "Tell me your symptoms."

Alec nodded to Sam. "She can't talk, not anymore." He hadn't discussed what he intended with her before, and hoped that she caught on in time. "She said it was like her insides had grown tight and painful." Alec pointed to her throat. He needed something that would be believable, but something she wouldn't be able to inspect. Smoke inhalation was potentially fatal, but not something she would be able to check on if he told the truth. They already believed they had been burned, so this wasn't *too* much of a stretch.

The woman twisted Sam's face, forcing her mouth open. She looked in for a moment and then shook her head. "I don't see anything, and you were able to make it all the way here from…"

"Callesh." It wasn't a highborn section, but relatively high class. It would be believable of them to have the money necessary for healing.

The woman's eyes narrowed. "The Callesh section is quite a walk. If there was a significant problem, it would have appeared by now. That it hasn't should reassure you."

Alec made a point of nodding vigorously. After overhearing the two physickers speak, he had a sense of what they expected out of him. They wouldn't expect him to know anything, and they would expect him to listen, but he had plenty of experience with those seeking healing to know how they pressed when they felt they weren't listened to.

"It's been getting worse since we left," Alec went on. "She said it feels like her throat is closing and she can't swallow anything."

Sam allowed a trail of drool to run down the side of her mouth, and Alec suppressed a laugh. At least she was playing the part.

That last should be enough to trigger a deeper investigation, but the woman would have to be interested in the supposed illness for her to care. Alec wasn't certain she was.

The woman glanced over her shoulder toward the door. "If you sit here, we can observe. If any intervention is needed, we will be able to offer it then."

"Where are we supposed to sit?"

She motioned to the floor. "You can sit anywhere in this room. You will be checked on periodically. When she's felt to be sufficiently stable, we'll release you."

Alec didn't get the chance to argue, or even ask for a chair. She slipped out of the door faster than he could speak up, leaving him staring after her.

This was how the physickers worked? At least his father offered a cot, even if not such a cozy room. This was more like a cell.

How long would they give them?

"That's it?" Sam asked.

"Well, she *is* right. There's not much to do for smoke

inhalation other than give it time. Though, I have seen a few cases where—"

Sam shook her head. "It doesn't matter, not right now. We need to get out of this room. Do you think it leads to the rest of the university?"

"It would have to." At least, he hoped that it would. If they got in, and he led Sam astray... Alec didn't like to think about that. Disappointing Sam bothered him.

When they'd been left alone for a few minutes, Alec reached for the door, unsurprised to find it unlocked. They would have no reason to lock them in this room. Most who came to the university for healing would remain as patiently as needed for the hope of what the university could offer. Most had spent enough to get here that they likely felt they had no other choice.

Alec pulled the door open and slipped out. Sam followed close behind.

The hallway was empty. No one moved, though he heard the soft voices coming from the other small rooms. He hurried away and reached a narrow hall with a row of long, gray jackets.

Alec slipped one on. If he were spotted, he could try to pretend he belonged. The lie wouldn't last if any thought to question him. He doubted he would be convincing to anyone who actually *was* from the university.

"We can pretend to escort you to a different part of the university," he whispered when Sam eyed him strangely.

"It suits you," she said.

Alec flushed and then hurried along the hall to the steps at the end.

When they reached the top of the stairs, they were in a much different part of the university. Pale white walls rose around him, all smooth marble. Hidden lamps glowed softly, giving the entire hall a serene sort of light. The soft sound of bells tolled distantly, a steady and gentle sound.

Alec hurried along this hall. If they were caught now… He didn't want to think what would happen were they caught now. Without the gray jacket, he could claim ignorance, and state he was lost, but without it, he would draw more attention.

The hall led to another set of stairs, and they hurried up these, as well.

"Do you recognize anything here?"

Sam looked around. The landing here was wide and the marble inlaid with decorative strips of gold. More lantern light created a soft calming effect, almost coming from everywhere around them. He suspected hidden mirrors helped with the light, but the effect impressed him. Heavy oak doors lined the hall, each closed. At the end of the hall, another stairway led up.

"I think… there." She pointed to the stairs.

The faint sound of voices drifted down the hall, and Sam grabbed him, pulling him against the wall, wrapping her cloak around them. He glanced over to her, but she brought a finger to her lips, silencing him.

"She grows weaker by the day," a hushed voice said. It came from the other end of the hall, and near the stairs. Were they talking about the princess?

"Soon she will pass."

"We can't allow her to pass here. She needs to be returned to the palace."

"They need to know we've done all we can to help her."

"And have we?"

"There are limits to what we can do without access to the book."

One sounded like an older man, and he had a hard edge to his voice, even hushed as it was. The other sounded more like a woman. If they were talking about the princess and the fact that she was dying, at least these two seemed concerned.

"There's no way to find the book in time."

"Then she really is gone, isn't she?"

There was silence, and Alec thought they were now too far away for him to hear, but then the man spoke again. "She's not gone yet, but all too soon, she will be."

The voices disappeared, and didn't return.

He stood next to Sam, feeling a chill wash over him. The physickers he'd seen in the lower level hadn't displayed any real caring, but these two had. If more of the physickers were like them... There seemed a profound sadness from them about the fact that they couldn't do anything.

"Come on," Sam urged, taking his arm and pulling him along the hall and toward the stairs.

He didn't resist, allowing her to pull him, and they climbed the stairs. With each step, they went further and further into the university, and further and further into the kind of trouble Alec had never dared risk before. He couldn't shake the troubling thought that if they were caught, any chance of him ever entering the university to study would be lost.

21

FINDING THE PRINCESS

The halls around her were familiar, and Sam guided Alec with more urgency. She was thankful that he had agreed, and the look of disgust on his face when they had reached the intake room troubled her. Had he thought that the university would be any different from anywhere else in the world? Could he really have believed that they wouldn't favor highborns over lowborns?

It was almost enough to make her regret dragging him here. Almost.

Now that they were here, she needed to get into the room with the princess and then see if there was anything Alec could do.

They reached a landing. The air had a familiar foul stench to it that reminded her of the danker parts of the canals, and she guided Alec down the hall. His eyes widened, and he paused periodically, sniffing, almost as if he *wanted* to inhale the stink that came out.

"This one," Sam said, motioning to one of the doors.

She tried the knob and found it locked. She glanced up at him, hating that he would see her breaking into the room, not wanting him to see that side of her, but she'd already proven that she was a thief. She debated using her knife, but she still had the slivers of wood she'd made when she escaped that would work better.

Slipping the slivers out of her pocket, she made quick work of the lock, and it popped open. Sam looked inside the room, but it was darkened, and she couldn't see anything.

The smell, though… that was awful.

She jerked her head back, gagging.

"Tissue rot," Alec said.

He reached a hand beneath his jacket and pulled out a roll of waxed paper, and ran his finger along it. He took this finger and smeared it beneath her nose. Instantly she smelled only the heady aroma of mint. The rot fought to get through the mint, but whatever he applied seemed to hold most of it back.

After applying a smear of the paste under his nose, he rolled it back up and stuffed it into his pocket. "My father taught me to keep some with me since we don't always know what we might encounter. I didn't expect to need it here."

"Helpful."

Alec shrugged. "You get used to all but the worst. For that, you need a little reprieve."

Sam shook her head. "I don't know that anyone can get used to stink like that."

Alec met her eyes. As he seemed ready to say something else, a moan came from within the room.

He rushed past her and into the room.

Even though it was the reason they were here, Sam reluctantly followed, hoping the mint paste would prevent her from smelling the awfulness of the room. For the most part, it worked, but she had a whiff of more, like a memory of it, that she couldn't completely shake.

Alec made his way toward a large bed occupying the middle of the room. As she watched, he peeled back the sheets to reveal the princess, a young woman with blonde hair and pale skin, so different from Sam's darker skin and hair. Alec was seemingly unmindful of the fact that he left the woman fully exposed. Beneath the sheets, she was naked. Was that the way he had treated her? Likely he had, needing to do so to save her from the crossbow bolt in the arm… and the glass in her belly.

"Can you help her?" she asked.

Sam approached more carefully than Alec had, ignoring the way he tipped his head to her chest and then stomach, again trying not to think about his examination of her that night. Practiced hands ran along either side of the woman's neck, and her chest, then her stomach. He lifted each arm, then her legs, studying them as if they could tell him secrets. The princess let out a soft moan, but didn't seem in pain.

Her cheeks were hollowed, and her eyes seemed sunken. Up close, even her flaxen hair seemed more like straw than silk. Bones were prominent, and her breathing had a ragged quality with each breath.

"This… This is strange," Alec said.

"What happened to her?" Sam said.

Alec paused in his examination, lowering the woman's

leg back down to the bed. "That's just it. I can't find anything wrong with her. It's some sort of rot, but usually with this…"

"Smell?" Sam filled in for him.

He nodded. "With this, there's a wound and an infection festering. I can't find anything. It's almost like whatever is happening is within her."

Sam stared at the princess. It was awful, what was happening to her, but she had a hard time generating any other kind of sympathy. The highborns, and all of those descended from them, had done nothing to help those like her from the outer sections. They didn't care, so, why should she? The only reason she was here was to help her brother.

Alec stopped at a small table resting next to the bed. Sam had missed that when she first came in, but noted now how Alec sorted through the various vials, holding them up and looking within. A few, he unstoppered and sniffed, before setting them back down. As he worked, he shook his head, slowly at first, and then with increasing intensity.

"None of this would work," he said softly.

"What do you mean?"

Alec held up the vial he'd just been sniffing. "This. It's a burgworm root. This would help with appetite, and given the way she's wasted, I suspect they intend."

Sam noted the boniness to the princess's arms. "It seems so."

"But in combination with this"—he held up another vial, this one looking like it held a few leaves—"it robs the burgworm of its potency."

"They would know that."

Alec nodded. "I think they would." He lowered his voice and pulled her away from the princess.

Sam didn't resist, feeling a growing sense of unease standing so close to her. If the princess could get poisoned and not healed by physickers, what would happen were *she* to catch it? She doubted there would be nearly the same effort spent trying to get her well.

"I don't think it's contagious," Alec said, almost as if reading her mind.

"How can you be sure?"

"Well… I can't. But if it *were* contagious, I'd expect there to be some sort of barrier in front of the room, and a film placed over her mouth. More than a sheet."

"A barrier like a locked door?"

Alec shook his head. "That's no real barrier. Anyone with a key can open it."

Sam looked past him and fixed her eyes on the princess. As much as she didn't feel empathy for the woman, she couldn't help but feel something. She was human, after all. "Is she suffering?"

"I thought you didn't care about her."

"I don't care about *her*, but I wouldn't want anyone to suffer needlessly. That's not completely true. I wouldn't have any trouble if one of the brutes suffered, especially after they put an arrow in my shoulder." She rubbed the spot as she spoke. There was always a soft throbbing in the shoulder, one she couldn't completely shake. "But I need her to come around. Tray needs her to come around."

Alec glanced up, meeting her eyes before looking back down at the princess. "I don't think she's suffering."

"How can you tell?"

"She's mostly quiet, for one."

"She's moaned twice so far, and we haven't been on the floor all that long."

Alec went back to the tray and started sorting through the different vials. There were also some uncovered bowls, and a thick brown paste was smeared around a plate, looking more like uneaten gravy than anything curative.

None of the vials or bowls were labeled. How did they even know what they used on the princess?

"It's not all about the moaning. With suffering, you'll see a few signs. A sheen of sweat on the brow. A racing heartbeat. Rapid breathing. She has none of those."

Sam had to trust that he knew what he was talking about. He'd healed her, so he obviously *did*, and it wasn't that she really cared whether he did anything for the princess. "She reminds me of some of the underfed strays I've seen in the Caster section," she said softly.

"If I can't do this…"

"If you can't do it, then I'm going to find the tunnels that connect between here and the palace and use those to get into the prison."

"Do you… Do you really think that would work?"

It wasn't her best plan, but it was all she had. Go from here and into the palace, from there, find the deep tunnel to the prison, rescue Tray, and be gone. Maybe then they would even risk leaving the city. It would be difficult, but what choice did she have?

She doubted she could even accomplish the first part of that plan.

"I don't know."

"You're probably a good thief, but I doubt you'll make it very far," he said. "And I don't know that there's anything I can do. Even if I had supplies…"

"You don't need supplies."

"If I'm going to help her, I need something. What they have here isn't going to be enough."

Sam dipped her hand into her pocket, pulling out the piece of paper that Bastan had given her. She didn't even know if it would work, but it was the entire reason she had come, the reason she had grabbed Alec, thinking that the two of them could make this work.

"What is that?" Alec asked.

Sam held out the folded sheet of paper. "Here," she said.

"What is this?"

"This is how you're going to heal the princess and how I'm going to get my brother back."

The surprised look on his face was priceless.

22

THE MAGIC IN PAPER

The look on her face made Alec think she was serious, so he smiled, trying to soothe her. She'd been through enough already, and he didn't want to upset her by telling her that *paper* wouldn't be the key to helping the princess.

The layer of paste under his nose itched, but he refused to scratch at it. The odor of necrotic flesh was potent, more so than anything he'd ever experienced. There was probably nothing he could do for the princess, but with the collection of medicines next to her bed, he doubted the physickers were getting anywhere, either.

There was a certain familiarity to what they used. Not the vials or the bowls holding them—those were far nicer than anything they would have had in the apothecary—but the cut of the leaves and the choice of berries or grasses… With healing, even the cutting could matter. That was something his father had always told him.

He took the offered sheet of paper, recognizing the

quality and the texture as similar to the one she'd had with her when he'd healed her before. That strange paper had required blood ink to write. Why would she try to give him paper?

"I don't think it will matter if I document her symptoms," he said.

A smile spread across her face, so out of place in this room where illness lingered and death chased. "It does. All you have to do is write them down."

"Sam—"

"This is what they're after, Alec. They want this paper because there is something special about it. They call it easar paper. I don't fully understand, but you've discovered the secret to writing on it. And it has power."

"Power?"

She nodded. "When you write on it. You figured out the secret."

"It was blood. That's not really a secret."

"You wrote on similar paper that night. Did anything unusual happen?"

"You mean other than you running out of the apothecary? Or the man who must have been chasing you who came and burned the place to the ground?"

Sam touched her shoulder, rubbing the spot Alec knew the crossbow bolt had pierced. There *had* been a poison on it, and hadn't the man been surprised that she had survived?

"You asked if there was anything strange that happened?"

Sam nodded.

"You."

Sam stopped pacing and faced him, crossing her arms over her chest. "Now you're saying I'm strange?"

"Not like that, but what happened with you *was* strange. You'd lost a lot of blood and there was poison in the arrow."

"Bolt."

He shook his head. "I used a salve that would have helped the skin heal, but it really *shouldn't* have made a difference when it came to the poison. But here you are. Still alive."

Sam pulled her shirt back and looked where the *bolt* had gone in. She tugged her shirt back, moving the cloak to the side so he could see. The skin was clear, free from any sign of the injury, from any scar. "That's what I'm talking about. The paper has power. It *healed* me."

He gasped and hurried over to her.

That shouldn't be. There should be some sort of evidence of the wound, even if it were subtle. He might have stitched her well, but he had still stitched her. No one healed that quickly, or even more alarming, with no sign of the original injury. No one other than Sam.

He touched her skin, noting it smooth and warm. "How?" he asked her.

She met his eyes, and he realized he was still holding on to her shoulder, cupping it gently. He pulled his hand away, and Sam gave him an amused expression.

"There's magic in the paper. That's why they want it back."

"I don't understand."

Sam shrugged. "I don't, either. Was I the only one you wrote about?"

He thought about what he'd written on the page. There had been Hyp's symptoms—which he and his father had long thought were more imagined than real—and then Mrs. Rubbles.

He recalled being somewhat surprised by her improvement. When he saw her after the fire, she was quite hale. Strong.

She had come to him initially with concern about a glandular issue. Alec had offered her what help he could think of, enough to tide her over until his father returned, but she had recovered far more than he would have expected. Even the achiness of her joints had seemed to calm… but hadn't he written about that, as well?

He eyed this new piece of blank paper with surprise.

Could that have made a difference?

Alec didn't believe in the old stories of magic, and didn't believe in anything but what he could observe, and what he could test, but what if Sam was right about this?

If it could help the princess, did he dare *not* try?

"There *was* something, wasn't there?" Sam asked.

He nodded slowly. "Other than you, I documented symptoms of two others."

"What happened to them?"

"I only saw one of them after I did, but she was better."

"Better?"

He looked over and saw her studying him, a line in her furrowed brow as she did, and he nodded. "Better."

He unfolded the paper carefully and made his way to the table next to the princess. Alec shifted everything on the table, moving it all to the side so he had room to work. A scrap of paper had been tucked beneath one of the plates, and he stuffed it into his pocket to look at later. Likely, it was the physickers' notes. "I'll need a pen," he said.

"There are none," Sam said, speaking over his shoulder.

"I can't do this without... Let me have one of those sticks you used," he said.

Sam shrugged and pulled one of the narrow lengths of carved wood from her pocket, handing it to him. Alec ran his thumb along the edge. All he needed was something that would write on the page. For that matter, he could use his finger if needed, but that wouldn't be neat enough. This should work.

"Your knife."

He held his hand out, and Sam passed her knife over to him. It was a strange blade, with a hook on the end, but sharp. The metal was a dull black, as if she'd left it in a fire for too long, charring the surface. Alec took the bowl that sat on the table and tipped out the flasn berries that had been in there. They wouldn't have done anything for the princess, anyway. They left a dark stain along the inside of the bowl.

Holding his hand over the bowl, he ran the knife across his palm, wincing as he did. Blood pooled in his palm, and he tipped that into the bowl, letting it run out.

With his other hand, he dipped the stick into the blood. This time, he wouldn't dilute it. There would be no purpose, not when it had seemed like the blood itself had been the critical ingredient rather than anything else. He pulled the stick free and brought it to the page.

As he wrote, he held his breath.

Princess Lyasanna Anders. Wasting. Thinning hair, sunken cheeks...

The words formed on the page, but began to fade, not holding as they had before.

"Kyza! What are you doing differently?" Sam asked.

"Nothing. When I wrote on the other page before, I used blood."

"*Your* blood?"

"It was mine..." Alec frowned. *Had* it been only his blood? He'd wiped the page with the cloth that had been stained with Sam's blood, too. Could that be the key? "Not mine. Yours." He turned to her. "Hold out your hand."

Sam shook her head. "What are you going to do?"

"If this works, and we can save your brother—"

"You need to save the princess first. Then *she* can save my brother."

"That's what I'm trying to do."

"Why do you think my blood matters?"

"Because it matters. When I did this before, maybe it wasn't *my* blood but *yours*. It was an accident, but it worked. And now we need to try it again."

"We. Sounds more like me."

Alec pointed to the blood congealing across his palm. "I already tried my blood. It doesn't work."

Sam held her hand out and turned away.

"It will hurt only for a minute."

"That's not it. I don't like blood."

Alec suppressed a smile as he made a quick slice across her palm. To her credit, she barely flinched. When enough blood pooled, he tipped the bowl to the side, emptying his blood from it, and let hers drip inside where it mixed with his. After two dozen drops, there was enough for him to work with, and he clenched her hand into a fist.

Working quickly, he started the same way as he had before, beginning with the princess's name.

Princess Lyasanna Anders. Wasting disease. No external source. Skin intact, but cheeks sunken and muscle has deteriorated.

Alec waited, watching to see if the ink would hold.

A moment passed. Then another. And another.

The blood remained on the page.

"It worked!" Sam said.

Alec smiled. It *had* worked.

"Why was *my* blood important?"

He had no answer for that. "What do I do?"

Sam shrugged. "Do the same as you did the last time. What was that?"

"Nothing more than documenting what I observed."

"Then do that."

Alec stared at the princess a moment and then began writing once more.

There is a heavy odor of necrosis, but none evident. I question whether this is an internal illness, as none is visible. Heart is regular, and her lungs are without rattle or wheeze. Skin is thinning, and there is a faint discoloration to it, though one I would not expect from blood loss.

"Alec?"

He noted an urgency in Sam's voice as he continued documenting.

Attempts have been made with willowleaf, episth paste, flasn berries...

"Alec!"

He looked up then, holding the makeshift pen above the page as he did. "What is it?"

"How much longer will this take?"

"I don't know what I did the last time. I'm trying to document everything I can. If it works... Why?"

She nodded to the door, and that was when he noticed a soft thudding against it.

They were about to have others join them.

23

THE FIRST AUGMENTATIONS

The change to the stillness of the room came suddenly. Sam listened as the steady scratching of the wood splinter moved along the page, trying not to think about what it meant that *her* blood had been the key to the writing remaining on the page. Had Marin known that when she asked her to break into the highborn house and steal it in the first place? Sam now recalled Marin's words that first night by the canal when she wasn't the best person for this and that Sam was a good fit to go after it. Why? Had she known it when she tried to help Sam escape before the brutes arrived?

Alec studied both the page and the princess with equal attention. He wore a determined expression, and every so often would pause, raising the end of the splinter to his mouth before resuming. Words flowed in her blood across the page, formed in a neat script, and remained there.

None of that had disturbed the quiet of the room.

No, that had come as he continued to work and as someone appeared at the door to the princess's room. From the way she heard footsteps on the other side of the door, and the heavy breathing that drifted through, she feared the brutes had found them.

And all she had was her knife.

With the crossbow, she would have been more capable of defending them, but even with that, she wasn't sure it would have protected her enough from the brutes. They were strong, and they were quick, and she was simply inexperienced when it came to more than brawling.

It had taken a few tries to get Alec's attention off the princess and the paper, but the puzzled look on his face faded as he seemed to realize they had company. "Try to hurry," she urged.

If this worked—and Sam was *not* sure that it would—they would need to work as quickly as possible to save the princess. If she woke, then they could explain what happened, and share with her why they'd broken in. Maybe they'd have time to explain the Thelns and how Tray had nothing to do with them, that *neither* of them were Theln sympathizers.

Sam stood near the edge of the princess's bed. Had the smell gotten better, or had she gotten to the point where she no longer noticed it anymore? Probably the latter. Alec claimed she would get used to it, and as much as the smell disgusted her, she suspected he was right about that.

The door sprang open.

Sam took a step back as the brutes entered.

Not just one, but three.

Two carried crossbows, and the memory of the last

time she'd been shot stuck with her, regardless of the fact that Alec had healed her. Poison. That was what Marin had said, and a kind that would be particularly fatal.

The other was the brute who'd questioned her when she'd been captured in the highborn house. He carried a long sword, and his eyes narrowed as he flicked his gaze from Sam to Alec.

There would be no questioning here. From the looks on their faces, the brutes had come to kill.

"Did you think you could hide from me? I warned you that I can *smell* you," the brute said.

"Come on. I don't stink *that* bad," she said, trying to decide what she would do.

The others held their crossbows ready, but didn't aim them.

Alec would be no help for her here. He might have saved her—twice—but he wasn't a fighter. And she might know how to fight, but she was out-armed and out-muscled. Even if the princess woke, there wouldn't be anything she could do to save them.

Had she come this far to fail?

Maybe there was one other thing they could try.

"Alec," she said in a whisper, drawing his attention to her, "if what you write on the page comes true, see if there's anything you can try."

He blinked and looked over at her. "Like what?"

"I don't know! Write that these three die or something."

He shook his head. "I can't—"

"Then give *me* the ability to stop them."

He stared at her then turned back to the page.

Sam rounded the bed and put herself between the princess and the brutes. If nothing else, she could stop them from reaching Alec. Maybe not stop, but delay.

"What are you doing here?" she demanded.

The lead brute glared at her. "Years of waiting will end today. Vengeance will be mine. You have been an interesting diversion, but a diversion, nonetheless. Now move as I claim my prize."

He waved his hand, and one of the brutes aimed his crossbow at her.

Sam spun, jumping and sweeping her leg around, kicking it as he fired. The bolt sailed high, striking the ceiling and sinking into the stone.

She kicked, and the man fell backward, but bounced back to his feet quickly.

The other aimed his crossbow, this time at Alec.

Sam jumped, but she wouldn't be fast enough to reach it.

Alec wasn't sure what Sam expected him to do. He couldn't harm another—that went against everything that he'd trained for with his father—but could he try something else as she suggested?

He still wasn't sure he believed the paper had special powers, but he *had* healed her, and then there was Mrs. Rubbles…

Sam needs speed and strength.

He wrote it as quickly as he could, his heart pounding wildly in his chest as he did.

It wouldn't work. How could it? There wasn't any real magic in the world, and what she suggested required magic.

But what had healed her? Not his salve. That wouldn't have worked nearly as well as what he'd seen. *Could* there be magic that had healed her?

What if he documented as if he were recording her symptoms? Would that matter?

He watched as Sam kicked the crossbow out of one of the massive man's hands, but the man bounced up faster than he would have expected possible. Given his size, there was no way that Sam could overpower him. At best, she would manage to delay them.

Compared to the others, reflexes are delayed. Strength diminished. Endurance low. Expect metham seeds to help with energy, and epigen leaves could help with reflexes.

Alec didn't know if anything he added now even made a difference. Probably not, but *if* there was anything to the paper and *if* it could help, he needed to try.

He looked up in time to see a crossbow pointed at him. The massive man holding it fired. Alec was frozen, unable to move.

Sam jumped, reaching for the crossbow as the brute fired it. There was no way she could reach it in time. Kyza, but she hoped Alec was smart enough to get down!

The jump carried her soaring across the room, farther than she should have gone. She *saw* the bolt streaking through the air and kicked at it, diverting it back toward the brute now looking at her with a strained expression on his face.

The bolt changed direction and soared toward him, catching him in the neck.

He went down in a spray of blood.

Sam landed, making a point of not looking at the man, trying to keep from vomiting.

Looking back, she saw Alec watching her, his eyes wide. At least he was alive.

But... how?

How had she managed to reach the crossbow in time to save him? The brute had to have been five paces from her, and then she had managed to kick the bolt out of the air. Not only kick it, but redirect it with enough force to take down the man down?

"A fully trained Kaver. I thought we had moved fast enough to avoid them," the brute with a sword said. He swiped toward her, and Sam jumped back, barely moving fast enough.

The brute swung again, and she rolled, noticing the other crossbow brute aiming once again at Alec. Not her. That had to be important.

As she rolled, she reached into her boot and pulled her mother's knife out. She flung it at the crossbow brute. He was the danger to Alec. The other brute came at her.

The knife sailed true, whistling through the air.

The brute seemed to notice, but too slowly.

He ducked, but she'd compensated for that. The knife struck him in the eye.

Sam turned her attention to the last brute, mostly to avoid looking at the blood spilling from the other two. He stepped back, swinging his sword more cautiously now, eyeing her with something bordering on concern.

"Whatever you're doing, keep it up," she said to Alec.

The brute smiled. "Perhaps *not* fully trained."

Swinging with more speed and energy than she would have believed possible for a man his size, he jumped at her.

Sam rolled again, but she wouldn't be fast enough to avoid him for long.

Could it really have worked? Alec didn't know how it was possible that writing on the page would have influenced Sam in that way, but there was no question that she reacted faster than she should have. Now two of the massive men were down, one with an arrow through his neck and the other with a knife in his brain. Neither injury was survivable.

Strange that even though he knew they had aimed at him, he struggled seeing them down like that. The urge to heal went deep into his core, and seeing others suffering, especially if there was something he could do about it, was difficult.

The remaining man moved quickly as he swung his sword. He was faster than Sam, even with whatever magic the paper provided.

Alec couldn't believe he actually thought the paper had any magic.

What else could have changed Sam?

She called on him to keep up what he was doing.

There wasn't anything he could think of that would make her any faster or stronger, but was there something he could do that would slow the last man?

The paper seemed to respond to listing of symptoms. Would it work in reverse?

Hyperactive reflexes, accelerated speed, abundance of strength. Would decrease all of the above with seven parts opium with one part vilen.

The princess's bed suddenly slid across the floor and into his chair, sending him toppling to the floor. The makeshift pen went clattering to the floor, as well. The tray spilled and the bowl holding Sam's blood splattered, cracking as it struck.

The massive man jumped *over* the princess's bed and landed in front of him.

"What did you write?"

Alec clutched the paper. Somehow, he'd managed to hold on to it when he'd fallen. "Nothing," he managed.

The man stalked toward him, starting to raise his sword, when he faltered.

His eyes widened.

"Sam! He should be—"

The man's boot caught Alec in the stomach, knocking the wind out of him before he got a chance to tell Sam the man was slowed. Would she know?

24

SAVING THE PRINCESS

"Alec!" Sam yelled. She wasn't sure what he'd tried to tell her, but knew she had to get to the brute before he could harm Alec.

Sam barely got out of the way before the brute collided with the princess's bed, sending it crashing into Alec, who tumbled off the chair and lost the pen as it skittered across the floor. The brute jumped, and it carried him over the bed as he turned his attention now to Alec.

She scrambled toward the nearest brute, unsheathing his sword and hefting it. The sword was heavier than it looked—heavier than any normal steel sword—and she swung it as she circled the end of the princess's bed.

The brute raised his sword to attack Alec.

She lunged, but missed.

The brute kicked Alec and he doubled over, whatever he tried to say cut off.

Had the sword faltered?

If so, it might be the opening she needed.

She jumped in front of him, catching his sword with the one she'd taken, knocking him back.

The brute staggered, his jaw clenched as he tried swinging his sword around, but she caught it before he could. Either she'd sped up... or Alec had somehow slowed him.

The wide-eyed look on the brute's face made it clear which it was.

"That's how it works? Writing in blood?" she asked, swinging her sword around, knocking his from his hand so it clattered to the ground.

"You will never get a chance to understand."

"No? I think he's already learned enough for us to figure out the rest. You can't move like you could before, can you?"

The brute laughed. "This is temporary. Soon enough I'll be restored, and you... you will fade. Then this will be finished."

She jabbed at him with the sword. He twisted, so rather than piercing his stomach, the blade only went through his side. He grimaced but said nothing.

Sam swung again, this time bringing the sword slicing up.

It grew heavy—too heavy for her to hold.

The brute grinned. "As I said. You fade."

Sam pulled on all the strength she could and kicked, catching him in the chest.

He went flying across the room, crashing into the wall. His eyes remained open, watching her. Somehow, he managed to say nothing when she'd hit him.

"Alec?" she asked.

She could feel whatever he had done seeping from her. It went slowly at first, but then more quickly. She had experienced enhanced strength and reflexes, but that seemed gone. And if what he had done for *her* was gone, then whatever he had done to the brute would soon end.

The brute watched her, and a dark smile spread across his face, as if knowing her thoughts.

She circled around the princess's bed, and picked up one of the crossbows, taking a bolt and nocking it, while pointing it at him. "Explain this."

He laughed. "You won't fire. I've seen it in your face."

"Why are you here for me?"

"For you? I'm not here for you."

Sam looked over her shoulder, noting the princess. Would she recover or would the effect fade for her as well?

But whatever Alec had done to help heal Sam the first time had worked, why wouldn't it work now? Why wouldn't her speed and strength remain?

"You cannot hold what was never meant to be," the brute said. "You can augment, but it fades. *You* fade. Much like you cannot take away what has been given. Eventually it returns."

"Like what you did to the princess?" Sam didn't even know if the brutes *had* done anything to the princess, but it seemed the most likely answer.

"You begin to see."

"I don't see anything. You said you can't take away. What did you do to her?"

The brute began to push away from the wall, flexing

his arms and wrists as he did. "Some still know the old ways, and they know how to make such changes linger, especially when written in the book." He waved toward the princess's bed.

Alec held the crossbow out and risked a look over. The princess seemed to be breathing more easily now, and if anything, her color had improved. Did the smell remain? She only noted the mint from the paste, and nothing more.

"He's healed her. She'll recover."

"For now. Once you're gone, I will finish her myself."

Sam fired the crossbow.

The brute caught the bolt as it flew toward his face.

With a smile, he threw it to the ground and started toward her.

Sam needed Alec to do something. If he could only write on the paper again, somehow slow the brute once more, they could get away. But she'd seen the blood spill and the bowl crack on the ground. There would be no more writing.

She threw the crossbow at the brute.

He smacked it away.

Sam had to draw him out of the room. If she could, she could give Alec a chance to escape. Or better yet, the princess a chance to awaken so she could help him.

Scrambling backward, she still had some residual speed, but nothing like she'd had before. She grabbed her knife out of the fallen brute's eye, trying not to gag as she did, or notice the squishing as the knife pulled free.

She held it out toward her attacker. The brute eyed the knife before flicking his gaze to her face.

Sam reached the door and stepped into the hall.

The brute laughed. "You won't find safety there, Kaver."

With a jump, he reached the door.

Sam darted back, across the hall, and her back pressed into the stone. The brute stepped into the hallway, blocking her from leaving.

Whatever she did, she was trapped.

"Why?" Sam asked.

"You can never understand."

He took a step toward her.

As he did, Sam heard feet pounded along tile, almost thundering toward her.

The brute seemed to notice it too.

She looked past him. Five soldiers marched along the hall, all armed with swords. The highborn who had captured her was with them, watching her with an amused expression.

The brute noted them, then turned the opposite way and casually strode to the end of the hall where he disappeared.

She quickly shoved her knife into her boot. If they didn't catch her with a weapon, she might get away with only prison. Might.

Now she stood in the hall alone, the guards each watching her with swords drawn, as if they hadn't seen the brute. With the way he'd turned and left at their arrival, she didn't think he worked with them, but how would he have managed to hide himself from them?

"Do not move," the nearest guard said.

Sam held her hands up. "I'm not moving."

After everything she had planned, she had found her way into the prison. Only, this way, there would be no escape.

25

AN AWAKENING

Alec rolled toward the paper as Sam backed out the door. Was there anything he could even do to help? If he could only write on the paper again, he might be able to help augment her ability once more. How had it faded as quickly as it had? Then again, could magical paper explain how had she gained the abilities she had in the first place? Had he not seen it himself, he wouldn't have believed it possible. He still wasn't sure whether he *could* believe what he'd seen.

He smoothed the page across the floor. Without the blood and without anything to write with, there wouldn't be a point of what he tried here.

The brute stepped through the doorway after Sam. He had to do something—anything—to help her. Even if it involved magic that shouldn't exist.

The problem was that there wasn't any of the blood left. Even if he wanted to help her, and even if the blood *could* somehow work on her, he wasn't sure there would be any to even use.

The bowl lay cracked near him.

Alec crawled through the shards of porcelain, ignoring the way they poked him as he did. His hand caught a particularly painful shard in the middle of his palm, reopening the wound from when he'd cut his hand to try and see if the blood would work on the page.

He bit back a cry of pain, looking up long enough to see that the huge man had the advantage on her. He had to hurry. Using whatever magic the paper possessed, he'd been able to speed her up and make her stronger; she had been able to counter him, but even that hadn't been enough to succeed. It had taken him figuring out a way to slow the man, only then had she a chance. Alec doubted he would have stood much of a chance had it been he who had to face the brutes. Sam at least had fighting skill. He had… well, not fighting skill.

His skill was what she needed right now.

He reached dried blood. Sam's blood.

With the bowl tipped, the blood had congealed quickly. It flaked free, and remained sticky in places, but attempting to smear it with his finger was useless.

Could he liquefy it in some way? The idea seemed grotesque, and something he would never have even considered, but this was a desperate time, and he had to try anything that could help her.

Alec chose the largest section of clotted blood and peeled it from the floor. Thinking fast, he wondered if there was anything he could mix with it to make it so he could write with it. Saliva came to mind, but he didn't relish the idea of putting blood in his mouth. If he found a cup or another bowl, he could spit into it and mix the two, but all such bowls and vials from the tray had been destroyed.

The only option involved spitting into his hand.

Dropping the clotted blood into his palm, he spat.

Using his index finger, he began swirling it in his palm. The combination of the saliva and the clotted blood and—surprisingly—his own blood from the shard of the bowl that pierced his flesh—all mixed together. As he reached for the paper, the sound of boots thundered across the tile.

Alec looked up to see a pair of palace guards hurrying into the room. They were dressed in the formal, deep blue jackets and pants, and each carried a sword unsheathed. The lead man, an older man with a long, weathered face and a soft chin, surveyed the room quickly before his gaze settled on Alec.

"You, physicker. What happened here?"

He glanced at himself, clutching the page tightly in his fist so he didn't lose it. He still had to find a way to help Sam. But then, if the guards were here, did it mean the massive man had been chased off? That might be the best outcome, especially for Sam.

"There was an attack." He started to stand but at a look from the other guard, he sank back to the ground. They weren't interested in him getting up. Not that he could blame them. If he were a guard and came upon a scene like the one in this room, he would think the princess had been attacked. Possibly even that Alec had been involved.

"I can see there was an attack. Why are you not trying to help these men?"

Alec managed to stand and peered over at the fallen men. Even dead, they were terrifying. They were massive, the enormity of their size imposing. There had been something about them, a certain supernatural speed and agility, almost as if they had been enhanced by the paper, only permanently so. If he could discover how, he might be better able to help Sam.

"They're dead. There's nothing I can do to help them."

Alec rubbed his eyes, trying to think through what he knew. These men had tried to attack Sam and Alec. They were somehow implicated in what had happened to the princess—he knew that much. But how? What was the connection? And now the palace guard seemed more concerned about these dead men than about what had almost happened here.

"There was a woman," Alec said.

"We captured her."

"She was—"

He didn't get the chance to tell them that Sam had helped the princess, and that without her, they might not have been able to do anything to help her. The princess coughed, and the guards rushed over to her.

Alec could only watch as she sat up. The color had returned to her cheeks, much more than he would have expected to have happened so quickly. She was still thin, but less so than she had been and now looked like there was nothing wrong with her that a few dozen meals couldn't fix. The hollowness to her eyes was gone, leaving her with a less haunted expression. Even her hair had taken on more of a luster, leaving her looking, if not healthy, at least somewhat well.

"Where am I?" the princess asked.

"The university, my lady," the lead guard said. "You've been deathly ill. The physickers saved you!"

The princess looked over to him, and Alec wanted nothing more than to shrink back into the wall and hide. The physickers hadn't saved her. Something impossible had. Alec still didn't know whether he could believe it.

"What happened?"

The guards looked to him for answers. What could he say that would placate her? What did she need to hear now, and what would be better for her to hear when she was well? He might be able to give her something. He probably *had* to give her something.

"A wasting illness, princess. Your body was rotting from the inside."

"I remember… I remember seeing a man who told me the same. He left thinking he could find help."

Alec nodded. She had probably seen all the physickers while she'd lain here nearly dying. Would she survive? With the way her skin appeared, and the way she seemed to recover even as he watched, each breath growing stronger, he thought that she might. Though it seemed impossible to think that she would, especially after seeing how sick she had been, but he couldn't deny it.

A sickening sense came to him then.

What if it faded, much like the effect of the magic had faded on Sam?

He would have to keep writing. That was all he could do.

"My lady?" the guard asked.

"I need food. And a bath. I should like to see my father."

The guard nodded, waving the other guard out of the room. Alec assumed it was to go for her father.

It was then the princess seemed to realize there were two bodies in the room with her. Her eyes widened, and she stared at them a long time, before looking to the guard for answers. He paled slightly.

"My lady, there was a woman found here. We think she killed these two and intended to come after you, but we arrived in time to thwart her."

Alec didn't even dare argue. What would happen to him if he did? But if he said nothing, Sam would be placed in prison. Maybe worse.

"Where is she now?" the princess asked.

"We've taken her to the prison. She carried a knife with her and…"

Possessing a knife in the same room with the princess would mean more trouble for Sam than she deserved.

"She helped you, my lady," Alec said.

The guard shot him a look full of anger, but Alec ignored it. If he didn't speak up, it was becoming clear that not only would Sam end up in prison, but she might be executed.

The princess looked over to him. "She did what?"

"Helped. Those men attacked. I think they might have been responsible for your illness. She came to let me have a chance to heal you."

As he said it, he realized he had said too much. The princess had been sick for too long, and now he made claims of poisoning and a claim that these men—men she wouldn't know—had been responsible for it.

"These men?" She studied him in a strange way. "You know them?"

Alec shook his head. "I don't know what brought them here at this time, but I know what I saw, and I know what they attempted. They wanted you gone."

The princess's face paled slightly. "I…"

She sagged, and Alec hurried toward her, but the guard rounded on him, sword raised. "Do not touch her, physicker. I will see we call the master—"

Alec pushed the man to the side. "Call who you would like, but I'm going to make certain that she's unharmed."

He reached the princess and touched her lightly on the neck. She breathed, but it was slow. Her pulse was not as regular as it should be. Had the healing begun to fail already?

Somehow, he needed time to help her. That meant attempting writing on the paper.

"What was that?" he asked.

The guard looked toward the door.

"Go!" Alec urged. "I'll stay with her and see that she gets the care she needs."

The guard looked at him, shooting him a hard warning glance, before racing off into the hall.

Alec pulled the sheet of paper out and didn't hesitate as he began writing on it, using his finger. The mixture of blood and saliva in his palm remained liquid. What would he write to help the princess? Somehow, he had to add something that would make the healing hold—or he had to write something that would hold long enough for him to find a way to fully heal her.

With the guard gone, Alec crouched on the floor next to the princess, thinking of what he could write that would help her.

Wasting illness, he started, the blood smearing across the page in great looping letter that were less clear than they would have been with a pen. He didn't risk taking the time to find the makeshift pen he'd dropped, not when he didn't know when the guard would return. *General improvement, but now regressed. No longer coherent. Generalized health returned. Would suggest provilin seeds and penac oil to help.* The last he added as things he *thought* might be able to help the princess, but didn't really know.

Alec watched her and was relieved to see her breathing ease again. The blood ink held on the page, thankfully the mixture that he'd formed had been enough. Would it stay? The first attempt hadn't lasted, and the massive attacker had seemed to know that it wouldn't, but how could he ensure that it *would* last? Somehow, he had to help the princess so he could help Sam.

The sound of footsteps started toward him from outside in the hall. The guard still hadn't returned. Alec rolled the paper back up and stuffed it into his pocket. After checking on the princess, noting her breathing continued to ease, and the color had once more returned to her cheeks, he left her.

Staying only meant more questions. Staying meant he would need to find a way to get not only Sam to safety, but himself. Staying meant the physickers would discover his lie.

Alec fixed the jacket, tugging it down, and hurried into the hall. He quickly retraced his steps, heading down through the halls and back into the healing rooms. He paused there, noting the line along the bench, shaking his head as he thought about how little the physickers would be able to really help these people, and hurried out. He paused when he realized he'd forgotten to take the jacket off. When he reached the gate, he hurried through. Someone called after him, but Alec didn't pause, quickly losing whoever might be chasing him in the crowds.

26

THE INSIDE OF A CELL

The inside of the prison was damp, and there was barely enough light for Sam to see. Sounds disrupted the stillness, but she couldn't tell where they came from. There was a steady dripping somewhere, and occasionally someone would shout or cry out or even moan. Otherwise, she was left with the occasional sound of a creature crawling through the walls, a scratching sound that broke the silence more than anything else.

Her hands and legs were free, but that wasn't surprising since the door to the cell held her completely confined. There was no escape.

Somewhere in the prison, she'd find Tray.

Now that she was here—and trapped—she realized what a fool she'd been. And she realized what a mistake it was to involve Alec. Now she was responsible for his rescue, as well. How had she ever expected to make it into the prison, find Tray, *and* get out again?

They had left her dressed in her clothing, including

her boots, though they *had* taken her cloak. And that meant they had her staff as well. Her mother's knife remained tucked into her boot, and she slipped it out, noting the blade had no dried blood on it. Thankfully, they had missed it when they'd hauled her off to the cells.

Also tucked in her boot, she hoped she still had the sheet of paper she'd taken from Bastan's table, and if she could reach that… she might be able to use whatever abilities the paper granted to get herself free. But that meant she needed to figure out what Alec had done with the paper, and how he'd made it work, if only she could do the same. It had been *her* blood after all.

Sam pulled her boot off and shook out the insole. Buried within was the folded piece of the paper. She took it out, put her boot back, and unfolded it in front of her.

What was it about the paper that gave it the special abilities? Why did it work, and why did the brutes seem to know so much about it? They were questions for which she didn't have answers, but she wanted them. First, she had to escape from this cell. Then, she could track down Tray—and Alec. Afterward, she would look for answers.

But first, if she wanted to try to make the paper work for her, she had to draw blood.

That was the part she didn't relish, but there wasn't any way around it.

She opened her hand, choosing the same one Alec had cut, and ran the knife along her palm the same way he had. Blood quickly flowed, and as she cupped her hand, it pooled briefly in her palm.

What had Alec done?

She'd seen what he'd written when describing the

princess's illness, but not what he'd written about her. How had he enhanced her speed?

Dipping her finger into the blood, she wrote her name: *Samara Elseth*.

Using only the tip of her finger, the markings were thick and without the tidy flow Alec managed, but it was still something. She waited, wondering if the blood would soak back into the page. When Bastan had tried, the blood held on the page for a moment before fading. Would it do the same for her?

She needed some way of writing more neatly than she managed with the tip of her finger. Sam glanced at the knife resting on the ground in front of her and held it like a pen as she dipped it into her blood. Hesitating over the surface of the paper, she considered the way Alec would have written. When trying to heal the princess, he'd described the symptoms. What symptoms did she have other than she was too slow, weak, and small?

Maybe that was all she needed.

Writing below her name, she added those words. *Slow. Weak. Small.*

Sam sat back, waiting.

The blood in her palm had congealed, no longer flowing as it had. She wiped her hand on her pants, and clenched her hand tightly, staunching the bleeding. After sliding the knife back into the sheath hidden within her boot, she waited.

And waited.

The blood stayed for a few moments, but then faded into nothing.

She slumped to the ground, staring at the page. Whatever Alec had done had been different. Or maybe *he* was the key. Either way, she wasn't going to get out of here without help. Tray wasn't going to get out of here.

They were so close... but trapped in the cell as she was, it seemed as if might as well be on the other side of the city.

A pounding on her cell door startled her from a sleep. She'd been sitting upright, her head slumped against her chest, and had somehow managed to sleep. When she came around, she looked at the walls, trying to remember where she was. Then it came back to her. Trapped in the prison.

Sam stood and waited. Realizing the sheet of paper remained on the floor, she grabbed it quickly and crumpled it in her palm.

The cell door opened.

A pair of guards entered, both carrying unsheathed swords. They were normal guards, not brutes, and they watched her warily.

"You're going to come with us," the nearest said. He was tall and had a muscular frame much like Tray. The leather helmet he wore looked scuffed, as if he had seen a few battles. The sword he pointed at her appeared sharp, and the metal gleamed.

"Where?"

He jabbed the sword at her again. "No questions. Put these on."

He tossed chains at her feet, and Sam stared at them.

"Put them on or we put them on you."

Taking the chains, she eyed them a moment before sliding the cuffs around her wrists. The metal was cold, and when she clamped them closed, she felt as if she were sealing her fate.

Sam looked up at the guards when the chains were locked on her wrists. "What now?"

"Follow us."

Her heart hammered. There was only one reason she would be able to leave the prison, and that was if they intended to carry out her punishment. She'd been discovered in the princess's room. Her, a lowborn. There was only one punishment she *could* get.

Fighting would only get her killed sooner, and there remained the distant chance they weren't marching her to her execution. If they were, wouldn't they say something about it?

Probably not. She was lowborn. There was no purpose in telling her anything more about her fate.

They led her down a long hall lined with other cells. As she walked along here, she realized she wouldn't even have known which cell to find him in. Might she be passing his cell even now? If she called out, she'd only get them both into more trouble. Bastan must have known how hopeless her idea was, which was why he hadn't been willing to do anything.

The guards guided her through a few more doors and down a set of stairs, twisting and turning as they went. Sam lost track of where they led her, knowing only that she wouldn't be able to find her way back if she needed to. There would be no rescue of Tray. She wondered if there had ever been any real chance to rescue him, or she'd simply kidded herself, thinking she could find a way to free him.

They led her beyond another door, and the walls changed.

The darkness that had surrounded her shifted, now a paler sort of stone, and with none of the smells she noted before. The walls were smooth, and though no windows lined them, there was a faint light coming from some hidden source.

The guards continued, taking her down the hallway until they reached another door, where they stopped and pointed for her to enter.

Sam hesitated.

"Go," the lead guard said. His tone made it clear he didn't agree with what he'd been asked to do, but did it, anyway. "Tell Marin we're even."

Sam looked over at him, frowning, but he pushed her forward and through the door. Then she found herself outside. She could see the city beyond. A man awaited her. And she noticed he held her cloak.

The guard grabbed her wrists and quickly unlocked her cuffs before leaving and closing the door behind him.

When she turned back to the man, he silently held out her cloak to her. She was amazed, but took it from him and put it over her shoulders.

"Marin sent you?"

"Quiet," he whispered. "Not here." He led her away from the prison. After crossing a bridge, he waved her away.

Because of Marin, she was free. Why did she feel even more trapped than before?

Sam walked slowly as she returned to her section of the city, crossing one of the canals, and then another, pausing briefly as she did, mostly to ensure she found her way safely to the other side.

Marin had freed her. Which meant she still lived.

Why hadn't she gotten Tray out sooner? If she had that sort of connection, Marin should have used in for Tray, not for Sam.

Sam barely paid any attention to the streets as she walked. The buildings slowly shifted from the stone and brick fronts to the less permanent wooden structures, many already starting to fall.

The sounds in this part of the city changed, as well, shifting from the calm and almost heavy silence she'd experienced near the prison to the more active chaos found near her section. There had been a comfort to the silence, but also a loneliness, especially now that she wasn't sure she'd be able to do anything to help Tray as she had intended. All Sam could do was sigh.

When she reached the street with Bastan's tavern, she hesitated. The tavern wasn't even there anymore. Nothing was. With the explosion and the fire, all that remained was rubble and ash. There was nothing here for her anymore.

She thought she could find Bastan in his new hiding spot, but did she want to?

Not until she knew whether Marin had done the same for Tray as she'd done for Sam. Not until she knew *how* Marin had survived the Theln attack.

When she reached Marin's home, she stood outside, looking up at the empty window. A faint light glowed behind the curtain. It was pale yellow, and had it not been dusk, and had she not been watching, she doubted she would even have noticed it.

As she started toward the house, she had the vague sense of movement. She spun, but there was no one there. Was that her imagination... or were the brutes after her still? One of them—the lead brute—had survived.

And Marin had known him.

With her mind racing, she hurried into the front door and up the stairs. She tried to move silently, but hope that she'd find her brother surged through her. If Marin had managed to get *her* free, surely she had to have done the same with Tray. Right?

At the door, she paused and listened.

She heard heavy breathing, a steady and labored sound that wasn't familiar.

Had she made a mistake?

There was another option about who she might find at Marin's home, and one she should fear: the brute. He'd disappeared from the university, but that didn't mean he was gone. And if he knew she was out of prison, she was sure he would find her. His words echoed in her mind. *I can smell you.*

She wished she had something to protect herself. She had her mother's knife, but that was all. Even a canal staff would have been helpful, though it might be too long to be of much use here.

Slipping the knife from the sheath in her boot, she leaned against the door frame, listening. The breathing was steady and regular, but there was a quality to it that didn't sound like it came from the brute.

Working cautiously, Sam cracked open the door.

"Hello, Samara."

"Marin?"

ANSWERS

"It's good to see you, Samara."

"It's Sam." Sam glanced around Marin's small room, eyes taking in the rows of shelves that seemed somehow undisturbed. Hadn't the brutes destroyed the room when they'd chased her? Wasn't there more destruction here?

All of that seemed to have disappeared, or at least to have been repaired.

Marin smiled and shook her head. "You've always fought the name your mother gave you—that fits your heritage."

Sam frowned. "I don't know anything about my heritage," she said. "My mother died before she was able to share that with me. All I know is what you told me, and I don't even know if that's true."

"It's true."

"What happened?" she asked. "When I saw you last, the

brutes were chasing you. I thought you were dead. And one of them knew you."

Marin let out a long breath and stood. Sam realized that Marin was shakier than the last time she'd seen her. The woman grabbed what looked like one half of a canal staff and leaned on it as she made her way toward her. "I was nearly dead," Marin said. "I'm still not recovered, but there is the hope."

"Marin?"

The woman stopped in front of her, leaning on her makeshift cane. She smelled strangely stale, if that were possible. Her eyes were hollowed and sunken back in her face. Up close, Sam could see the way her hair had thinned, and her skin had a yellowish tint to it.

"What did they do to you?" she whispered.

Marin blinked. "What do you mean?"

"You're sick, aren't you?"

"Ah, Samara, always so observant," she said, with more sarcasm in her voice than what Sam thought she would manage.

Did she share with Marin, explain that she'd seen something similar with the princess, or didn't it matter to Marin? Now that she was sick, and now that she seemed to be wasting away the same way the princess had been, would it even matter if she told her anything? Without someone like Alec and his magic, she doubted there would be anything she could even do.

But Marin needed to know. If there was anything that could be done for her, she needed to know. If it were Sam, she would *want* to know.

"How do they do it?" Sam asked. "This is the work of the brutes, isn't it?"

Marin sighed. "Not the Thelns, but near enough."

"Who is he? I heard you use his name when he came to your house."

"You should sit, Samara. And I will provide the answers you seek."

Sam took a chair near the window. There was relief in knowing that she could escape if needed even if she no longer thought that Marin would try to harm her. As sickly as the woman seemed, Sam wasn't sure Marin *could* harm her, though she probably could still manipulate her into doing things for her. That might actually be worse, in some ways.

"How did you know I was in prison?"

Marin watched her. "I learned you were there and used all of my resources to get you freed."

"Me? Not Tray?"

"Tray will be released in time. You were the one in greater danger."

"What happened to you?" Sam asked again. She had no answers yet, and wasn't sure that Marin was interested in providing them to her. "Why are you sick? And why are the brutes here?"

Marin sank into a chair, keeping the staff near her. "So many questions, and you deserve the answers. As to the first, when we were attacked, I managed to escape. I am not without skill, Samara."

"I never—"

Marin raised her hand and offered a slight smile. "No. I know that you would not. The Thelns attacked me in my home, a place I have managed to hide from them for many years."

"What do you mean?"

Marin leaned on her staff and shook her head. "Your second question is more difficult. Why am I sick? I suppose it's because they discovered me and that I have nothing to offer them."

"What does that mean?"

"The answer is complicated, Samara. To better understand, you need to fully understand the role our kind has played."

"Our kind? You mean lowborns."

Marin smiled and leaned forward. "I mean something else entirely. You should wear your heritage proudly."

"Proudly? I'm lowborn. We're looked upon as worse than anyone else in the city. We live in this filthy section. And we aren't allowed into other parts of the city without sneaking. I would say there's no pride in being lowborn."

Marin sighed. "It wasn't always the case. There was a time when our kind served an important role, and it was one others could not. That has… changed over time. Now we are little more than lapdogs." She said the last with a whisper that trailed into a cough.

"What was that?"

"We opposed the Thelns."

Sam started to laugh but realized that Marin was serious. "What do you mean?"

"The Thelns fear our kind, Samara. With our connection to a particular kind of power, we can oppose them."

"What kind of power?"

"The kind you're born to."

Sam controlled her breathing, trying to understand. "And is it connected to the easar paper you had me steal?"

"Where did you hear that term?"

"From one of the highborns. That's what you sent me after, but why?"

Marin sighed. "That paper should never have been stolen."

"*You* had me steal it!"

"Only because those in the palace stole it first. They are the reason the Thelns risked coming to the city. The reason Ralun risked coming."

"He's the main brute?"

She sniffed. "Something like that. A powerful Theln in many ways."

"And the highborns stole from them?"

Marin coughed, covering her mouth but not before Sam saw bloody phlegm. "They made a mistake. And now they are responsible for returning a conflict that has been quiet for a decade. That paper is dangerous. All it does is draw attention. The Thelns discovered what they did and came after it."

"Why did you want *me* to steal it?"

"Because I could not."

"What?"

Marin shook her head. "I thought that you would have a better chance at getting in and back out. The Thelns shouldn't have been in the city, not yet, but I miscalculated."

It was a rare admission of fault from Marin. "But why? What did you want to use the paper for?"

"The Thelns possess a book that I have only seen a few times before. The paper can counter it."

Sam thought about the book she had discovered in the highborn house, and how the pages all had markings in the bottom corner. The marking had been the only thing permanent about the page she'd taken from it before being captured. It was that page Alec had used to heal her. "Why does the book matter?"

Marin stood and leaned on her staff. She had grown weaker in the time that she'd been sitting there, and now barely managed to stay upright. "The Thelns use that book—well really, *many* books—against those who oppose them."

"If you wanted me to grab a book, why send me after the easar paper? Is it because the paper has power?"

"Yes. And you made a mistake selling those sheets to Bastan. I intended to use them for a different purpose."

Sam flushed. "Well, had you *told* me what you were after, I could have grabbed the entire Kyza-cursed book rather than one page!"

"You saw the book?"

Sam blinked. "It was there when I went back. Bastan wanted to figure out how to write on the paper and now he has it…"

Marin leaned more heavily on her staff. "The pages are the only way we have a hope of countering the Thelns."

"I don't understand. What do they have to do with the book?"

"We call it the Book of Maladies. The Thelns have a different title for it, though it's one more important in their language. For us, it has always been the Book of Maladies."

"Why?"

Marin reached the window and stared out, her eyes taking on a forlorn expression. "That's what they've used against our kind and others who oppose them, Samara."

"Was the book why the princess is sick?" Marin looked over at her, frowning. Sam took a deep breath. "I saw her, Marin."

Marin approached her, her eyes shining brightly. "When you broke in?"

Sam nodded.

"What did you see?"

"The princess was nearly dead. She was…" She considered how to describe it, not wanting to offend Marin, but could she share with her that the princess had looked like she did now? "She was weakened. Wasted. The healer I was with said it was like she rotted from the inside."

"You were with one of the physickers in the university? And they let you reach the princess?"

"Not a physicker. An apothecary. He's the same one who helped me when the brutes attacked the first time and shot me with that poisoned bolt."

Marin tried to stay standing, but she sagged, leaning more heavily on the staff. How sick *was* Marin? How much time did she have? Marin struggled as she turned to Sam, her mouth pinched in a frown as she seemed to consider. "An apothecary? Why would there be a healer in the university?"

"He wasn't. We paid our way in hoping to reach Tray. His name was—"

She didn't have a chance to finish.

The door to Marin's room popped open.

Sam leapt to her feet and spun, knife already coming free as she readied to throw it at the attacker. If the brutes had followed her here, she would be ready.

When she saw who it was, she relaxed a little, but only a little. How had Alec found her here?

28

SEARCHING FOR A FRIEND

A lec paused long enough to return to his section. Unlike earlier, when he and Sam had left for the university, the streets were now busy with people making their way toward work, some pushing carts along the streets as they came from the canal ports, and others pushing carts laden with items to ship on the canals.

He looked into Mrs. Rubbles' store and noted her still moving quickly behind the counter, seemingly still well. If writing on the paper had helped with *her* healing, why hadn't it worn off the way that it had seemed to for the princess?

He considered going into the store, but decided against it. What he needed were answers, and he didn't think he would get them from Mrs. Rubbles.

Alec started away from her store, his mind racing through what he'd seen. The paper *did* have magic, and with it, he was able to help heal not only Sam and Mrs. Rubbles, but he'd helped the princess. But it was the healing of the princess that hadn't held. The others... whatever he had done for both Sam and Mrs. Rubbles... they had seemed to remain.

What answer was there for that? Could it be that with both Sam and Mrs. Rubbles, they would have healed eventually, and all he needed was to get them through the worst of their illness? That was a possibility. There was another possibility that troubled him more. What if the massive man was still poisoning the princess somehow?

If they had a way to reverse what Alec did, and over-power the magic in the paper, it was possible the princess's condition would continue to deteriorate. And if that were the case, how could Alec stop it?

He had wandered toward the south end of the section. From here, he could see the edge of the city and was aware of the dark and brooding presence of the prison rising up in the distance. Had he come here on purpose or had his worry for Sam led him here?

Before thinking too much about what he was doing, Alec had crossed several sections until he stood outside the prison wall, careful not to get too close. He'd heard stories of people cutting themselves on the metal embedded in the wall, and he didn't need another injury. His hand still throbbed where he'd cut it, and where the glass had pierced it.

He pulled the paper from his pocket and rolled it out, looking at what he'd written on the page. There was the neat script from when he'd had the narrow length of carved wood he'd used as a pen, and the description of not only the princess's illness but of what he'd written in an attempt to help Sam fight the brutes, and then there was the thick, flowing script from when he'd written it with his finger. They looked like two different people had written on the paper. Both remained visible, the blood ink almost brown now, not appearing crimson at all, nothing like what it *should* look like considering the source.

Was there anything he could do to help Sam now? Not even knowing where she was in the prison, or what they were doing to her, he didn't see how.

Not without more of her blood. That was the key.

Alec circled around the prison, stopping opposite the massive barred doors leading inside, before moving on. What must it be like for her inside? It must be torture, and though he had seen her be tough, he didn't expect her to make it out of the prison.

Finishing his circuit around the wall, he noted a man waiting opposite a narrow door in the wall.

Alec frowned.

The man wore a long gray cloak and had gray hair shorn close to his scalp. The hilt of a sword peeked out from beneath the cloak. He held a bundle of some sort in his arms and faced the door.

Waiting.

What would he be waiting for?

Alec tried hiding in the background, remaining as much in the shadows as he could. With the bright sun overhead, there wasn't much he could do to hide.

As he watched, the door opened.

He almost gasped.

Sam emerged, escorted by a guard. Her wrists were bound in shackles and she appeared weakened, but otherwise well. A deep bruise surrounded one eye, and several other injuries marred her exposed arms.

The guards handed her over to the waiting man. He handed her the bundle he'd held, and when Sam took it, Alec realized it was her cloak. After she slipped it on, the man took her over the bridge, but then stopped, waving her to go away.

Alec watched as she walked toward the city, debating what to do, but the answer was clear to him. He *had* to catch up to her. He had to tell her that it was *her* blood that was the key to the paper. If those brutes were still after her, he needed her blood so he could augment her strength. But he could only get it if he caught up with her. He still had the sheet of paper, and it still had some blank areas on which he could write… He had hope he'd be able to do something.

Once the man was out of sight, he made his way toward the bridge. He had to hurry so as not to lose sight of her.

Alec turned the corner just as Sam entered a simple two-story building, all of wood construction, and the kind he wouldn't have found in his section of the city. Most of the buildings there were brick. Even that hadn't stopped the apothecary from burning. Narrow windows lined the face of the building, but all were drawn. No light escaped from inside. Alec had an ominous feeling as he approached, and he suppressed a shiver.

Why would Sam have come here?

This section was so different from the city he knew. The streets were narrower and the buildings dirtier, but surprisingly, that was where the differences really stopped. The people he passed had the same sense of urgency as they made their way through the streets, some going to work, others moving wares in carts away from the canals no differently than they would in his section. There was a strange vibrancy here that there wasn't in his section, and he didn't know if that was imagined or real.

The styles of the buildings were different as well. Many were plain, much like he would find in his part of the city, but there were enough with ornate decorations, though faded and now deteriorating, that he could tell this had once been a prosperous part of the city. How long ago must that have been and why would they have allowed the section to get so run down?

He reached into his pocket and touched the paper. That was the secret to helping Sam if she was in danger. If needed, he could write something similar to what he had before, then he could again augment her strength and speed and let Sam do the work. Together they could see what they could discover about helping the princess and finding a permanent solution to her illness.

But to do that, he needed her blood.

When Sam had entered the building, she'd done so without hesitation. Without knocking, as if she knew this place. Had this been home to her or just some place she had frequented? He knew little about where she came from, only that she had come from the lowborn section. Now he was here, he worried that maybe she wouldn't want him to try to help her. What if these were people she knew?

It didn't change the fact that he needed to help the princess. To do that, he needed Sam.

Alec approached the door and pulled it open. The massive wooden stairs on the inside led up, the steps now worn and cracked, but he could tell they had once been polished and majestic. If they were refinished—if most of the building were refinished—it would rival most he found in his section. Lanterns set into the wall were unlit, but were equally ornate, made of iron with glass housings. The railing leading up the stairs was a similar iron, and of a similar design, set with patterns he couldn't quite make out.

Where would she be in this building?

No light came from under the doors on the lower level. Alec paused to listen, but didn't hear anything to make him think she'd be on this level.

Up?

He ran his hand along the rail as he made his way up the stairs. With each step, he worried that he was making a mistake. Did he really want to risk coming up here, especially since he didn't know what he might find? What would he do to help her anyway? It's not as if he would be able to rescue her in any way if she were really captured. He might only end up caught next to her.

The door from the street opened, taking away his choice.

Alec hurried up the stairs, trying to be as quiet as he could. At the top of the stairs, a wide hall opened. There were sections of the floor that were discolored, long straight lines where it looked like the walls had been moved. Alec hurried down the hall, glancing at each of the doors, trying to think through what he could do. Feet sounded on the stairs, and he would be forced to make a decision. Alec started checking doors, but found each of them locked. At the end of the hall, he stopped before the final door. This one was unlocked.

He glanced over his shoulder and saw a figure stepping out into the hall.

He twisted the handle and hurriedly stepped inside.

Inside the room, Alec was taken aback when he saw Sam leaping from a chair, her knife in hand.

His immediate reaction was relief, to know she was unharmed, but the knife made him take some involuntary steps back before stopping himself. There had been someone outside, hadn't there? That was why he had risked entering the room in the first place.

He glanced into the hall, but didn't see anything. Maybe it was only someone who lived in the building.

When recognition came to Sam's face, she lowered the knife. "Alec, what are you doing here? How did you find me?"

After closing the door, Alec turned back to Sam and surveyed the room.

The inside of the room reminded him of his father.

The thought hit him with a strange certainty he didn't know how to put into words, but there was no other way to explain what he felt. The rows of shelves, all made of a stout wood and richly stained, filled the space to his left. Books were stuffed into the shelves, more than he could quickly count, and enough that were this any other circumstance, he would have turned to the shelves and lingered.

As he pulled his attention away from the books, he realized he and Sam were not alone. A woman, obviously ill and quite weak, stood by a low table near the window overlooking the street, leaning on a staff that was nearly taller than she was. His mind immediately began working through symptoms as he looked at her.

Sallow skin. Hollowed eyes. Thinning hair. Still has some strength remaining. A wasting disease like with the princess?

He shook away the thoughts and turned his attention to Sam. "You were captured. I tried to find you, but they wouldn't let me—"

"I *know* I was captured," she said.

He tried to hide the hurt he felt at her words. He hadn't wanted anything more than to try to first help the princess, and then to help Sam. It seemed he'd done neither.

"I tried to find you, but I couldn't," he said. "They had escorted me out of the university, and by the time I made my way back to the prison, someone was leading you out. I followed you…"

Sam's expression changed, some of the darkness and the heat leaving her face. "You went to the prison?"

He nodded. "I would have augmented you again, but I ran out of"—he turned to the woman leaning on the staff and wondered if he'd said too much— "ink. There wasn't any left after I tried helping the princess again."

The woman leaning on the staff took a step toward him and started to sag. "What did you do for Lyasanna Anders?" she asked.

Alec couldn't help but note the woman's familiarity as she said the name. Not *the princess*, but her full name. He wouldn't dare consider such informality when speaking about the princess.

"She's sick."

"Was," Sam said. She rubbed her shoulder as she did. Was it the same one the arrow had pierced?

"Is," Alec corrected. "Whatever I did was temporary. I don't understand it, but after you left, a couple of guards came—"

Her face darkened. "I know."

"The princess awoke, and I thought she might recover, but she failed again. I used what ink I had remaining, but I worry she'll just fade again like she did the last time."

"She will," the woman said.

Alec noted the way her arms trembled. She wouldn't be able to hold on to the staff much longer. As he watched, her grip slipped, and she dropped to the floor.

Sam beat him to her.

Alec checked her pulse and tipped his head to listen to her breathing. It was shallow but regular, though her heart beat was slower than it should have been. She was much farther gone than she appeared.

"Hold out your hand," he said to Sam.

She frowned but did it, and without him asking, she used her knife to draw a single line across her palm, letting blood begin to flow.

Alec reached into his pocket and found the rolled-up paper, and smoothed it on the floor in front of him. Dipping his finger into Sam's palm, he used the blood as he began writing. He paused a moment and looked at

Sam. "Her name." When Sam frowned, Alec nodded to the woman. "What's her name?"

He didn't know if it mattered, but suspected it did at least a little. The healing would need to be tied to someone for it to work.

"Marin," Sam said.

"What's her last name?"

"I don't know."

Alec looked to the woman to see if she had anything she could offer, but she was unresponsive.

He turned his attention back to the page and started writing, beginning with her name.

As before, the blood took to the page, darkening slightly, becoming more brown than maroon, before lingering on the page. Exhaustion worked through him, and he sank back onto his heels, waiting to see if the healing would hold.

"What happened?" he asked Sam as he waited.

"You know what happened. I was chased into the hallway by the brute."

"The augmentations had…"

"Faded," Sam finished for him.

He nodded. "Faded. I suppose that's as good a term as any." The words on the page hadn't faded, though, so why should the abilities have done so? Then there was the healing that he'd added to the page. The princess's healing had also faded. Why should it not remain when the healing he'd done for Sam and for Mrs. Rubbles did?

"The guards appeared. There were enough of them that they chased him off."

"What happened then?"

"They took me to prison, Alec. That's what happened."

"How did you get out?"

"Marin managed to get me released," she said, pointing to the fallen woman.

"When did Marin get sick?"

"I don't know. She wasn't sick the last time I saw her."

"When was that?"

"Only a few days ago."

A few days? That wouldn't have been long enough for any sort of wasting illness to take hold, and certainly not for it to have progressed to the point where it left her this weakened.

"I have been sick for barely a day," Marin said without opening her eyes.

Sam lifted her and propped her up before Alec had a chance to inspect her and see if the healing had worked.

Marin studied him, almost ignoring Sam completely. "What did you do?"

"I—"

Sam saved him from needing to answer. "This is the apothecary I mentioned to you. Alec helped me when the brutes attacked me the first time."

"And he's the one who helped heal the princess?"

"I didn't heal her," Alec said.

"She was getting better," Sam said.

"The healing faded. Like almost everything else I've written on this page."

Marin glanced down to the paper now covered with words written in blood ink. Her eyes widened slightly. "The healing will fail."

"I thought this paper was magical?" Alec asked.

Marin smiled slightly. "Magic? Perhaps it is."

Sam tipped her head to the side, frowning. Alec had seen the expression before, and wondered what she might be hearing.

"Why wouldn't it work? It worked on Sam when I healed her the first time. And it seemed to work for the princess before it began to fade."

Marin sighed and lifted her staff, using it to push herself up. "What is happening to me—and the princess—will always fade unless you can counter the source."

"The source?"

Now standing, she nodded and started toward the window, throwing back the curtains. "A shame this place has none of the protections it once did," she said softly.

"What source?" Alec asked.

Marin looked at him. "The Book of Maladies." She closed her eyes, tipping her head much the same way that Sam did. When she opened them, she nodded to the window. "You, Samara, are descended from the ancient Kavers. And it appears your apothecary friend is a Scribe."

"What does that mean?" Sam asked.

"The combination is important. Together you are more potent than alone."

"Together?" Sam asked.

Was that why it took *both* of their blood on the paper to have an effect?

He didn't have a chance to question. Marin tapped her staff on the ground, and said, "Now it's time for us to go."

Alec heard footsteps outside the door and remembered the figure he'd seen coming up the stairs behind him. Would it be the men Sam called the brutes? Something worse? In this part of the city, he didn't know what to expect.

Sam grabbed him and tossed him toward the window.

Marin stopped her. "No time. Scribe. What else can you do with that paper?"

29

ANOTHER AUGMENTATION

Sam's heart raced as she watched Alec dip his finger into the blood from her palm again. He started writing, and she tried not to pay attention to the blood pooling in her palm. She just hoped it would be enough. If it was the brutes who approached, and if they were as powerful as the last time, she wouldn't be strong enough.

Marin stepped carefully to one of her shelves and reached behind it, pulling out two slender rods and tossing them to her.

A canal staff.

"What is this?"

"That," she said, holding up half of her own staff and reaching for the other half, "is a weapon, Samara. Perhaps our most traditional one at that. If your Scribe is success-ful, these can balance the strength differential."

Marin shot Alec a look, but he was busy writing.

Sam wondered what he wrote that was different from

what she'd tried when she had been trapped in the prison cell. Would it be enough? How long before it faded again?

The door thundered as it splintered open.

The massive form of one of the brutes filled the doorway. Marin jumped forward, her staff spinning, moving more quickly than Sam would have expected her capable given how sick she'd seemed only a few minutes before. Now it was as if she were completely healed. More than that, as if she were *better* than healed.

Sam glanced at Alec. His head sagged forward, as if he were weakened.

Did using the paper take something out of him?

How could that be? Why would writing on the paper require both of them?

Another brute appeared in the doorway. This *still* wasn't the same one she'd fought in the university. That meant he was still out there, and likely directing these.

Ralun. The main brute.

A powerful Theln.

Sam knew that he was. Would she be able to withstand another attack?

Marin faced off with one of the attackers, her staff spinning quickly, hitting the brute with sickening smacks over and over again. The other brute held a sword in one hand and raised a crossbow with his other.

Sam took a deep breath—hoping that Alec had managed to augment her again—and jumped forward to join the fight.

Years spent leaping the canals had taught her to use the staff at its full length, but this was different. Within Marin's home, there wasn't the same amount of space to navigate, and she was left using the halves of the staff. At first, she fought with only one end, hitting the brute's hand so he couldn't use the crossbow on them, but realized after watching Marin that she could use both ends of the staff.

As she fought, her steps felt light.

That was the only way she could describe what she experienced. It wasn't that she was quicker—though it seemed that she was—but that she moved as if there was no resistance. Each step flowed faster than she'd ever imagined moving, and the staff struck with more force than it should.

The brute focused on her, blocking with both his sword and crossbow, but neither was able to stop her as she continued to fight. She spun, the staff catching his arm, then his wrist. It snapped, and he dropped the crossbow.

Sam twisted around, moving as if in a dance, and she flicked the staff at him again, this time, catching his other arm, once, then again. The sword dipped, but she didn't have the same effect that she'd had on the other side.

She was slowing down.

"It's fading!" she called to Alec.

"It will always fade, Samara," Marin said far too calmly. "Your power is temporary, especially when using easar paper."

The brute smiled.

She noticed the injured arm seemed to heal itself, the twisted arm mending the longer she faced him. How was it possible?

How could he stay so strong—and even seem to heal himself—while her strength faded?

She smacked him again with the staff, this time hitting his face, then sweeping toward his leg. She would have to do more than hurt him; to stop him completely, she'd have to kill him.

The brute blocked her next attack, then her next. Sam's strength and speed were disappearing, and with them, her advantage.

Closing in on her, the brute caught the end of her staff in his fist and jerked.

Sam went flying.

As she rolled, she neared the dropped crossbow.

In a fluid movement, she brought it up and fired.

The bolt struck the man in the face, sinking through his eye and going completely through his skull, sticking into the wall with a sickening *thunk*.

The brute fell.

Sam shivered and scrambled to the fallen brute, trying not to think about how close she was to him. If she somehow *hadn't* killed him, all it would take was for him to reach out for her, and he could grab her arm, or her neck, or…

She pulled two crossbow bolts from the quiver at his waist and rolled away from him. Reloading the crossbow, she aimed it at the other brute, who now held Marin in a tight grip, practically crushing her.

She fired.

The bolt caught him in the shoulder.

He released Marin, and she jumped back, swinging her

staff around at the same time, catching him in the injured shoulder.

Sam reloaded again and fired quickly. This time, she caught him in the other shoulder.

"Just kill him already!" Marin said. She struck the brute again, this time hitting his face, then swung the staff up and around to crash between his legs.

Sam reloaded a third time. Taking careful aim, she struck him in the stomach.

The brute grunted, finally falling.

Sam reloaded as quickly as she could and aimed the crossbow at him. "Where is he?" she demanded.

The brute kicked, but there was none of the same force to it he'd had before. Sam easily dodged it.

Marin swung her staff, catching him in the stomach, driving the newest bolt deeper. He grunted again as blood began pooling around him, staining the floor of Marin's home.

"Answer the question, Theln," Marin said.

"You can't hope to survive. You took his prize from him. He knows you're here, he *smells* you—"

He cut off as Marin hit him again, this time on the side of his face.

"Where. Is. He?" Marin emphasized each word with a smack against his legs.

"He will find you, Kaver."

Marin glared at him for a moment, smacking him with her staff once more until his eyes rolled shut, before turning her attention to Sam. "It's not Ralun we need to find. It's the page from the book used to poison the princess. Without the book…"

The book had hundreds of pages. "How will we know which page?" And why had the book been at the highborn house?

"It will be marked in some way, different from the others. It signifies that it has been used."

Sam's breath caught. The one she'd torn from the book had an extra marking that made it different from the others.

"You won't be able to save the princess until you find that page. It must be destroyed and then the Scribe can help her."

"Kyza," Sam whispered.

"You've seen it."

It was the page that Alec had used the very first time he'd healed her. But if that page was in the shop, wouldn't it have been destroyed in the fire? "When I went back to the highborn house, I saw the book... and that page." She went to Alec, leaving Marin standing over the brute with her staff ready to strike. "Alec?"

He looked up at her, his eyes glazed. After blinking a few times, he managed to focus on her, though it wasn't with as much clarity as he'd looked at her before. "Sam. Did it work?"

"It worked," she said, motioning to the two downed brutes. The one pinned to the ground still had his eyes closed but considering how quickly they healed, she didn't expect it to last.

"I should help him," Alec said, starting to stand.

"Help? Let the bastard die. He and the others tried killing us already."

"Samara!" Marin called to her.

Sam glanced over, and saw Marin leaning on her staff, studying the brute. She looked weakened again, as if the effect of the healing that Alec had used on her had already begun to fade.

"Alec, you have to heal Marin again," she said, holding out her hand. There was still some slick blood there, but it had begun to clot.

Alec nodded weakly and dipped his finger into the blood and started to write on the page.

"No!" Marin said with more force than Sam would have expected from her. "The Scribe needs to maintain his strength, otherwise he cannot help you."

Sam looked from Marin to Alec. "You're dying, Marin."

"Find the page. Destroy it. Then I'll be better."

"Marin?"

Marin managed to stand and swung her staff at the brute, catching him on the side of his face. He stopped moving. She turned toward Sam and calmly said, "There's only one way to heal me—*and* the princess, from what you've told me. You need to find the missing page from the book, and you must destroy it. Do that, and I can recover. The princess can recover. Then we can regroup." Marin approached Alec and leaned toward him. "You must do this, Scribe. Are you strong enough?"

Alec nodded, the glaze to his eyes fading, and his strength seeming to return, as well. "I can do this."

"Good. Because more than you know depends upon it."

30

SEARCH FOR A PAGE FROM
THE BOOK

Alec trailed Sam, watching as she held tightly to the long staff the dying woman had given her. Sam carried it as if she had always held it. They hurried from the woman's home, leaving her sitting in the chair holding tightly to her own staff, with the loaded crossbow resting on her lap. Alec had wanted to try using the paper to help her, but Marin had refused, telling him he'd only weaken himself. He couldn't deny the fact that he was tired, but that shouldn't be from writing. Sam and Marin had been the ones doing the fighting, and Sam had been the one whose blood he'd used.

Outside the building, he noted three bodies lying in one of the alleys they passed.

"Sam," he said, motioning to them.

Sam paused, and they hurried into the alley. Alec went to each one and checked for a heartbeat. None of them had one. Two had their necks snapped violently, and the third had an arrow through his neck, reminding Alec of what Sam had needed to do in order to save them from the men she called brutes when they were with the princess, and again at the woman's house.

"Did you know them?"

She nodded. "Bastan's men, but why would he have sent them here?"

"Who is Bastan?"

Sam squeezed her eyes shut. "My boss. Maybe a friend. I don't even know."

Alec wiped his hands on his pants and stood. "Where now?"

"We need to find the page you used when you healed me. You said it was in your apothecary?"

"It was. You saw what's left. Burned to the ground. One of those men—"

"The Thelns."

He nodded. "The brutes, as you call them, came to the apothecary," he went on as they headed down the street. There was nothing they could do for the men, and it didn't make any sense for them to remain there. "He was looking for you. I didn't know where you'd gone and told him that, but he started searching through the papers. He wanted to find my notes on how I treated you. I tried to keep him from your page, but I don't know if I did. Either way, it would have been destroyed in the fire."

"Are you sure?"

Alec hadn't checked. When he had gone back, he had been focused on what had been lost of his father's shop. Since most of the contents were now ash, he'd not thought to look, but then, not everything had burned. Maybe that page *had* survived.

"I'm not."

"That's where we need to go, then."

Sam led him through the streets, navigating the narrow paths much better than he would have managed. At times, she'd pause, and would lean her head to the side in the way that she had, almost as if she were listening for sounds. Then she would continue onward, guiding him ever closer to the canals. As they neared, Alec could smell the change in the air, and noted the stink from the canal.

"How do you know where you're going?" he asked.

She glanced back at him. "You spend enough time in the streets, you get to know them pretty well. If you don't, then you end up getting hurt."

They reached the edge of the canal. Sam eyed it and then looked to Alec. "Normally, I'd just jump, but there's a bridge at the end of the street."

"You'd *jump*?"

She offered her staff, holding it out to him. "Canal staff. Used for leaping over the canals."

He must have stared at her with incredulity in his eyes because she took a step back and tipped the staff into the water, springing *over* the canal, before landing neatly on the other side. She flashed a smile and pulled the staff free from the water before repeating the process and landing next to him again.

"See? That's how I reached the university the first time. Lowborns aren't allowed to go beyond these sections, so the bridges would have been closed. With the staff..."

"The canals there are twice as wide!" Alec said.

"Yeah, I didn't say it was easy. I might have gotten wet. Good thing the canal eels didn't come for me."

He shook his head. "The eels aren't real."

"If not the eels, there's something in the water."

They hurried down the street and reached the bridge arching up and over the canal. She took the steps two at a time and then hurried back down equally quickly. Somehow, the staff didn't get in the way as she moved.

On the other side, they were in a section nearer to his, but still a bit out. The streets were wider here, and the buildings had a newer feel to them. Many were brick, though there remained some of the wooden structures, many with the same style that he'd seen from Marin's home. There was something almost regal to the design, a flair he wouldn't have expected to find in one of these outer sections.

They passed a few people in the streets, but for the most part, Sam made a point of weaving around others in the street or changing streets as to avoid others altogether.

When they reached the next canal, Alec was surprised to realize his section was on the other side.

"You can cross, but I'll have to jump," she said.

"Even if you're with me?"

She motioned to herself and shrugged. "Lowborn. Not lowborn," she said, pointing to him. "This is fine. Just meet me at your apothecary."

With that, she planted her staff in the middle of the canal and leaped over the water. Alec still marveled at how easily she managed to do it. When she landed safely on the other side, she seemingly made a point of unscrewing her staff and separating the two halves, hiding them within her cloak.

Alec hated that they had separated. With Sam, he felt as if he were capable of something more, almost as if he were capable of being someone more. Without her, he was left with the same doubt and insecurity that had always plagued him. It was that doubt his father tried to remove, but Alec had never managed to get past it completely.

Realizing he stood alone in one of the outer sections, he shivered and hurried toward where Sam promised he'd find the bridge. It was there in the distance, close enough that he began to feel a sense of relief working through him.

Would it really work to heal the princess if he destroyed the page? Was that all that it would take?

Marin seemed to think so, and she seemed to know more about the paper than he or Sam did. There were secrets she knew, and that Alec *wanted* to know, and answers he wanted from her, such as why she referred to him as a Scribe.

As he neared the bridge, Alec thought he heard something and turned.

There were only shadows.

He would feel better when he reached the other side of the canal. When he did, he would not only be able to search for the missing page of paper—and hopefully the answer to healing both the princess and Marin, but he would know the streets. Sam might *tell* him the others in this part of the city wouldn't harm him, but everyone knew the outer sections were dangerous.

There came a sense of another shadow.

Alec spun again, this time his heart racing.

There was nothing there.

Why hadn't he at least grabbed something to use as a weapon? He might not know how to use a sword, but he would have felt better at least pretending. Anyone who thought to harm him might think again if they saw he was armed.

He reached the stairs leading up to the bridge arching over the canal.

This time, he could swear he *heard* something, only it seemed to come from the other side of the canal. Alec hesitated at the top of the stairs, not sure whether he'd really heard something or not, before continuing on. There had been nothing, but he began to hurry.

He was overreacting, and he knew that he was, but it didn't change the fact that he felt uncomfortable. As he started down the stairs, he took a few calming breaths, determined to slow his heart rate.

There was nothing here.

This side of the canal immediately felt better. The streets were wider and paved with cobblestones, and the buildings were like those he had known his entire life. He started forward, and as he did, he thought he saw a shadow moving out of the corner of his eye.

Alec paused, and turned toward it.

Too late, he realized he'd been followed.

One of the brutes—the same one he'd seen in the princess's room at the university—swung the flat end of his sword at Alec's head. When it struck, Alec crumpled, his sight fading into blackness.

31

AN ATTACK IN ASHES

Where was Alec?

Sam found the burned husk of the apothecary and waited outside, wondering how long it would take him to cross the bridge and reach her here. Jumping canals *did* make it easier to move between sections, but once she was here, she feared she'd be out of place. Having the cloak back seemed to help, but it only obscured her, and didn't hide her completely. She didn't feel as if she could walk openly, not even in a merchant section of the city.

Were it not for Marin's illness, she wasn't sure she would care enough about trying to help the princess. Did it matter if the highborns suffered and failed? But Marin... Marin had answers that Sam needed. Without Marin, would she ever understand what happened to her mother? Would she ever learn about herself? And Marin had promised to get Tray out of prison. Saving the princess hadn't even done that.

But if what Marin said was true, it meant she *was* something other than lowborn.

While waiting for Alec, she started into the ruins of the apothecary. Piles of ash inside the building marked where the shelves had been. Would the page still be here?

It couldn't be, could it?

After a fire like this, there didn't seem any way the page would remain, but she didn't think it was already destroyed, otherwise the princess would have been healed by what Alec had done. For that matter, Marin would have been healed. Neither was.

She made her way toward what had once been the back wall of the shop. This was where he had placed her on the cot, and had done what was needed to help her recover. Without Alec, she probably would have died.

No... there was no probably about it. She *would* have died without him. It had been more than the salve he'd used on her, but that didn't change the fact that Alec had been responsible for her recovery.

A few remnants of paper remained scattered atop a blackened frame of what had once been a bench. She remembered waking to see Alec working at the table, and had laughed at the meticulous way he documented everything in the way his father had trained him. Now, she acknowledged that meticulous hand had been the reason she recovered.

A Scribe. That's what Marin had called him.

And how had Alec learned it?

That might be the better question, she realized. Had he not known how to document on the paper, she would never have been augmented and they would never have escaped the brutes.

As she looked around the remains of the apothecary, she wondered... could his father have been a Scribe, as well?

Marin might know the answer to that, if only she could recover. Which meant destroying the page that remained, if they could find it.

Where was Alec?

He should have found her by now, shouldn't he?

Sam made her way toward the street and noted movement there.

Pulling the cloak around her shoulders, she ducked into where shadows coalesced around the street, joining together. With the cloak, she'd be able to remain hidden. She reached for the canal staff, wanting to pull it from beneath her cloak, wanting the reassurance she would get from having it in hand, and pulled only one end free. Screwing the two ends together would only draw attention to her, and she didn't want to do that, not unless she knew what was out on the street. It was possible it was nothing more than one of the other merchants who lived on the street. Chances were good Alec knew them.

As she hid, she heard a steady breathing, deep and coarse. She'd heard a similar sound before and remembered it from when she'd faced the brute in the princess's room.

They'd been found.

Sam wanted to move, to get anywhere but where she was, needing to hide so the brute wouldn't find her.

Without any augmentation, there wasn't anything she could do to fight him. It was better to run and get the chance to fight again later than to risk herself here.

But if he was here, it meant that he thought there was a possibility he might find the missing page.

She needed to find it first.

Doing so risked discovery, but *not* doing so risked him obtaining the page first, which meant that not only was the princess going to continue to waste away, but so would Marin and any hope of Sam finding out more about what she was—and what she could do.

Slowly, she lowered herself behind the brick wall that almost toppled over. Simply bumping into it might bring the wall crashing down. For now, it provided some protection, and she needed it. Moving back into the apothecary, she went straight for the table where Alec had sat. If the page would be anywhere, wouldn't it be at the table?

She reached into the ash but found nothing more than that. There was no sign of the page, nothing that would make it seem the paper had survived the fire.

Sam swore to herself and backed up a little, trying to get closer to the wall. She might need the cover if the brute made his way into the shop and started searching. As she did, she realized he wasn't alone.

Another figure slumped in a heap in the middle of the street.

Sam recognized the still form of Alec.

The brute had found him.

Even if she didn't find the page, she couldn't leave Alec lying here. That would be abandoning him to the brutes, something she wasn't willing to do. He'd helped her too often for her to be willing to leave him to the brutes.

"Find the page."

Sam tensed when she heard those words. The brute wasn't alone.

She didn't see anyone else with him, but then, she didn't risk moving and exposing herself yet.

"The place was burned, Ralun. If the page remained here, it would have been destroyed."

Maybe *he* would have the book.

If they couldn't find the page in the ashes, maybe there would be something in the book that would allow them to heal Princess Lyasanna.

"We know it wasn't. Lyasanna fails. We need to control the page until she's gone. Then my revenge will be complete."

It really *was* the way that Marin claimed. They wanted the paper because it was somehow responsible for poisoning the princess. Which meant it was the same one that was responsible for poisoning Marin.

Footsteps crunched along the burned remains of the building and came closer to her. She needed to move now, or she'd be discovered.

Crawling forward, she glanced into the street, looking for Alec.

He was gone.

Kyza!

Had the brute moved him?

She ducked back down. As she did, something grabbed at her cloak and jerked her up and around.

Ralun stared at her with his dark eyes. "You've been

hiding from me long enough. You should have been eliminated long before now. That you haven't been is my fault. It is a mistake I will correct now—"

She didn't let him finish.

Jerking the two halves of the canal staff free, she smacked him in the stomach with them, bringing the narrow lengths of wood up and around to connect with his arms. They struck loudly, but he didn't drop her.

Sam pulled back again and hit him one more time, pushing more effort into it. It struck him, but he barely made any expression that it hurt.

He looked at her with amusement and casually threw her to the side. "Without your Scribe, you are nothing, are you?"

Sam scrambled backward, her back crashing into a remaining section of brick wall, and it toppled over. She continued pushing herself back, needing to get away, and needing to find out what had happened to Alec. Where had he gone? What had they done to him?

Ralun stalked closer to her, his sword now unsheathed. "It's time I finish this. Even untrained, you have been troublesome."

He swung, and she raised the staff rods up to block, but she knew it wouldn't be enough to stop him.

Somehow, she managed to catch the sword with the staff, and deflected it to the ground.

Sam jumped out of the way of his next blow, thankful that she still seemed able to do that much.

"All of this over paper?" she asked.

"If this were only about the paper, I wouldn't have come myself."

"This is personal for you?"

Sam rolled out of the way of his next attack, and the sword whistled past her head, almost close enough for her to feel the cold coming off the blade. A moment later, and the sword would have split her in two. It was almost as if he played with her.

With a sinking sensation, she knew *why* he seemed to be playing with her. Because he was. There had been another brute with him at the apothecary.

Almost too late, she spun, bringing the staff around, and she caught the second brute in the head and in the leg with more force than she should have.

An augmentation.

The brute dropped briefly to one knee, his eyes going wide and looking to Ralun, then looking out into the street, as if seeing that Alec was gone. "The Scribe. Where did he go?"

Sam could think of only one reason why they would care about where Alec had gone, and it was the same reason that she would seem able to stop their attack.

Had Alec woken and found a way to write on the page?

Where would he have gotten some of her blood?

Ralun rounded on her and she jumped, needing to test if anything had changed.

Sam arced up and over him, coming to land behind him. As she did, she swept the staff toward his legs, and caught him in the back of his calves. Ralun slipped and righted himself quickly.

He spun, coming around to face her.

She would have to be faster. Would whatever Alec had

done be able to help her get faster than she was now? She would need speed to stop Ralun.

But she detected the other brute behind her.

She would be caught between them.

Ralun smiled a predatory flash of teeth.

Using the staff, she leaped into the air and pushed off. As she did, she swung the staff up and caught the other brute in the head, sending him flying backward. Sam brought the staff around as she landed, and it crashed through his chest.

She tumbled off to the side and yanked the staff free. The brute didn't move. Given the way the staff had pierced him, she didn't think he would.

That left Ralun.

Unless there was another brute.

Sam jumped to her feet again, worried that the augmentation would fade. The last time Alec had managed to augment her strength and speed, it had disappeared fairly quickly. If the same thing happened again, she wanted to be able to stop Ralun first.

He watched her, his eyes glittering with dark anger.

"I will kill you quickly, but I will take my time with your Scribe."

He flicked something from beneath his cloak.

Without thinking about what she did, Sam pressed off with her staff, sending herself into the air. The crossbow bolts had been poisoned, so she had every reason to believe that any other weapon they'd use on her would be, as well, so she needed to get *above* it.

Ralun reached beneath his cloak again.

She flipped the staff in the air, swinging it down, catching it forcefully on his arm.

The bone splintered.

Sam landed and swung the staff around again, catching him in the back and sending him sprawling. With another swing of the staff, she hit his head with a heavy thud, his face smashing into the floor. Ralun didn't move.

She needed to finish him off, even search him for evidence of the book, but the sound of movement disrupted her thoughts. It came from the street.

Was that where Alec was?

She ran into the street, nearly tripping over her feet as the augmentation faded and speed left her. She should have grabbed Ralun's sword and run him through before leaving, but she needed to see to Alec first.

She found shadows in a nearby alley.

Stalking toward it, her staff ready, she prepared to attack if needed.

One figure hunched over something on the ground, but there was another beside him who didn't move.

Sam paused.

Hadn't Alec been the one to augment her skills? He was the only one to know how to do it, wasn't he? But that wasn't Alec leaning over the paper writing with a long quill.

"Kaver," a man with a deep voice said as he looked up.

"Who are you?"

The man set the quill down, his gaze darting to the end of the alley before returning to Sam. "The Thelns. Where are they?"

"One is dead. The other is out. Might be dead." She glanced back, thinking she needed to return to finish off Ralun, especially now that she knew that Alec wasn't in any danger. "Augment me, and I'll go back and make sure he's finished."

"That's not possible."

"It *is* possible. You must have been the one who did it before, especially since Alec is still out." She didn't know who this man was, but he must understand the Scribes and the Kavers, for him to have managed to help her as he had.

"I'm out of ink," he said, holding up a vial.

"Use mine, then."

The man shook his head. "It doesn't work like that. Scribes are keyed to their Kaver."

Sam tipped her head to the side, noting movement.

She spun, readying her staff, but there was nothing. Had Ralun disappeared?

If so, she might have lost her chance to find the book and the necessary page to help the princess and Marin.

Without them, the princess would die.

Marin would die.

"Who are you?" she asked, turning back to the man.

He ignored the question, folding up the page and stuffing it into Alec's pocket. Sam wondered why he hadn't put it in his own. Then he lifted Alec, hoisting him to his shoulder.

"You know what I am, which means you must know Marin. Who are you?"

The man sighed and turned to her. "Such death. This is

why I have hidden for so long, and now you've brought Alec into this." He took a deep breath. "As to me... I am his father."

32

UNEXPECTED HELP

S am helped Alec's father carry him to the remnants of the apothecary. From the expression on his face, it seemed he hadn't known his shop had burned until now. Sam hadn't noticed before, but he wore a long brown cloak, and beneath it looked to be a canal staff. Other than her mother and Marin, she hadn't known anyone else to carry a canal staff.

"How do you know me?" she asked.

"I don't know you. I know of you." He grunted as he said the last, lowering Alec to the ground. He seemed to make a point of keeping Alec away from the fallen brute, and for that, Sam was thankful. As she had feared, Ralun was gone.

After defeating him, she had still lost.

"You know the secret of the paper," Sam said. "You know of the Thelns."

He nodded as he began looking through the apothecary, shaking his head every so often as he went, making a soft whistling sound from time to time. "I know of a great many things."

"You're a Scribe."

He paused and turned to her. "I am no Scribe. I understand the power of the paper, but that is all."

He began sorting through the ash, as if he would find the page that was missing.

"What are you looking for?"

"The same as you," he said, moving a hunk of charred table out of the way. When he set it back down, ash drifted up into the air, and he waved it away with his hand.

"The page isn't here. It must have burned in the fire."

"It could not."

Sam smiled. "It's paper. It would have burned."

Alec's father looked up at her and met her eyes. "Why do you think the Thelns used fire here? They've been granted access to the book, and they would have held that responsibility almost sacred." He kicked at a pile of debris, sending it flying across the room. "Fire will not harm pages from the book. So that is what I'm looking for."

"How will we destroy it then?"

He paused again and looked over to her. "The pages in the book are powerful, and the magic used to hold that power protects them, but there are other ways to destroy them than fire."

"What is the book?"

Alec's father sighed. "A relic of a time long past. A reminder of a war that should be over."

"I don't understand."

"And you shouldn't. For now, help me search so we can be done with this."

Sam used the canal staff to sort through the remains of the apothecary, but she didn't expect to find the page here. If it were here, why wouldn't the brutes have seen it before? How would they have missed it?

"Will Alec be okay?"

Alec's father looked back to where Alec lay. He hadn't moved since they'd brought him into the apothecary. Even destroyed, it seemed better to have him here than lying on the street. "He will recover. The Thelns would have wanted to use him. They could not have done that were he dead."

"How would they have used him?"

"The same way you used him."

Sam blinked a moment as the accusation settled. "I didn't use him."

"No? You didn't draw him into a battle he was never meant to be a part of? You didn't drag him into a fight that has been over for years?"

Sam laughed bitterly. "Over? Whatever it was doesn't seem to be over. From what Marin said, the Thelns continue to attack. What makes you think the war is over?"

Alec's father shook his head and a troubled expression crossed his face. "The battle *was* over. The attempt to steal more paper changed that." He watched her for a moment, the way he did reminding her of the measured stare that Alec managed, before turning his attention back to searching through the debris. "There is nothing here."

"That's what I said."

"Then the Thelns have it."

If the Thelns had recovered the page, then it meant that the princess and Marin would die. There wouldn't be anything they could do to stop it. Alec had slowed their decline, but the effect faded.

"Why can't we reverse the effect permanently?" she asked.

"The book—"

"The Book of Maladies?" she asked. He nodded. "What is it?"

He sighed. "A rumor that turns out to have been real."

"Rumor?"

"The Thelns have long been rumored to have such a book but none has ever seen it. It is power. Written on pages of power, the book details ailments. Many are real, but many are imagined, horrors that could not be possible without the book."

"Why can't you use the paper and reverse it? Why does it have to fade?"

"What is written in the Book of Maladies is etched with more permanence. There is something about the writing Scribes have not discovered, though they have tried."

"But Alec healed me."

His father glanced to where Alec lay before answering. "You were not afflicted by the book, so the healing is different. There is a connection between the Kaver and the Scribe. That connection grants him the ability to heal you."

"But he augmented me, as well, and that didn't last."

"Augment. An interesting term."

"What would you call it?"

"I suppose augment would work. They fade, though, because sustaining them would require too much strength otherwise."

"The Thelns don't seem to fade."

"No. They do not."

"Why is that?"

"The Thelns have a different connection to power. They do not have need of Scribes."

"Alec was able to slow Ralun."

"He slowed him?"

She nodded, thinking to the attack in the princess's room. "I don't know what he did, but it gave me a chance."

"I don't know what he would have done. I have not seen an attack like that work on the Thelns, though I admit I haven't faced them myself."

"If you're not a Scribe, how do you know all of this?"

He looked around the street before turning his gaze on her. "You don't have to seek power to desire understanding." He sighed and tapped his staff on the floor. "We will lose the princess now. I had thought..."

"Were you at the university?" Alec asked.

Both Sam and Alec's father looked over when he spoke.

"Mrs. Rubbles gave me the note you left her that told me you once trained at the university. Were you there?"

His father hurried over to him and ran hands along his neck, and then listened to his heart and lungs before leaning back. "You're unharmed."

Alec coughed. "That's all you can tell me?"

"I had been harvesting, but when I heard the princess

was sick, I went looking for a different kind of help. I... I failed."

"What do you mean you went for help? Why won't you tell me more?"

"Because at this point, that's all that matters."

Alec looked to Sam, and his eyes narrowed. "How did you escape? He was coming for you."

"Your father augmented me."

"My father?" When Alec turned his attention to his father, he looked away. "How is it you know how to do that?"

"I was the one to write the words, but I was not the one to create the augmentation. The ink I used belonged to another pair."

Alec stared at him for a long moment. "Another Scribe and Kaver?"

His father nodded. "They left me with a gift, a powerful one. Were there ever a need, I could use their blood—their ink—if only I had the proper documentation."

"Who were they?" Sam asked. Could it have been her mother?

"Someone who was lost long ago."

"Were you going to share any of this with me?"

"There wasn't the need. I intended to protect you from all of this as much as I could."

"But you must have the ability to serve as a Scribe!"

His father sighed. "Perhaps I did once. Now... now I have a different task."

Alec stared at his father a long moment and turned away from him.

"Where are you going?"

Alec didn't bother looking back to him. "To find the missing page, so we can save the princess."

Sam hurried up to him as he reached the street, and Alec's father followed behind. "You know where it is?"

"I have an idea."

"I thought you said it was here?" she said.

"That's what I thought, but there's another possibility."

"We need to find it," Sam said. "Not only for the princess."

Alec paused a moment and looked over to her, nodding. "Marin? I know you care about her. We'll find the page."

"It's not so much that I care about her. It's the answers she might have."

Though, now that she saw his father, she wondered if he might have answers of a different sort. He had known enough to use the paper, and he had blood ink stored, even if he claimed he was no Scribe. Who would he have taken it from?

"It seems we all have questions," Alec said.

33

FINDING A PAGE FROM THE BOOK

Alec hurried along the street, still shocked that his father had helped Sam. Not only had he helped her, but he had seemed to understand the trick to the paper before now. How much suffering would they have been able to avoid if only his father had shared what he knew about the paper?

All these years, he'd been taught that everything he needed to learn could be done through observation and study. Now, for him to learn that there was more—that there was magic he could tap into—he struggled with *why*.

None of his anger and frustration mattered. Not right now, anyway. What mattered was finding a way to destroy the page, and to do that, they had to reach it and then save the princess. They had thought they would find it in the burned husk of the apothecary, but maybe there was another place it could be. How would it be possible for the paper to survive the fire?

"Rubbles?" his father said as they turned a corner.

Alec nodded, not wanting to share anything more than he had. Would it matter if he told his father about Mrs. Rubbles and her interest in ink? Was it possible, as he suspected, that she had likely found the page within the ashes of the shop? If she had, and they got ahold of it, would his father know of a way to destroy it when fire could not? If so, then maybe it would help the princess. Maybe she would survive.

He knocked on the door.

Waiting was the hardest part.

Moments passed. Then more.

Alec knocked again.

Finally, Mrs. Rubbles appeared in the door and slowly pulled it open.

"You went to the shop after it burned," he said to her without preamble.

"Alec? What are you—"

"The paper. Did you find it when you went to the shop?"

She looked from Alec to his father to Sam. "After the fire, I was sorting through the remains looking for what could be salvaged. When I saw it…" She looked at each again before motioning for them to enter. She breathed out heavily and went behind her counter and pulled out a leather-bound book, sliding the page out from within.

Alec took it, recognizing his writing and the marks in the two corners. Reluctantly, he turned to his father for answers. "How will we destroy this?"

"Destroy?" Mrs. Rubbles asked, clearly surprised by the idea. "Alec, paper like this should be preserved. That's why I went after it! This is a quality sheet of parchment. If I had another sheet—"

His father took the marked page and held it. "To think that I would hold one of the pages from the book…"

"We need to destroy it, Father. Do you know how? Fire didn't do it and"—he lifted the page and attempted to tear the sheet, and was unsurprised to discover he couldn't— "we can't simply rip it. What else can we do to destroy it?"

"Only a Scribe can do it, but in order to do so, we need to know what was originally written on it. Otherwise, anything we do won't last."

"How will we know?"

"That's the problem. We have to reveal the writing. We don't have anyone who can—"

Mrs. Rubbles grabbed the page from them and took it behind the counter. She pulled a vial of a thick liquid from beneath the counter and swirled it slowly. "This," she began, "should help enhance the writing. I've tried using it a few times since I retrieved it from the ashes," she told Alec.

Mrs. Rubbles took a brush and started wiping it across the page. As she did, letters and words formed in a spindly script of black ink. As the liquid faded, so too did the writing.

"Do that again," his father said.

Mrs. Rubbles brushed the liquid over the page again, painting it. The words formed once more, and remained while the page was wet. When it dried, the writing disappeared.

"I don't know what to make of it," Alec said.

His father's face paled. "I do. Alec, we'll need you to

mix ink from your Kaver's blood," he said turning to Sam. "I think we can save the princess."

Alec turned to Sam, and she said nothing as she took her knife and drew it cross her palm, then held her hand out to him. As the blood pooled, he started to say something but caught himself. There was really nothing he *could* say.

"Write these words," his father said.

Mrs. Rubbles handed him a quill and he began to write.

Sam sat with Alec near the canal. Neither of them had spoken.

"How is she?" he finally asked.

"Marin? I haven't been able to find her." Sam had left him after they'd destroyed the paper, but hadn't found Marin in her home. Sam hadn't wanted to stay away from Alec for long, not until she understood what had happened and was certain Ralun wouldn't return. She'd injured him, but now he knew about her—and Alec—and she was sure he would come back. And Marin needed to share with her *why*.

"She'll be fine," a voice said from a distance.

They turned, and she saw Marin watching them, leaning on a canal staff, but not quite as heavily as she had the last time they'd seen her.

"You destroyed it," Marin said.

Alec nodded. "We did. I haven't heard whether the princess..."

"My sources tell me she will be fine," Marin said. "She's still at the university, but she won't be for much longer."

"Ralun—the brute—escaped," Sam said.

"He would be difficult for you to defeat without any training. But you will have to learn. Both of you. Stealing the paper only renewed an old war."

It was more than that, Sam knew. "It was personal for Ralun," she said.

"Why do you say that?" Marin asked.

Sam shrugged. "Something he said. He said that he wouldn't have come himself if it were only about the paper. And he kept calling the princess his prize."

Marin's brow furrowed, and she looked away. What was she hiding from them?

Alec seemed not to notice. "What now?"

"Now you will train," Marin said.

"No," Sam said. "First, Tray—"

Marin raised her hand. "Your brother is free. He's at my place recovering."

"He's free?"

"After my recovery, I made certain to leverage my assets to see him freed. With the princess healed, there was no reason to hold him, and no proof that he was a Theln sympathizer."

Sam almost started crying. All of this, and now her brother was free. So much had changed while he'd been in prison. She wasn't even sure she was the same person she'd been before. "I need to see him."

"You can."

"Does he know?"

Marin shook her head. "He's never known. And he cannot."

"Why?"

"There are things you don't understand, Sam. Things you *can't*."

"Marin..."

"You take after your mother, Sam. You are a Kaver. Your brother, he takes after his father."

"And that means what?"

"He's different, as are you. Whereas you can work with a Scribe and perform great feats, your brother possesses a different ability."

Even before she said it, Sam thought she knew.

"He's a Theln."

She didn't need Marin's nod to know she was right.

Whatever he *might* be, he was still her brother. And right now, after all the time they'd been apart, she wanted to find him.

"Go," Alec said. "I have questions for my father. You find your brother. We'll talk again soon."

She sighed. What would she even say?

After leaving Alec, she crossed the canals between this section and hers, and reached Marin's home quickly. She hurried up the stairs and down the hall and through her door without determining whether it was safe. Everything she had gone through had been about getting back to him, about finding her brother. Instead, she'd found so much more. She didn't know what to make of all of it—including herself—but there would be time for that later.

All she wanted now was to see her brother.

When she pushed it open, she found Tray sitting in the room, staring at the window.

Sam raced forward and threw her arms around him.

His face was gaunt and had a haunted expression, but he was still her brother. Of all the things she'd thought about saying, the only one that came out was, "Kyza, it's great to see you again, Tray."

Her brother hugged her back, "You, too, Sam. You won't believe what I've been through."

She hugged him again, laughing as she did, knowing that she'd tell him more later. For now, they were back together.

Grab Volume 2 of The Book of Maladies: Broken.

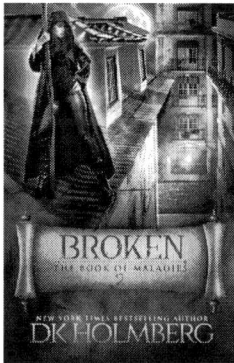

Decades of peace has ended. The real battle is still to come.

Sam and Alec work to understand their connected magic, but the limited supply of easar paper limits them.

Worse, Marin has again disappeared, leaving questions unanswered. How can they be ready for another Theln attack if they don't have an opportunity to train with their abilities?

New power complicates everything. Sam wants to use it to continue taking jobs that will eventually buy her way into the nicer sections of the city, but Alec sees a higher purpose to their magic. When an opportunity Alec thought he would never have is offered, he needs to decide whether to follow his heart or his mind. Sam feels like she should be more than a lowborn, but what is she without her Scribe?

Strange attacks in the city leaves her thinking she and Marin aren't the only Kavers remaining, but why would Marin keep that from her? Finding the answers she and Alec need puts both of their lives in danger but might be the key to knowing whether she'll ever be anything more than a lowborn. The safety of the city just might depend on it.

NAMES AND TERMS

People:

- Aelus Stross: An apothecary and skilled healer. Alec's father
- Alec Stross: an apprentice apothecary
- Bastan: a thief who essentially runs Caster
- Hyp: a moneylender in the Arrend section who frequents Aelus's shop
- Marcella Rubbles: owner of a stationary store in Arrend
- Marin: a thief who knew Sam's mother
- Samara (Sam) Elseth: a thief
- Trayson (Tray) Elseth: Sam's brother

Places and Terms:

- Arrend section: a merchant section

- canal eels: possibly mythical creatures living in the canals
- Callesh section: a merchant section
- Caster section: a lowborn outer section of the city
- Central Canal: the canal that separates the lowborn sections from the merchants and highborns
- easar paper: magical paper
- highborn: a term for the wealthier living in the center of the city
- Kyza: one of the many gods worshipped in Verdholm
- lowborn: a term for people living in the outer sections of the city
- Lycithan: a southern nation. Known for their skilled artisans.
- Narvin Plains: east of the city, thin stretch of land
- physicker: healers with specialized training at the university
- Piare River: connects to Ralan Bay and the canals
- Ralan Bay: a trading hub along the coast of Verdholm
- Sornum: Bastan's tavern
- Thelns: dangerous brutes
- Valun: a country known for various artifacts, including the stout rope Sam uses
- Verdholm: an isolated city situated near the

coast with canals running through it separating
it into different sections

- Yisl: one of the many gods worshipped in
  Verdholm

ALSO BY D.K. HOLMBERG

The Binders Game

The Forgotten

Assassin's End

The Teralin Sword

Soldier Son

Soldier Sword

Soldier Sworn

Soldier Saved

Soldier Scarred

Printed in Great Britain
by Amazon

12509245R00196